...to find my center. Arranging my hair so I was well covered, I got to my knees, then sat on my heels. "You know, last night, when you and Doc abandoned me, Norman became a huge pest. He kept at me, wanting me to dance with him."

Bella's "Um" irritated me. Annoyance tingled my exposed skin, running along my collarbone and down the insides of my arms.

"He wouldn't leave me alone. It was so gross." I straightened as angry lightning strikes marched down my back.

"Then he *insisted* I finish my drink because he wanted to buy me another. Bella, I thought I was going to have to decapitate him to get him to leave me alone. I decided to just take off and let you find another way home. But after I finished my drink—and I only had the one Doc bought me—I don't remember anything. It's as if I got lost in the night."

I gathered my fury like a fiery orb in my chest. "You *know* I never have a memory lapse except during a blood moon phase or if I lose control. I wasn't that angry." A simple full moon hadn't done that to me since I was three years old.

"That son of a cur must have slipped me a roofie. Why else would I have been out of control?" I allowed my rage to explode as I thought about the man putting a date rape drug in my drink. My body stung as the bristles burst through my skin, but I exalted in the sensation as my face narrowed, then lengthened. I loved the feeling of my body shifting from human to wolf shape. he power surge a

Other Books by Susan Shay

TO SCHOOL A COWBOY
BLINDSIGHT
available from The Wild Rose Press, Inc.

Make Me Howl

by

Susan Shay

This is a work of fiction. Names, characters, places, and incidents are either the product of the author's imagination or are used fictitiously, and any resemblance to actual persons living or dead, business establishments, events, or locales, is entirely coincidental.

Make Me Howl

COPYRIGHT © 2013 by Susan Shay

All rights reserved. No part of this book may be used or reproduced in any manner whatsoever without written permission of the author or The Wild Rose Press, Inc. except in the case of brief quotations embodied in critical articles or reviews.
Contact Information: info@thewildrosepress.com

Cover Art by *Debbie Taylor*

The Wild Rose Press, Inc.
PO Box 708
Adams Basin, NY 14410-0708
Visit us at www.thewildrosepress.com

Publishing History
First Black Rose Edition, 2013
Print ISBN 978-1-61217-885-1
Digital ISBN 978-1-61217-886-8

Published in the United States of America

Dedication

To the men in my life:
Gary, Danny, Matt and Brad.
You're the beat of my heart and the depth of my soul.
Through it all—
the beautiful good times and the saddest of the sad—
you've always found a way to Make Me Howl!
Love you little. Love you big.

Chapter One

Even a man who is pure in heart and says his prayers by night, may become a wolf when the wolfbane blooms and the autumn moon is bright.

"Jazzy Cannis, you're late!" My twin sister, Bella, was furious when I got to the Halloween party. "And you know how important this fund raiser is." As Princess Fiona, Bella's green-painted face almost glowed in the dim light beneath the pink cone hat.

"Are you're responsible for that?" I waved a hand at the old "Wolf Man" movie, flickering on the big screen TV.

She had the sense to look sheepish as she tossed a glance at the film. "It's a classic. We'll be running them all night long."

I snorted in reply as we moved away. "I can't believe this party was your idea."

"You know we're going to need a lot of money to build the new surgery wing for my babies," Bella murmured as she looked around the room. "Can you think of a better way to kick it off than by letting people pay to have fun?"

She had a point, so I shrugged. "With the way Texans like to party, it could be completely paid for tonight. But why didn't the powers-that-be build the surgery wing before they blew their wad on this overdone meeting room?"

"It's a multi-functional building—an ongoing resource for the park. Once people get used to it being here, there'll be a waiting list for weddings, family reunions—all kinds of celebrations." She nudged me with a hip-bump. "Besides, administrative and supervisory offices are here, and they're extremely necessary."

As my eyes grew used to the darkness, I glanced around. The colossal room was decked out like a haunted doll house, filled with costumed adults. The bar, created from several fake caskets, was being run by a witch whose costume was almost as low cut as mine—but not nearly as well filled.

The room was large and open with big windows on three sides. The wood floor looked smoky with ragged clouds of vapor, courtesy of a working fog machine. To one side of a designated dance area stood several tables, the tops shaped like old tombstones. Each one had a silly saying such as: *Here lies Lester Moore, Four shots from a .44. No Les No More,* and, *Final Drop Funeral Home, We'll be the last to let you down.* Shredded pieces of cheesecloth hung over the windows and draped along the ceiling. The corners held an assortment of rubber spiders, ghosts and maniac killers.

As I waited, a man dressed like a vampire towed a cowgirl onto the dance floor, slid both hands to her bottom and pulled her snug against him. Oh, yeah. People in our area love to party. I leaned close to Bella. "Unless you want those *offices* to become multi-functional, too, you'd better be sure they're locked."

"Oh, crap! I forgot." With a gasp, Bella rushed away, her scarf flapping from her cone hat.

"A fund raiser at a drive-through zoo on

Halloween." I tightened the knot holding my blouse closed as the cowgirl jerked away from the vampire and stormed off. "And all the really wild animals are inside. Appropriate."

At the bar, I made sure I didn't get close enough for the Green Hulk in front of me to stomp on my Jimmy Choo stilettos. I'd spent all afternoon at the manicurist and I'd have to hurt anyone who spoiled my 'What's Your Blood Type' red pedicure.

The enormity of the bar, which spanned one side of the room and took four bartenders to run, amazed me. As I waited for my turn, I noticed the rank odor of what must have been really old cologne. Had someone found a way to dress up as the Fart Monster? Curious, I glanced back to find the dancing vampire, who'd just been mauling the cowgirl, standing as close as he could get without touching me.

His face puckered into a smarmy smile. He shuffled around in front of me, pretending to look at my costume as he coughed a phlegmy chuckle. "Hey, hey, darlin'. You a belly dancer? 'Cause you can dance on my belly anytime!"

I gritted my teeth to keep from snapping at him. "No." The best way to handle a man like that was to be short and to the point. Or eat his face.

"Too bad." He had the temerity to reach for the gold medallion dangling between my breasts.

Reacting automatically, I knocked his hand away.

"Oooh, that's a funny costume if you're supposed to be the Karate Kid." He tried to sound sarcastic, but he held his wrist close to his overgrown gut. "I'm an important man around here, baby. You've probably heard of me. I'm Norman Briderson, chief of animal nutrition. Why don't you let me buy you a little drinky?"

What would it take to get this guy to give it up? Seeing no one paying attention to us, I dropped my focus to his groin and gave him a microscopic smile. The need to heave hit me, but I took my time. Very slowly I lifted my gaze over his beer belly and narrow chest until I stared into his heavily-jowled face. Then I removed every bit of expression from my face, lowered my chin, narrowed my eyes and concentrated.

I kept my growl low. Even my deep-in-the-heart snarl was nearly below human hearing. After a moment, the blood drained from his face until he was nearly the same color as Bella. Sweat poured from him, making him glow even brighter than she did.

With a backward step, he tripped over a man walking toward us and fell to the floor. Scrambling to his feet, he rushed out of the room.

"Hello." The new man, dressed in a flat brimmed cowboy hat, black boots and a dark suit, looked me over then frowned. "What's your costume?"

I glanced at the TV screen, and seeing where the movie was—at the gypsy camp—I nodded toward the young woman with the tambourine. "Isn't it obvious? I'm the Gypsy dancer."

"Nice to meet you, Gypsy Dancer." The man hooked his jacket behind a holstered pistol. "I'm Doc Holliday."

Dark, almost black hair, a decent width to his shoulders and legs long enough to put a smile on a girl's face. And no beer belly. Doc might just put some life into Bella's Halloween party.

As if my thoughts had conjured her, Bella

reentered from the far side of the room, a look of relief on her face. After a moment, she saw me and started over. When she noticed Doc Holliday, her face brightened. "Jazzy, I see you've met Chase."

"Well, I met Doc Holliday here." I watched Bella to see what kind of relationship the two of them had. No way would I cut in on a man Bella had her sights set on—unless I had to. "Do you two work together?"

Judging by Bella's easy chuckle and her manner, she had no feelings for the man, and I was glad. He was too fine not to get to know. "This is Dr. Chase Holliday, the other veterinarian here at the park. Chase, this is my sister, Jazzy."

He dipped his chin a bit when he smiled. "Maybe you two should have come as nuns."

"Nuns?" I couldn't keep from rolling my eyes. "You'd rather we were wearing long, black robes that hide everything but our faces?"

His gaze met mine then, and I could feel...something. I'm not sure about him, but there was a definite tingle on my end. Besides, he was hot. He had dark blue eyes, a square jaw, hair that was just a little too long and a way of focusing that made me wonder if I should attack or run.

And I never run.

As he moved closer, my heart did this flip-flop thing. I thought for a moment he was going to whisper in my ear, but instead he spoke in a tone both Bella and I could hear. "I didn't say I'd *rather* see you hide all that, but on a night like tonight, you might be safer from men like Norman Briderson if you had."

Bella chuckled with him as if they had a private

joke, but I didn't think Norman was funny. Rather than comment, I decided to change the subject and make Doc uncomfortable instead of me. Because he was still so close, I skimmed my fingers over the grip of his pistol a couple of times. "Hey, Doc. You got a hair trigger on this thing?"

Capturing my hand, he held it under his palm and studied me for a long, breathless moment. Something dangerous flashed in his eyes. Finally he released me, pulled out the firearm and held it out for us to look at. "It's very well balanced, and when loaded, it's deadly. But it doesn't have a hair trigger."

"Doc's an avid gun collector," Bella murmured. "How old is that gun, Doc?"

He thought for a moment. "A little over a hundred years old, from the original Doc Holliday's era."

"Could it have been his?" Bella asked, wonder in her voice.

"Probably not. I didn't pay enough for it to have real historical significance." He flipped the gun over his finger as easily as a percussionist twirls his drumstick before sliding it back into its holster.

"What'll it be?" the overworked witch at the bar asked as the group in front of us moved away.

Touching our elbows, Doc moved to the bar between us. "So, Princess Fiona, Gypsy Dancer, what would you like to drink?"

Together we glanced at the list of available beverages and their common name equivalents. Corpuscle Cocktail—Bloody Mary, Monster Blood—Margarita and Bottled Witches' Brew—Lone Star Beer topped the list. After making our choices, we took our drinks to a recently vacated table, which read: *Here lies*

Butch, We planted him raw, He was quick on the trigger but slow on the draw.

Doc read the tabletop then glanced at the one next to us. "Bella, where did you find these things?"

Bella took a sip. "Hey, in the Metroplex, there's very little you can't find if you know where to look."

Honest admiration for Bella was plain on Doc's face. "And you would know where to look."

"Of course. I'm a woman, aren't I?"

As they chuckled, Norman returned to stumble then sprawled onto the empty chair next to me. "Hey, Doc. I have a joke for you. Ready?"

I edged as far away as possible.

With a small shrug, Doc answered, his voice tight. "All right, Norman. What's your joke?"

"What did one worm say to the other worm in the cemetery?" The man's inebriated speech shortened the last word to two syllables.

"I don't know. What did one worm say to the other?" Doc asked obligingly.

"Let's go make love in dead earnest." He looked around the table. "Get it? Get it?"

"Yes, we get it, Norman." Doc's tone grew hard. "Now go get a cup of coffee. You've had way too much to drink. If you don't sober up, you'll have to pay for a cab to—"

Raised voices at a side door cut Doc short then a man dressed in denim and work boots rushed to our table. "Doc, Dr. Bella, it's Sheba. She needs you. Now."

"Damn." Doc jumped up and followed the man out the door, but Bella paused.

"It's the Mexican Gray wolf I've been telling you

about." Taking off her cone hat, she dropped it to the table. "Her first litter and she's apparently having trouble. I hope I'll be back before the party's over, but if you're ready to leave before I come back, go ahead and take the car. I'll get Doc to drop me off."

"Don' worry about Bella." Norman swayed toward me as my twin rushed away. "Doc takes care of her. Real good care."

I glanced after Bella, wishing I were with her. I should have volunteered to boil water for them. Anything to keep from being left at Norman's mercy.

I almost chuckled as I thought what Bella's answer to that would have been. *As if you've ever been at anyone's mercy.*

****

The next morning, Chase Holliday knelt nearby as the strange wolf in the isolation cage attacked the bars. His fascination with the species stirred in his gut. This one was a real beauty. Powerfully built, long and sleek, it obviously had never seen captivity before. But how had it gotten inside the heavy duty fence surrounding the Safari Land property? And how had it found its way inside the compound's enclosure without anyone noticing?

Shutting his eyes, he drew a long breath. Sometimes he could catch a scent from the wild ones.

There it was. The nearly unnoticeable underlying odor that meant she hadn't been eating the vitamin enriched meat provided by the park. She was wild.

As he waited, his eyes burned. He tried to blink the sand from them, but long hours of helping Sheba safely deliver pretty much guaranteed that wouldn't be happening. Not today, anyway.

Bella left the delivery room to wander over. Dark shadows beneath her eyes were evidence of just how exhausted she was. "Why do you have that wolf locked up?"

At least she'd washed off the ghastly makeup and changed out of her froufrou costume before she'd gone into the delivery room. Otherwise, Sheba might have become really upset.

"It—" He took a second glance—"*she's* not one of ours. Wandered into the compound last night. Aren't her eyes an odd shade of green? I don't think I've seen a wolf with eyes that color before."

As Bella looked at the wolf's eyes, her face paled. She must be exhausted, too. "So what's she doing in there?"

"She had Norman treed on top of his car. After he rescued Norman, Tony put her here until he could find out what to do with her." With a chuckle, he looked again at the wolf who'd stopped attacking the bars and was now in a low crouch. Growling. "You should tell your sister about that. She'd probably get a laugh out of it."

Bella blinked a couple of times then glanced at him. "Yeah, I'll do that. Next time I talk to her."

"Next time? I thought you two lived together."

She nodded then flipped her hands, palms up. "You know how it is. The life of a fashion consultant is almost as hectic as a Safari Land veterinarian's. We live together but don't see each other much."

"And I imagine she dates quite a bit." Damn, why had he said that?

The wolf chose that moment to stop growling. Sitting back on her haunches, she howled.

"She goes out some, but hardly ever with the same guy twice." Bella glanced at the wolf, letting her gaze linger.

He thought about the woman he'd met the night before, waiting her turn at the bar. Her shoulder-length hair gleamed, even though the room was practically dark. Her eyes had been huge and tipped upward at the edges. But it was her costume that had made it hard for him to breathe. The top had been snug with only the knot between her breasts holding it together. The skirt hung low on her hips and was made to look as if the hem had been torn in several thigh revealing rips. Her legs had been long and tanned, and he was fairly positive they rose all the way to paradise.

He had to swallow before he could speak again. "Tell me more about her."

"Well—" she drew out the word while making the dimple low in her cheek indent— "we're twins, but not identical."

"So that means you know what she's thinking, but just can't hear her thoughts?" he teased.

She chuckled then nodded. "Something like that."

"Wish I could do that with my brothers." How could he find out what he wanted to know without actually asking?

"It comes in pretty handy for us, but it's almost too much for my dad. He moved out for a while when we were two, but I don't really remember it. He was back for our third birthday."

He couldn't put it off any longer. "So, is Jazzy engaged or dating...?"

Bella smirked that women-have-intuition-and-men-drool smile. "No, there's no one in her life. Never has been, at least for very long."

"Why not?" he asked before he considered his words. "With her looks and body, I'm surprised she's not married or something."

Bella's superior smile disappeared as her brows drew together. She shook her head, then, more concerned than he'd ever seen her, she shrugged. "She just hasn't found the right—uh—man. But when she does, I have a feeling she'll never let go."

Bella's words warmed him inside. "Do you think she'd mind if I called her?"

All but laughing, Bella turned away from the wolf to focus on him. "Why's that? Do you think one of your brothers might be interested?"

Surprised by her question, he frowned. "One of my brothers?"

"Well, yeah. I know *you* wouldn't have time for a woman. You're too busy with your research to actually spend time with a female. A human one, at least."

He shook his head at her teasing. "I went to your party last night."

"For how long? Fifteen minutes? Thirty?" Folding her arms, she chuckled. "And that's probably the longest you've spent in a social setting in months."

"Hey, my work is essential. Wiping out that gene is way more important than spending time at local watering holes, sniffing for a mate."

"If you say so. But there are millions of singles out there who wouldn't agree with you." She pursed her lips. "You never did tell me exactly what you were doing in your research."

He glanced away for a moment as he thought about how much he should tell her. "I'm trying to isolate the

Syzygia Gene. It's relatively obscure, so most geneticists haven't heard of it. Humans coming into contact with an animal affected by it usually understand the need for its destruction."

When Bella nodded, he forced a grin. "That and five dollars will get you a good cup of espresso."

"I could use one right now." Bella yawned then waved at the wolf. "So what are you going to do with her?"

"If she stays calm while she's in there, we'll release her somewhere off the property." He gazed at the wolf, trying to get a handle on what it was that roiled in his gut. After a moment, he gave up with a shrug. "We don't have the right to keep her locked up for very long. There's something about her that's different from our Safari Land wolves, and I'd hate to see her lose that."

****

Cool air stirred my hair, tickling the back of my neck and down my spine as I slowly drifted toward consciousness. I was a bit light-headed, and my eyes were all but glued shut. And the really bad part, my mouth tasted as if it were full of downtown Dallas dirty cotton.

The morning was fragrant with a light scent. Wildflowers? Unable to imagine where I was, I rolled over then stretched the kinks out of my arms.

Another breeze wafted over me, swirling over my naked breasts, down my belly and along my thighs.

"Jazzy?"

Hearing Bella whisper my name, I was tempted to pretend I was still sleeping. "Um?"

"Jazzy, look at me."

After working a moment, I was able to open my eyes. I tried to look at Bella, but her face kept going in and out of focus behind the bars.

Bars?

Abruptly I sat up, my head swimming at the sudden motion. "Bella?" I practically coughed the word, my throat hurt so.

Her gaze was filled with concern. I hated that look, as if as the moments-older twin, she was responsible for me. "Are you okay?"

"No, I'm not okay." I paused to control the bristle prickling down my spine. Then I whispered between my clamped jaws, not bothering to use telepathy since there was no one around. "What am I doing here? *Naked?*"

She reached through the bars to brush back my hair, now at its longest length, so she could touch my shoulder.

I jerked away. "Answer me. Where am I? Who put me here, and *where are my clothes?*"

As her anger flamed to match mine, she narrowed her eyes. Not a good sign. "You're in the isolation cage here at Safari Land. And I don't know where your clothes are."

"*Who put me here and why haven't you gotten me out?*" I would have shouted, but my throat hurt too much. That should have been a clue, but I couldn't begin to imagine it.

"Tony locked you up until the zoo officials could decide what to do with you." She lost all her anger, then looked to her right and left. "And you aren't out because this is quarantine. Doc has the only key."

Although I'll never admit it to Bella or any of the

rest of my family, a werewolf's adjustable hair length isn't always a good thing, at least for me. When I let my hair out to its longest length, I'm not always the sharpest stiletto on the shelf. When I draw it in all the way, I get a little fuzzy minded, so it all evens out as Grandma used to say. Today was one of those dull stiletto days. But like Lady Godiva, I needed the hair on my head to be long at that moment for modesty's sake.

"Why did Tony lock me up?"

"You treed Norman on his car."

I tried to comprehend her words. And I have to be honest, it took a moment. Or two. "I'm sure he deserved it."

As she nodded, her face clouded until I thought she was going to cry. "Tony thought you were a wild Mexican Gray."

"I must have had Jose Eber go too heavy on the highlights the last time." I gave a quick shrug. "It could have been worse. He could have thought I was an Arctic."

That infuriated her. "How can you make jokes at a time like this?"

I have to admit, my temper was a little short this morning. "What do you want me to do? Bite someone?"

Then we heard voices.

Bella's mouth dropped open and her eyes grew wide with horror as she looked around. "Doc's coming back and Norman's with him. You'd better go primal. Quick."

As if it was that easy. I couldn't just wiggle my nose like some TV witch—I had to allow myself to release. And after a lifetime of learning control, that wasn't easy.

I took a moment to settle myself, to find my center. Arranging my hair so I was well covered, I got to my knees then sat on my heels. "You know, last night, when you and Doc abandoned me, Norman became a huge pest. He kept at me, wanting me to dance with him."

Bella's "Um," irritated me. Annoyance tingled my exposed skin, running along my collarbone and down the insides of my arms.

"He wouldn't leave me alone. It was so gross." I straightened as angry lightning strikes marched down my back.

"Then he *insisted* I finish my drink because he wanted to buy me another. Bella, I thought I was going to have to decapitate him to get him to leave me alone. I decided to just take off and let you find another way home. But after I finished my drink—and I only had the one Doc bought me—I don't remember anything. It's as if I got lost in the night."

I gathered my fury like a fiery orb in my chest. "You *know* I never have a memory lapse except during a blood moon phase or if I lose control. I wasn't that angry."

A simple full moon hadn't done that to me since I was three years old.

"That son of a cur must have slipped me a roofie. Why else would I have been out of control?" I allowed my rage to explode as I thought about the man putting a date rape drug in my drink. My body stung as the bristles burst through my skin, but I exalted in the sensation as my face narrowed, then lengthened. I loved the feeling of my body shifting from human to wolf shape. There's never anything better than the power surge as it filled my muscles. It's exhilarating.

That morning, the only downside was the sharpening of my senses. I could smell Norman a long time before I saw him. He smelled of his breakfast, last night's strong cologne and sex. The only odor I picked up on Doc was soap and fresh coffee.

At that moment, I could have killed for a cup.

Focusing on my need for caffeine, I lifted my chin to howl. When I stopped for a breath, Norman stood directly in front of me, staring. I howled again—a bloodthirsty wolf who'd scented prey.

Then I rose to my four paws and stormed the length of the enclosure. When Norman stepped closer to the cage, I hurled myself at the bars.

"Good morning again, Bella," Doc said softly.

"Good morning," she answered as she turned to walk away.

"Don't leave on account of us." Norman was such a dweeb.

As cool as January in Aspen, Bella shook her head. It was easy for her to be cool since I was the one who'd gotten the Lycan blessing. The worst thing she'd inherited was straight hair. "I've got to go. I have some things to take care of."

Norman turned to watch Bella's rear as she walked away then moved closer to my cage. "He's a mean one, Doc. Maybe we should test him for rabies."

Doc didn't answer Norman as he gazed at me. His blue eyes were dark this morning, almost midnight blue, which made me wonder if he'd had a rough night.

He took a long breath then blew it out as he shook his head. "She."

"Say *whut*?

"This is a female wolf. A bitch." His tone of voice as he said the word made the anger inside me explode. Did he just enjoy saying the word that describes female canines and nasty women?

Unable to bear being so near Norman, I paced in front of the bars. Exhausted and thirsty, I wanted nothing more than a drink of cool water and to lie down for a nap—just not while they were watching.

"So what are we going to do with her?" Norman asked. Hunkering down like a caveman, he poked the end of a choke stick into my cage to see if I would go for it. What kind of idiots did he think wolves were? As if a wild animal didn't know the difference between an inanimate object and a walking, talking man? Besides his poking, the tone of his voice, the way he said the words, even his breathing irritated me.

How would his blood taste as it spurted from torn flesh to pour hot across my tongue and down my throat. Salty? Tart? Nasty because of his ancient aftershave?

I was tired of Norman's staring. Licking my lips, I lowered my head and stared at him as I had the night before. After a moment I started a low growl deep in the back of my throat then very slowly crouched as I lifted the hair on my back.

He started sweating, his face drained and, again, he turned ogre green. Scrambling to get up from his squat, he dropped the pole as he landed on his butt in the dirt. Just where he belonged.

Rolling clumsily to his knees, he got to his feet and hurried away. Now I turned my stare on Doc. For all his good looks, I'd grown tired of his company, too.

But he just continued to look at me, even when I upped my growl decibels. "You are something to look at, Beauty. You go right ahead and growl if it makes you feel better. Being caged must be hard when you're used to the wild."

After several incredibly long moments, Bella strolled back to stand near Doc, but from the way she was breathing, I knew she'd run all the way there. While she was gone, she'd put on a white smock that said Veterinarian Bella Cannis over the pocket.

Too bad I couldn't ask her if that was so she wouldn't forget who she was.

"What do you think, Doc?" Bella's voice was huskier than usual. Worrying over me, her sister-in-the-can must have been a little much for her. "What are we going to do about this wolf?"

"Do?" He shook his head. "She doesn't belong to Safari Land just because she came around to make our party more exciting."

"So we turn her loose?" Bella looked at me while she spoke.

"Yeah, we turn her loose."

But Bella pushed the subject. "Do you think she might have come from Lost Canyon?"

Doc frowned, probably trying to figure why always-busy Bella cared. "That's as good a guess as any, and it's not that far as the crow flies, so it makes sense. I'll tell Tony to take the old mail route and release her near the canyon. If that's not her normal territory, she'll find her own way home."

"Why don't *we* take her?" Bella asked. I wondered if he could hear the desperation in her voice as well as I could.

"You want to drive all the way to the canyon with her, rather than letting Tony do it?"

"Sure. Why not?" She nodded until I was afraid her head had come loose. "It's a gorgeous day and we might get to see some more of her pack."

"Fine. I'll get the key to the truck." He strode away.

While he was gone, Bella rushed to the cage door. "When he releases you, stay close. I'll come back for you just as fast as I can."

While it's hard for a wolf to pout, over the years, I'd perfected the art. I spoke in her mind. *Yeah. You do that.*

When Doc returned, he picked up the choke stick where Norman had dropped it. After adjusting the stick's noose, he moved it between the bars and fitted it around my neck. He put a key in the cage's lock, made sure Bella was out of the way, opened the door and stepped inside with me.

I had to make it look good, so I put up a token resistance before settling down.

It just took me a moment to adjust to the foreign object around my neck—like an old lady wearing a tight necklace. But I didn't want to look like a trained pooch on a leash, so I kept myself in a near crouch, ready to spring or run.

He led me to a tiger striped truck and locked me in a cramped cage in the back. I just prayed I wouldn't get car sick in that airless, miniscule box.

When he removed the noose, I wanted to rub the chaffed place, but thought better of it.

Riding where I was, I could tell Doc had to be the absolute worst driver in the world. In a relatively short distance, he hit every bump, bounced in and out of every rut and quite possibly found every rock in every road we were on. I wanted to spew. Bad.

Finally, the truck came to a stop. Both Doc and Bella came to let me out, but he made her stay back when he opened the door. Unable to stop myself, I had to show off just a little.

Taking a fantastic leap from the cage—if I do say so myself—I ran a few yards, then stopped and braced my front feet on a small boulder. Raising my chin, I howled at the top of my lungs, and waited as if I expected an answer.

"Go on, Beauty. Have a wonderful life."

I gazed at him for a moment, lifted my head high, turned my tail toward him and charged into the nearby woods, where I hid in the underbrush.

He stood there for a long time. Then, as if he'd suddenly remembered Bella was with him, he turned back to the truck. "We'd better go."

After they left, I paced through the trees for an eternity while I waited for Bella. What could she be doing? She knew I was waiting and in need of a cup of coffee.

A dull headache pounding in my skull, I moved to a nearby jumble of boulders that looked as if a baby giant had used them for building blocks. At the base was a small crevice. Not a cave, really. It wasn't large enough for that. But it had a stone floor and one rock had fallen on another, leaving an opening just big enough. I squeezed inside and put my aching head against the cool rock to sooth the pain.

And not only would it help my headache, if I fell asleep and shifted back to human form, I'd still be naked. In my stone cubby I wouldn't be as easily spotted as if I were in the open.

I lay there for some time, unable to sleep because of the pain in my brain. After what seemed like hours I scented her, coming through the trees. Inching out of my hole in the rock, I ran to her.

"What took you so long?" I snarled.

She frowned hard at me then whipped off the smock. "Shut up and put this on. I had to lie to Doc and tell him I had an errand in town. And you know how I hate to lie."

Sitting down, I drew into my cool center and tried to think calming thoughts. It wasn't easy when I'd rather tear something or someone to pieces with my teeth than go calm, but I had an appointment with one of Fort Worth's wealthiest matrons.

After several cleansing breaths, I was no longer vertically challenged.

Bella glanced at me, a smile playing around her lips as she helped me into her smock. "All these times I've seen you morph from woman to wolf and back again, and I still am dumbfounded each time you do it."

"At least I don't chase chickens anymore," I answered before she had a chance to torment me with her favorite memory jab. We walked back to her car. "I used to tear off their heads and eat them, feathers and all, just to watch you gag."

"What two-year-old wouldn't?" She chuckled at the memory as we got into her Volvo. "And poor Dad. Grandma Maleva always said she tried to warn him, but he wouldn't listen."

"I have a feeling she didn't use the word werewolf in that conversation." I chuckled, too, as I remembered my favorite grandmother. "There's no telling how people will react."

"I miss her," Bella whispered softly.

"Me, too."

Thirty minutes later, Bella dropped me at the apartment and went back to work while I turned on the shower. Thank goodness I hadn't made the appointment any earlier. As it was, I would have trouble getting to my office on time.

After I swallowed a couple of aspirin, I rushed through my shower. I let my hair out to its full length to hit it with shampoo a couple of times before drawing it back to the most manageable and, at least for me, flattering length.

Trying to make quick work of it, I squirted shower gel directly on my body, then grabbed the hippo-shaped scrubby Bella had put in my stocking last Christmas. I enjoyed the light brushing sensation on my skin until I got to my rear end. As I touched my right buttock, a sharp pain shot through me. I glanced down to see an angry, black bruise on my ass.

I got out of the shower, dripping like a crystal pitcher on a humid, Texas day, and looked in the mirror. The bruise covered most of that cheek, and there was a small scab exactly in the middle.

The realization hurt almost as much as my butt. Someone had shot me with some kind of tranquilizer, and Bella had been too chicken to tell me. Screeching my outrage, I grabbed a towel, wrapped it around myself and marched to the telephone. When her cell went directly to voicemail, I opened the personal phone book we shared and looked for her work number. The hard part was deciphering it. Why hadn't someone told her in the beginning that just because she was a doctor, she didn't have to write like one?

After dialing the number, I tapped my almost dry foot to expend some of the pent up anger. When someone finally answered, it was Doc. His deep, sexy voice almost melted me into the floor. "Clinic."

After a heart-pounding breathless moment, I said, "This is Jazzy Cannis, Bella's sister—"

"Gypsy Dancer?" he teased, his voice a bit softer but every bit as fascinating.

A thousand thoughts darted through my mind. Why was it simple words, even from miles away, could turn a girl on?

I pictured his mouth, full and well defined, and imagined the words coming from them. I loved the way he smiled and laughed, which made me wonder, would his lips be soft, yet warm? Firm and sweet?

I couldn't keep myself from smiling. "Yes, the gypsy dancer. I was trying to reach my sister. It seems her cell is either turned off or she has a dead battery."

"Want to leave a message with me? She's in surgery so she can't talk. "

Brain going numb, just like it did when Bella started speaking vet, I decided to break off. "Sure. Tell her I might be late tonight. I have to meet with the models for the fashion show later this month."

After hanging up, I hurried to get dressed. I had to look good. After all, I had an appointment. But with the way my head pounded, I needed comfort more. So I did a quick makeup job, except on my eyes. There I had to pull a couple of tricks out of my bag to keep the hangover from being obvious. Next I pulled out my Scarlett Johansen ensem. Designed as it was, the body skimming fabric and dip-down-to-there neckline kept people from noticing, without a waistline, it was as comfortable as a bathrobe.

Too bad I couldn't do that with my shoes. For some reason, women who could afford to hire a fashion consultant expected them to have fabulous footwear. Or maybe I was just known for having shoes to die for, but anytime I tried to go easy on my feet, my ladies whined.

Extremely grateful for condo garages so I wouldn't have to go outside, I grabbed my bag, put on my sunglasses and rushed to ours where I slid into my Z4. Starting the car and shifting into gear, I took off for the office.

Although the drive to the high-end mall where I kept my office was, in Texas terms, just around the corner, getting there seemed to take forever. And the line at the drive-thru at Starbucks didn't help matters.

What is it about a hangover that can stretch time?

Naturally, after I chipped a nail in my rush to get the office door unlocked, there was a message on my voicemail, canceling the afternoon appointment.

Irritated enough to bite the furniture, I stormed to the desk and flicked on my laptop so I could check my calendar. Nothing for the entire day until that evening, when I had a meeting with the models for the fashion show.

Since most of my afternoon was open, I decided to do a little reading. Online. When I clicked on the Internet, my browser opened to the *Dallas Morning News*. I read through a story about the party at Safari Land and what a roaring success it had been—apparently that stupid pun was intended. A related story announced a dedication dinner in a few weeks, where Dr. Chase Holliday would be the main speaker.

Then I tried to remember the name of the wolf gene he told Bella he wanted to eradicate and decided to Google it. After spelling it about every possible way, I found it. The Syzygia Gene was the topic of an article about a doctor in South America. From the way it was written, the reporter thought it was a joke, calling the gene that caused lycanthropy mythical.

I stared in disbelief at the screen as realization penetrated my still cloudy brain.

Doc Holliday—a werewolf hunter.

Chapter Two

Anger poured over me, flamed my veins, scorched my lungs and filled my heart with fire. I could hardly breathe, much less think. I was so furious, my nails curved into claws. My muscles tensed with energy as the fury grew. Unable to sit, I prowled the office from my desk past the loveseat and chairs to the door and back, into the next room with its mirrored dressing space, then started over.

Most people didn't realize Lycans actually existed. Now the first man I was truly attracted to in eons, and he wasn't just a werewolf killer. He was a destroyer. Not satisfied to rid the world of them one at a time, he wanted to completely eradicate them.

Throwing myself into my desk chair, I closed my eyes for a moment and thought about the sexy gunslinger from the night before. Taller than me, even in my stilettos, he had to be over six feet tall by several inches. He was smart, easy to be with and, unless I was mistaken, knew how to have a great time.

Damn him!

Unable to sit still a moment longer, I sprang out of my chair, snatched my bag from the desk drawer and stormed out of the office. Maybe a little shopping would make me feel better.

My trip through the mall might not have helped my mood, but it helped the Texas economy. The first stop was at Saks, where I loaded down my Visa, and the next was at Nordstrom's. In the shoe department, I maxed out my American Express and, in bags, my Mastercard. By the time I hustled back to my office for my meeting, I was exhausted.

I'd just put away my bags when the door whooshed open and I was greeted by the high giggle of female voices. The hackles on the back of my neck rose at the sound.

Rather than acknowledge me, the trio of young women kept their heads together and whispered. Shoving my irritation with their rudeness away, I strode toward them, a smile firmly fixed on my lips. "Emily? Hannah? Madison? I'm glad to meet you. I'm Jazzy Cannis."

"We saw the sign." The blonde with very long, straight hair slid a glance at the others, then in a pseudo whisper said, "But I thought it was the door's name."

The giggling started again, so I walked back to my desk and looked at the list on my clipboard. "Which one are you?" I asked the blonde.

She looked away from her friends, her mouth turned downward while she shrugged one shoulder. "Hannah."

I nodded, focusing on the next girl before Hannah could make another stupid joke. "And you?"

The girl next to Hannah looked at the floor, turning her double chin into a quadruple one. "I'm Emily." I couldn't tell if Emily had really narrow eyes or if her cheeks had so much fat on them, they just crowded everything.

"And you must be Madison," I said to the third girl.

She shot me a self-confident smile. "I must be." With a toss of her head, she sent her curtain of shining brown hair sliding behind her shoulders.

At least one of the girls might make it all the way to the end of the runway without getting rug burn.

"All right. I have names on the clothes you'll be wearing, hanging outside the dressing rooms off the next room. I'd like you to try them on."

While two of the girls started to shuffle toward the dressing room, Madison planted her feet and ditched the smile. "What do you mean?"

"What is it you're unclear about?" I shot back.

Madison narrowed her eyes as she lifted her chin. "I thought *we'd* pick out what we're going to wear."

I gave a soft laugh. As if I'd trust a college girl to choose what she'd wear in one of my shows? "No. You can help me decide if what I've chosen fits you well and is flattering to your coloring, but I make the choices."

"What if we don't like them?" the girl with the fat cheeks—Emily—whined.

"Then you don't have to buy them." More than a little irritated, I got out of my chair and walked to the front of my desk. "This event isn't so you can do some extra-curricular shopping. It's so the stores in the mall can get their fashions out for our audience to see. And to be honest, college girls aren't the target clientele for this mall."

Nose wrinkled as if she smelled something bad, Madison raised an eyebrow. "Maybe we should be."

Leaning a hip against my desk, I nodded. "I see. How often do you drive over here to shop?"

"If they had anything I liked, I'd probably shop

here every weekend," Madison said, then shrugged when Hannah gave her a sharp look.

"And how much disposable income do you have?"

"I get an allowance for clothes."

I kept my voice very soft. "The allowance you get is nothing compared to what the average woman who shops in this mall spends."

"How do you know?" Surprisingly, the question came from Hannah, and from the curious look on her face was sincere.

"Because it hasn't been that long since I was in college, with a set of very affluent parents who enjoyed spoiling me and my sister." I thought of telling them about our college graduation presents—my first BMW and my sister's Escalade—but thought better of it. "As much as we'd like to have you as regular shoppers, it's your mothers' business we really want."

Without another word, Hannah turned and went into her designated dressing room. After a moment, Madison did the same, and finally, so did Emily.

As they tried on the clothes, I took notes. Emily had lied about the size she wore and, not surprisingly, nothing fit.

After a very long hour, we were finished. "All right, girls. I'll see you the Friday evening before the show at six. Emily, you be here at five."

"Why do I have to come back early?" Emily asked, her whine becoming more pronounced.

"Because I have to find something in your size." I leaned close and whispered, "Next time, don't lie. It only causes trouble."

The girl gasped. "I didn't—"

"Don't." I held up a hand to cut her off before her

whine did me in.

"So why do we have to come back before the show?" Madison asked.

By that time, I had to dig deep for patience. "To practice on the runway so you'll know where to go and what to do."

Emily and Madison charged out of my office, but Hannah lingered a moment. "I think the practice is a good idea. Some of us might walk onto the runway and get lost."

I chuckled as she left. I could only wish—fervently—that the rest of the models would be more like Hannah and much, much less like the other two. But I didn't have much hope.

I was shocked to see the disaster the girls had left in the dressing rooms. The clothes they'd tried on weren't cheap by anyone's estimation, but no matter the cost, they'd all been thrown on the floor and looked as if they'd been walked on. At least I had a steamer to freshen them up. I spent half an hour picking up ensembles, sportswear and dresses and putting them back on hangers, sorting them between keepers and returns. Next year, no matter how badly the mall owner wanted to use the girls in her old sorority to model for us, I'd have to put my foot down. Professionals were so much easier.

After checking my calendar, I decided to finish up in the morning. I snagged my purse from its drawer, picked up my packages from under the desk, locked the office and headed for the parking lot.

Just as I stepped out the door, lot security pulled up in the official golf cart. Recognizing me, the white haired rent-a-cop offered me a ride to my car. Exactly what I needed after the exhausting night and day I'd had. Giving him my brightest smile, I climbed in. It took only a moment to get to my Z4, which was a good thing since I'd have fallen asleep if it had been much longer.

To be sure I'd stay awake I turned up the radio, rolled down the windows and let the breeze blow through my hair as I drove home.

I parked in the garage, so tired I was almost as giggly as the girls had been. Lack of sleep can do that to me. Thankful it wasn't far to our apartment, I dragged myself out of the car and over to the elevator.

Finally I stood at our door, which I'd painted red right after we moved in, much to the annoyance of the property owners. As I shoved the key in the hole, I remembered it was my night to cook.

I was lousy at it, but no matter how awful my food tasted, Bella wouldn't take over that chore. More than a little disgusted, I dropped my stuff, turned on the oven to preheat, hurried to the freezer and looked for something I could warm up. After pawing through freezer snow for a few moments, a burnt orange package caught my eye. Lasagna! Just what I needed.

Adjusting the oven temperature, I yanked the food out of the box, made a tent out of the metal lid, shoved it in the oven and set the timer. Then I crashed on the couch. So exhausted I didn't even turn on the TV, I dropped into the sleep of the dead until an incessant blaring woke me. I blinked several times, my eyes burning, but I couldn't focus. Finally I realized the room had filled with black smoke.

Understanding gradually filtered into my brain—dinner was on fire. Grabbing a magazine, I fanned at the smoke. When it had cleared enough to see my way into the kitchen, I turned off the alarm. I battled my way to the oven, opened the door and saw the lasagna was blackened beyond reclaiming, but at least it wasn't actually blazing, as I'd half expected.

Using a couple of turkey shaped potholders that Bella had bought in honor of the upcoming season, I took the dish to the sink and dropped it there to cool when I heard Bella's key in the door.

She was chattering before she had the door open. "Jazzy? I brought home a guest for din—" Although I couldn't see her through the fog, the first wave of smoke must have hit her because she stopped talking mid-word to cough.

"Bella, I'm fine," I called out, but apparently she couldn't hear over her fright.

"Jazzy! Where are you? What's on fire?" Just like our mother, her voice grew sharp with distress.

Before I could answer her, a large, very male form materialized in the dense haze. Fireman? I continued to fan as I considered the man, made blurry by the tears filling my eyes. There was no helmet, no center-stripe-yellow coat, no puss-in-boots footwear. He came straight to me, knocking my *Elle* from my hand. "Let's get out of here."

Doc! My heart did a triple beat as he slid an arm around me to guide me through the smoke. I took a breath, intending to tell him I was fine, but the smoke curled in my throat and I had another coughing fit instead.

Soon I found myself outside the apartment with Bella and Doc. After taking several long breaths of delicious, smokeless air, I could finally breathe without hacking like a nicotine addict. I leaned against the wall. "Dinner's ready."

Bella's face gleamed white. "What happened?"

At that moment, my nose started running to match my eyes. I gave a long sniff, so she reached into her purse and pulled out a packet of tissues, which she shoved into my hands. "Now tell me why our apartment looks like the inside of a smoker at a barbecue cook off."

I took my time, drying my eyes and blowing my nose before I tried to answer. When I thought I might be able to talk, my throat was as rough as if I'd been on a howl all night. I almost forgot...I had.

I swallowed hard, cleared my throat, and rasped, "I fell asleep."

"Fell asleep?" She repeated my words as if they were a new concept. "With dinner in the oven, you fell asleep? *Didn't you set the timer?*"

Closing my eyes—as much to shut out her face as to stop their burning—I nodded. "Yeah. I set it, but I must have slept through it."

Bella glanced at Doc, her eyes widening as if she'd forgotten he was there. "My car wouldn't start again, so Doc drove me home. I invited him to stay for dinner."

A vision of the three of us, sitting around the charred remains of the lasagna to dig in, popped into my mind. I tried to control the smile curling my mouth, but the more I tried, the funnier the image became. As I grew more and more tickled, Bella grew redder with anger.

If she'd inherited the werewolf blessing, she'd have gone animal right there.

Before she could find the words to gripe me out,

Doc gave us both an easy smile. "Hey, no harm done. I'll just take you out to dinner."

Bella glowered at me for a few more seconds, then without answering Doc or speaking to me, she turned and started toward the parking garage.

"Hey, Bella?" I called after her.

She stopped and, after a very long moment, turned toward me. "What?"

"Don't forget to lock the door."

We went to dinner at a nearby family restaurant, and were seated at a small round table. While Bella and I both ordered salads, Doc ordered a steak. Rare.

There's nothing on the menu of most restaurants that a werewolf likes better than rare beef, but I'd learned over the years that ordering it bloody would just make me hungry for more. Besides, seeing me tear into one might just make a Lycan hater grow suspicious.

Doc leaned toward Bella, a smile in his gaze. "Have you told Jazzy about the wolf pups?"

He obviously tried to get her to lighten up. She hadn't spoken except to order dinner since I told her to lock the door.

I put a smile on my face and tried to look interested. "The ones born during the Halloween party? Did they all survive?"

She gazed at him for a moment before heaving a sigh—a sure sign she would give in. "Not all of them. It was her first litter, and she slept on one of them. But the other five are fine."

I tried to think of another question. "Are they still in the nursery where you can watch over them?"

She nodded as she tried to retain her angry look. "Yes, they'll stay for two or three more weeks, until they're about ready to wean. But we leave them alone as much as possible, hoping to keep them from imprinting with humans. It is a *wild* animal park."

I chuckled, pretending she hadn't been mad enough to imprint me just an hour earlier. I knew she couldn't stay mad. Not at me. "If you need help feeding them, let me know."

"That would be a first." Bella shot me a bright smile. "You've never been fond of any kind of babies."

Thanks for reminding me. I rarely used our telepathic link because it gave me a grinding headache. Maybe I could use a headache to keep me from enjoying Doc's presence too much, and to help me keep in mind his life goal. I let my gaze drift toward him to make my meaning clear.

No problem. She gave me a miniscule, smug smile. *How's your head?*

When they brought the food, it was all I could do to accept the plate of vegetables while Doc's juicy roast-sized slab of meat put its wonderful smoky scent into the air. Dead vegetables or red meat? It was all I could do to keep from wrestling his plate away from him.

While he slathered his potato with butter and sour cream, I salted and peppered my greens. He reached for a chunk of bread nubby with seeds and herbs, and smelled of honey and heaven. I ignored the cellophane wrapped saltines in the ugly basket between Bella and me.

"Is your steak done enough?" Bella asked, her damned smile still hovering around her lips.

He cut into the beef and watched the red juices run before he stabbed the bite with his fork. "Perfect. Just right."

And it was. Seared on the outside, most of the beef was dark pink and firm. I was practically salivating as I lifted my fork to my lips. The greens were bitter. I picked up my cup of ranch—house dressing of Texas—and drowned my plate with it. If I couldn't have real sustenance, I should at least be able to have some good taste with my meal.

Bella shook her head as she dipped her fork in the dressing, then, with a sweet smile, stabbed the lettuce on her plate and took a bite. As she chewed, she closed her eyes, clearly enjoying the watered down flavor of veggies. The only thing missing from her performance was a heartfelt yummy sound while she rubbed her belly.

She always was Little Goodie Two-Shoes.

Bella and Doc glided into shop talk while I let my brain go numb. Instead of lasagna for dinner, I was stuck with lettuce and critter-speak, and nothing to look forward to but a bed that smelled of smoke. Good thing I didn't keep a journal like Grandma Maleva had because the entry for that night I would have had to write in boring beige.

****

I accepted the script the mall manager handed me and took my place in front of the microphone. Since this was a fund raiser for literacy, I hadn't expected much of a crowd, but I was surprised. The room was filled almost to capacity. Next year the organization would have to think about finding a larger room.

After the show had started and we were into designer separates, a woman made her way down the aisle to sit near the dais. Either she was going to climb up on the platform to help with my narration or the room was even more crowded than I realized.

As I talked about the fashions, tossing in a joke here and there to perk up the script, I found her watching me instead of the clothes. Since she looked well into her sixties, wore a Chanel suit and diamonds the size of my Z4, I wasn't too worried that she was a serial killer. At least I hoped she wasn't.

As I gathered my things to leave after the show, Chanel Suit woman stopped me. "Hello. I'm Beatrice Holliday."

"Holliday? Are you Doc's mother?" I didn't have my hair so short it made me fuzzy, but I couldn't figure it. I'd briefly met Doc a couple of times, and now his mother was checking me out?

Her laughter was almost musical. "Yes, I am. He mentioned having met you, and since I had an invitation to this show, I thought I'd say hello."

That didn't sound good. He hadn't looked like a mama's boy, but looks could be deceiving. "Does Doc still live at home?"

"Oh, yes. All my boys do." Her gray hair was drawn into a neat chignon at the back of her head. "When we built the house a few years ago, we made it like six separate houses that are attached—one for each of the boys, one for Sam and me, and then, of course, one for guests. We call it a wagon wheel. And the hub is a garden area."

"That sounds...interesting." What else could I say?

"It can be. Do you have time for a cup of coffee?" When I nodded, we walked to a small restaurant there in the mall, where we ordered Irish coffees. "Trouble is, as busy as my sons are, I hardly ever hear from them, much less see them. That's why I decided to come tonight. Chase must have been very impressed to call me and just happen to mention you."

How did I answer that? Yeah, he should have been? "My sister is the other vet there at the zoo. That's probably why he mentioned me."

Idly, she turned her cup on the saucer. "No. I understand they've worked together for some time now, and this is the first I've heard about anyone. Human, that is."

Wishing I could be alone to think over her words, I took a sip of my coffee. "He was very nice—what I got to see of him, that is."

"Well, he's one of the nicest of my boys." She picked up her coffee, but didn't drink. "The two youngest are wilder than March hares. They take after their father, while Chase and Spence are more like me."

Oh, goody.

"So tell me, dear. What do you do when you aren't officiating fashion shows?" Finally she sipped her coffee. I was halfway through mine and wishing I could chase it with a shot of Southern Comfort.

"I'm a fashion consultant and personal shopper. And I do a little legwork for buying offices out of New York now and then."

"Turned a vice into a career opportunity?"

I shrugged. "You know what they say. If life gives you lemons, twist mine and drop it in a martini."

I couldn't tell if her laughter was amusement or a sympathy chuckle. I decided to change the subject. "What are your other sons' names?"

"Besides Chase there's Spence, Drew and Mack." She finally took another sip then set her cup down with a *thunk*. "You'll get to meet them at the dedication dinner for Safari Land."

"Dedication dinner?" I thought for a moment, but couldn't recall an invitation. "When is it?"

"Thursday night in the park's multi-purpose building." She quirked a delicately arched eyebrow. "Didn't Bella tell you? She and Chase will both be speaking."

That explained it. Bella hated public speaking, and if she was absolutely forced to do it, she wouldn't want her little sister there. Laughing. "Oh, I'll be there, Mrs. Holliday. I wouldn't miss it for the world."

Mrs. Holliday checked her diamond encrusted watch. "I'd better head for home or Sam will send the hounds after me."

I glanced around for the tab. "It is late. You go ahead, and I'll take care of this."

She gave me a sweet smile then shook her head. "Oh, no, dear. It's my treat."

After she'd left a bill on the table to cover the coffee and tip, I walked with her to the main entrance, where she gave the valet her parking ticket. In just a few moments, a sleek red Mercedes stopped in front of the door. "It's been lovely, Jazzy. I'll look forward to seeing you next Thursday." With a wave of her hand, she slid into the leather seat, slammed the door and drove away.

Across the lot, about fifty miles away, was my car. Wishing my feet would go numb instead of my brain, I took off across the parking area.

When I got home, Bella was in bed, asleep. How could she sleep when I wanted to talk to her? And scold her about the dinner, which I was certain I should have been invited to. After all, I am her sister.

She'd need a new dress to wear, I was sure. Her only gown even close to appropriate was older than dirt. I would see to it she got a new one if I had to drag her shopping. I doubted she'd thought to make an appointment to have her hair done, and while we're there, we might as well have them do our makeup, too.

I tried to ignore the fact that I buzzed all over. I wasn't excited just because I'd get to see Doc again. I'd gone out with doctors before. I'd dated men with more money at their disposal than the United States government.

I'd just never met anyone who I was as anxious to see again. I caught myself as I realized the direction of my thoughts. It had to be the danger he carried with him making me quiver.

****

Chase looked in the mirror and tied his tie for the third time. If he didn't get it right this time, he'd be forced to hike across the garden to get his mother's help. Or Spence's. Why was it he could understand DNA but couldn't tie a bowtie? He should have bought the fake.

He almost winced as he thought of his brother's response if he walked into the room with an easy-does-it tie on. According to Spence, any man who couldn't handle neckwear wasn't any kind of man at all.

Chase thought about the time when they roomed together in college, when Spence had been so pissed with him that he was ready to fight. But rather than skin his knuckles before the formal dance they were both attending, he'd left before helping Chase with his tie.

Each time Chase had tied the bow, it looked as if it

had been knotted by a drunken sailor. He'd tied and untied the strip of fabric until it looked like a shoelace. Finally, he'd opened the collar of his shirt and let the tie dangle. When he'd walked into the ballroom, Spence had worn a superior smile because of Chase's less than stellar appearance. But for some reason, his casual appearance had attracted every girl in the room—including the one with whom Spence had been dancing.

Spence told him later that if he'd just forgotten to shave, he'd probably have gotten laid right there on the ballroom floor.

After checking his shoes to make sure they had a hard gloss, he went out his door and walked across the courtyard to Spence's.

With a light tap, he stepped into the kitchen, which was laid out just like his own. Instead of the utilitarian stainless steel sink, fridge and dishwasher like Chase had chosen, Spence's sink was stone, as were his countertops. The fridge and dishwasher looked like black glass, and his stove/oven unit, which took up much of his counter space, was a professional model. The cabinet doors all had glass fronts, and the cabinets were immaculate. In the middle of the kitchen was an antique butcher block, which had been their great-grandfather's, and above it hung a rack with pots dangling from it that each cost as much as Chase's first car.

From the looks of things, Spence could have been a gourmet chef at an exclusive restaurant rather than the financial officer in the family oil business. Of course, it probably took a truck load of money to finance that kitchen.

Spence stood near the butcher block, a long

stemmed glass of white wine in his hand. "You're the last one."

Chase grinned at his younger sibling. "You mean Drew and Mack beat me?"

"Hell, yeah." Spence grinned. His eyebrows, which were auburn just like his hair, dipped to a shallow frown. "After the way you talked about that gypsy dancer, they hurried on out to the zoo, hoping to cut you off at the pass."

Spence set down his glass, slid Chase's tie a bit to the left then began tying.

Tension caused Chase's gut to harden. "Talked about the gypsy dancer? I don't remember saying much of anything, except that I'd met Bella's sister."

Spence twisted and tugged at the bow, then started doing whatever he did to keep them from looking like pigging strings. "Maybe it's what you didn't say. They were convinced if they rushed on out, they'd have a vision to behold."

"Idiots." Chase glanced at the wine glass Spence had set down. "Got anything to drink besides that Kool-Aid?"

"Not for you." Spence took a step back, checked Chase's tie once more then gave a sharp nod. "Not only are you going to be driving in a few moments, you're speaking, too. I, for one, don't want you in front of a crowd giving away the family secrets."

Chase gave him an easy smile. "Why don't we just tell them that *you're* Chase the vet, and I'm Spence the money man? Then you could make my speech for me."

"You'd probably get more women that way. But as soon as they got close enough to smell the water buffalo spoors on you, they'd know better."

Alarmed, Chase lifted his sleeve to his nose and sniffed. "Is there someth—"

Spence's chuckle relieved him. "Sorry, Bud. Just yanking your chain."

"Damn brothers." Chase scowled, but it didn't affect Spence. "I should 'thank you' for that one."

Spence folded his arms and leaned against the counter. "Don't try to get out of this dinner by starting a fight with me. I'll just drag your butt down there, black eye, split lip and all."

"You boys stop it." Beatrice's high voice cut through the air. "You sound just like you did when you were four and five. Won't you ever grow up?"

"Probably not," Dad answered as he moved close behind her. "What's fun about growing up?"

Their mother's eyes twinkled just before she kissed his cheek. "I can think of a lot of things."

Sam took her hand in his—the habit of a lifetime. Sometimes Chase wondered if they even knew they were holding hands, they did it so automatically. But when Beatrice patted Sam's hand with her free one, he had the answer. They knew.

Beatrice glanced at her two eldest sons. "They clean up fairly well, don't they?"

Their father shrugged, a mischievous look on his face. "As well as can be expected I guess, considering the material at hand."

Beatrice gave him a nudge. "Stop teasing. You'll give them an inferiority complex."

Sam brushed a non-existent wrinkle from his own lapel. "After growing up around a father like me, if they don't have one now, they never will. Besides, you know a Holliday's never felt inferior in his life. Especially these two."

Clearly bored with her husband's rambling, Beatrice turned to the door. "Which car are we taking, dear?"

"How about the Hummer?" After her nod, he glanced at his two sons. "One of you want to drive? We're going to ride in back…where we can snuggle."

When Beatrice swatted Sam's shoulder, Spence chuckled. "I'll drive, Dad. I imagine Chase will need to go over his speech on the way."

After walking to the multi-car garage, they climbed into the Humvee. As they drove toward the park, Beatrice and Sam chatted together in low voices, leaving Spence free to irritate Chase as he drove. "So tell me more about this mystery woman. What's she like?"

Chase shook his head, wishing he'd never mentioned her. "You all are making too big a deal out of a passing remark. She's just a woman, who happens to be the sister of one of my co-workers. Nothing special." Not just a serious misdirection; that was a downright lie. He just hoped he wouldn't get struck dead for it.

Spence gave a sharp laugh. "Nothing special? Right. Must be why you bought a new tux for tonight. Or got your hair cut for the first time in a couple of months."

Chase wished he'd driven by himself. At least he wouldn't have to go through the third degree. "I got a haircut because I *hadn't* had one in a couple of months—"

"You were beginning to look like a shaggy dog," his mother interrupted from the backseat.

"And I bought the tux because my other one was too old."

"Funny you just noticed that after the Halloween party," Spence murmured with a sidelong glance.

"I hadn't thought of it until after the party."

Sam leaned forward and patted Chase's shoulder. "Don't mind them, son. I know it's hard for you."

Chase gritted his teeth. "What do you mean, hard for me?"

Sam shrugged. "I mean you're focused on your job, is all. You don't have time to think about much outside the clinic, or your research."

What else is there? he wanted to ask but thought better of it. No use upsetting his mother by talking about his view on life. He had the feeling his father had harbored the same outlook for most of his existence. Why else would he have spent so much time either working or thinking about working? If Sam had enjoyed living as his two youngest sons did, he would have spent more time doing it rather than increasing his earning capacity.

When they arrived at the park, Spence delivered them to the door of the multi-purpose building then parked the car. As they walked inside, the first person Chase saw was Jazzy, seated at the head table next to Bella. Then he noticed his little brothers, who'd taken the adjacent chairs so the women were bracketed.

Mack had his arm along the back of Jazzy's chair, practically sitting in her lap, while Drew gazed at Bella, looking as if he'd been kicked in the head by an elephant.

Knowing his brothers as he did, Chase realized they weren't above switching place cards in order to sit by the women of their choice.

He'd put up with their tricks all their lives. They'd pushed, finagled, tormented and bullied until they'd always gotten what they wanted. Well, not tonight. It was time he put his foot down.

Stiff with annoyance, he marched past the attendants at the door without a second glance. Approaching the table, he caught a small wave from Bella, but Jazzy didn't even look up from Mack's line of bull. Couldn't she see through his nonsense?

Irritation spiraling, he stormed to the table. Standing behind Mack, Chase doubled his fist and nudged his brother with it—a little harder than he intended. "Move."

Face filled with surprise, Mack jumped to his feet. "Hey, big brother. I was just chatting with—"

"I said move." Chase kept his voice low.

Mack blinked a couple of times then tried, unsuccessfully, to find a smile. "Sure thing, Chase. I was just…" Unable to finish his explanation, Mack rubbed his bruised shoulder a couple of times as he moved away.

While Chase had been focused on Mack, Jazzy must have gotten out of her chair. When he saw her, long and sleek in a shiny red dress with a deep vee neck and a slit up the leg, he forgot how to breathe.

"Hello." Her eyes glistened with unvoiced laughter. Her hair was shades of gold that warmed to not quite chocolate, making her look as if she'd spent her summer playing under the sun. Standing there as she was—so damned feminine and just plain hot—he wasn't sure if he'd be able to speak past the huge boulder blocking his throat.

"Hi," he croaked. "I hope my brother wasn't bothering you too much."

She gazed at him for a moment, her brows raised as if she had trouble understanding his words. "Oh, no. Your brother was doing me a favor. That weird guy from the other night, the one who said he feeds the animals, kept trying to get me to move to his table. Mack sat here with me to keep him away."

He forced himself to stop thinking about the way she looked long enough to remember. "Norman Briderson? Is he here tonight?"

Jazzy glanced pointedly toward the back. Following her direction, he saw Norman, sitting next to a young woman talking earnestly. "Well, he seems occupied for now. If he bothers you again, though, don't hesitate to report him to the zoo administration."

She nodded then looked past him to his parents. He introduced them and, while they chatted for a moment, he checked out the seating arrangements.

His seat was actually on the other side of Bella, where Drew sat. His father's place card sat on the other side of Jazzy. Not bothering to look around, he rearranged the seating to his own satisfaction.

Just let someone say something about it. Anything at all.

Chapter Three

When they were finally all seated, he smiled at Jazzy. "You look gorgeous, Gypsy Dancer."

She smiled, confident. "Not too shabby yourself, Doc. But I miss your holster and six shooter."

The tension that had been growing along his shoulders vanished as he chuckled. "My mother always taught us boys not to take our revolvers to the table."

"Your mother's nice."

He glanced to where his parents were chatting with another couple. "I think so, too. "

Jazzy tossed her head, sending her hair swirling around her shoulders. "We had a nice chat over coffee the other night."

He took a deep breath, trying to catch the fragrance of her hair. Had it been fixed like that at the party? He didn't remember it being that long. Ready for a little hands on—

Her words registered. "You had coffee the other night? With my mother? When?"

"A few nights after the Halloween party." Jazzy's smile broadened. "She came to a fashion show I narrated then invited me out for coffee. I really like her."

Chase slid a glance toward his mother as he held Jazzy's chair for her. How in the world had she known? With a light chuckle, he shook his head. The woman had radar when it came to her children. That was the only answer.

"What?" Jazzy asked as she lifted her gaze to his.

Again he shook his head. "I didn't say that much about you. Any time I go to that type of function, she always asks if I've met any interesting women. I do my best to describe one or two to her so she won't worry about me."

Jazzy's eyes sparkled as she laughed. "And I was the only one you met before you were called away?"

"Yeah." He shrugged, trying not to look like too much of a loser. "I must have gone a little overboard, describing your costume. Or something. I didn't want her to think I was totally oblivious."

He glanced up with a scowl as Mack and Drew all but attacked the chairs directly across from them. "What are you two idiots doing?"

Drew blew him off with a typical laugh while he sat, but Mack planted an elbow on the table, rolled his eyes and leaned toward Jazzy. "He's such an old man—has been since we were kids. If you want, I can move your place card so you're over here, between the two sexy brothers in this family."

Almost before he'd finished speaking, they heard a squawk. Carrie Everson, assistant to Judge Parker, the park administrator, rushed toward them. Wearing a dress that even Chase knew was years out of date, she propped her fists on her hips.

Her brown hair was pulled back by a clamp that sparkled as if it were covered with of every ounce of glitter from a Sunday school craft box. The hard shine of the clamp made her coloring even muddier, and with her hair skinned back, the length of her thin face was more apparent than usual. Her laugh, especially when near the judge, sounded like a neighing horse.

Wildly she flapped her hands in the air. "Have y'all lost your minds?"

What was she talking about?

When no one answered, she rammed her fists to her hips again. "You're not supposed to sit there—the Honorable Dora Hanson is." She bobbed the entire top half of her body toward Drew, whose mouth tightened and eyes widened in an effort not to laugh.

She stretched her already too long neck to look over him at Mack. "And Mrs. Hanson's escort is supposed to sit there."

Then she glanced at Chase's side of the table and her mouth dropped. "You're all messed up. Bella is the only one sitting where she's supposed to. Chase, you should be next to her, and…and…"

Clearly too exasperated for words, she opened and closed her mouth several times. Finally she got a grip then made the mistake of stomping closer to Mack. "Move."

****

I set down my glass of water when a woman started making a huge fuss about seating arrangements. Didn't she know how stupid she looked doing that chicken imitation? And what an ass she was making of herself? After all, we'd paid a hundred dollars a plate to be there, with the possible exception of Dora Hanson and her escort, who were invited guests. What difference did it make where anyone sat?

Mack looked up at the woman and simply answered, "No."

I almost burst my Spanx Power Panties right down

the side.

Everything on the woman's face opened—her eyes, her mouth, even her nostrils flared as far as they could. After a moment she regained control over her facial features, which would have looked better on a Shetland pony.

She started stomping her feet, first one then the other. If she hadn't been dressed like something out of my college fashion history book, I might have been able to keep my amazement hidden. But she had on a full length pastel yellow shirtwaist dress with a self-belt, printed with long cords, keys and locks, and a box pleated skirt. No kidding—a box pleated skirt!

She must have had the turnout heavily starched just that morning, because as she marched, very little moved. Oh, the skirt swung with her, but the pleats barely expanded.

Then Mack did the unthinkable. He caught her by the wrist and tilted her onto his lap.

That's when I lost it. And when I lost it, so did Chase, Bella and the rest of the table—even Dora Hanson, who'd taken a seat across from Doc's parents.

The way the woman sputtered, you'd never have guessed she just been given one of the best seats in the house.

After extricating herself from his lap, she glared at him for a moment. Then seeing someone across the room, she threw her hand into the air and took off in that direction.

I sobered long enough to ask Doc, "Who's that guy, hiding behind the white mustache?"

"That's Judge Parker, administrator here at the zoo. He'll calm Carrie down."

"Judge *Roy* Parker?" I gasped playfully. "The hanging judge?"

With a half grin, he shook his head. "You're thinking of Judge Roy *Bean*, down about Langtry, Texas. Judge Parker was the hanging judge, but he lived in Arkansas and his name was Isaac. "

I thought for a moment. "And what's your judge Parker's first name?"

His grin grew wider. "Judge."

"What are you?" I asked, trying my best to sound sweet, which I *never* am. "Some kind of history buff as well as a veterinarian and geneticist?"

"Are you kidding? I almost failed history in school." He slid down a bit in his chair. "I wondered the same thing you did, so I Googled him."

Charmed by his wit, I had to remind myself he was a werewolf killer. How much did a man have to hate a species to dedicate his entire life to wiping it out? What could have happened to make him hate us so? A fang scarred girlfriend sometime in the past? A brush with one himself?

As if drawn by an invisible thread, Carrie followed the zoo administrator as he moved to the podium. He leaned toward the microphone until it squealed. "I'd like to thank y'all for comin'," he said with a low-country drawl—the type that's usually embellished. "*Your* support is what's gonna make Safari Land a success. And I know it will be."

He turned to the bird dancing woman, and spoke in her ear. Face flaming so red I thought it might explode, Carrie all but flew out of the room.

Judge Parker smiled affably at the crowd. "Just a little mix up there. Carrie will be right back, I'm sure."

Make Me Howl

My mind wandered back to Doc and his research. How close was he to success? I could ask, but if I was too interested, he'd want to know why. He might even decide to do a little one-on-one eradicating. And I wasn't nearly ready to take the taxi to that big shopping mall in the sky.

Judge started to look a little uneasy, standing at the podium without anything to say. The entire room knew the instant he thought of something because his entire face lit up and his mouth dropped open as he sucked in a quiet "ah." "Let me introduce a few notables tonight. At the head table is the honorable Dora Hanson, past governor of the fair state of Texas. Across from her are Doctors Bella Cannis and Chase Holliday, who we're honoring."

He went on around the room, introducing everyone who worked at the zoo. When he spoke, his mustache hid most of his mouth. If it hadn't been for his chin bobbing up and down, I'd have thought it was a ventriloquist/dummy act. His matching eyebrows rose and fell like ocean waves. And when he was momentarily stumped for a name, he drove his hand through his hair, which made it stand on end.

Finally Carrie flew back into the room, skidding to a stop near Judge. He leaned away from the microphone again to tell her something. With her head bowed, she went to the nearest table and started handing out cards.

"Carrie is passing out volunteer cards for those of you who'd like to give more than just your dollars. They should have been at your plate when you got here." He shot a scathing look at Carrie, who ducked her head even lower.

"If you'll look at your card, you'll see there are

several areas where we could really use some help." Then as if people who could afford to pay $100 for a meal couldn't read, he started reading to us. "Docent—those are the people who can be counted on to give our visitors a tour of the facilities."

Duh.

"Primates—monkeys. We can use some help in that area." He looked up then one side of his mustache lifted as he gave us a half smile. "Those little guys can be a real handful."

I expected the room to groan as I did, but most everyone chuckled politely. To keep from throwing something at him, I tapped my fingers on the table until Bella gave me a toe nudge to make me stop.

"Groundskeepers," he continued. "Even though we're a new facility, we already have problems with wild animals breaching our fences. Why, just the other night we had a *wild* wolf that wandered inside our compound. Put quite a scare into some of our people, too."

I shifted in my seat and sent Bella a quick glance, but she gazed into space as if she weren't listening.

Carrie came to our table last. She slapped cards down in front of us as if she were killing fire ants. When she reached past Mack, he ran a hand down her spine. She jerked erect as if she'd been zapped by a cattle prod. Rather than finish handing them out, she released them so they scattered across the table. With a nasty look at Mack, she turned on her heel and stalked back to her table.

The card was exactly as Judge had read it. There was no blank for filling in if you had another idea. So I reached for my bag, which was so tiny I'd had to decide between my lipstick pencil and my lip gloss when I left the house. I did have a miniature pen, thank goodness. After I filled in my name, address and phone number, I wrote the word, OVER across all the volunteer suggestions. On the back I wrote, "Veterinarian Clinic."

Bella took my card before I could hide it from her. As she read, she lifted one eyebrow. "You gave them your office number?" she whispered.

"Well, yeah." I lifted one shoulder in a shrug so she would know how important this was to me. "I keep the answering machine there turned on so I won't miss the call." As if my cell didn't have voicemail.

"Right." Bella knew me too well. "You just didn't want to write down your mobile number where Norman might see it. And use it."

"Do you blame me?" I murmured as I smiled pleasantly at the other people at our table.

Then she turned the card over. "The clinic? You want to help with sick animals?"

With a small frown, I nodded, trying to look as if her question hurt me. Deeply.

"You know there's blood to clean up. And feces. And you have to actually *deal* with the animals. We don't just pet kittens in there."

"I know." Wanting to be sure no one else could hear me, I leaned closer. "But I want to get into Doc's lab. I need to know just how far he's come with his research."

"And you think you can do that while you're volunteering?"

I nodded once. "If they want my help, I'm going where it will do *me* the most good. I'll find out how far Doc is in his research…and I'll see what, exactly, I can do about it."

Bella frowned at me. "I'm not going to let you come in and destroy my career."

I turned, looking her full in the face. "But you'd let him destroy me?"

She blinked hard as if fighting tears. "You know if he'd talk about it, I'd tell you. But he won't. Not a word."

****

I dreaded Bella's talk as much as she had to. But when they brought the mystery meal, she ate hers as if she didn't have a care in the world. Usually when she had a speech to make, she didn't eat for the entire previous week. But tonight she ate, chatting with Doc's brother or staring into space. What was it with her?

Finally they brought the dessert—pecan pie. Although she normally didn't like pecan, she ate the entire piece. It was as if she were another person.

More than a little worried about my twin, I only ate a few of the nuts then shoved my plate away. Finally Doc got up to speak.

As he talked, I admired his blatant good looks and forgot all about my worries. Dark hair, a square jaw and broad shoulders were always a turn on for me, but a man who knew how to choose a tux and actually looked good in it finished me off like a short-on-minutes phone card and a long talk. While he spoke, he must have told a joke, because his eyes sparkled with mischief and everyone in the room chuckled.

That was when he focused on me. I forgot I was supposed to laugh. I may even have forgotten how to smile. It was all I could do to sit in that chair without sliding onto the floor. And talk about the buzz. It started up my spine, jumped to my shoulders and along my arms, and continued through all my bones, running in a stream throughout my entire body.

My first inclination was to drop my mouth open and pant, but I knew better. Instead I squeezed my hands tightly together under the table. I tried counting to get my mind off my body, but I kept losing my place. Every time he glanced my way, the buzz jolted up a notch and I lost the number I had in my head.

Finally his speech ended. During the applause, he looked only at me. Then he walked toward me and I knew in a matter of seconds he'd soon be in the chair next to mine.

I couldn't breathe. The air that was supposed to go into my lungs was suddenly too thick to force inside. My heart pounded while I thought I would die from the lack of oxygen.

Then he was there next to me and I managed to force a wisp of air into my lungs. His father said something to him and his brothers laughed, but the buzz had reached my ears, making it hard for me to understand anyone's words but his.

"Are you okay?" he murmured as he picked up his glass of water.

I nodded. Yeah, I was fine.

"Shh!" Spence hissed at us. "Bella's going to speak. Now maybe we'll hear something interesting."

Doc smirked at him in a brotherly fashion. Spence shook his head then turned to watch Bella while he leaned on his fist, with his middle finger raised slightly above the rest.

Bella smiled brightly. The dress I'd helped her find, a black satin that could have been created for a twenties movie siren, gave her face a glow I hadn't seen before. At least I assumed it was the dress making her sparkle. "I'd like to add my welcome to Safari Land tonight…"

She went directly to vet-speak, which numbed my brain like a shot of Novocain. Every now and then I heard a reference to "research" and "findings" until finally she said, "While we work very hard here, we also know how to play. To prove it, we've brought what we believe to be the best orchestra in Texas to play for you. And singing for us tonight is Dave Dorrell."

The lights quickly dimmed to total darkness, accompanied by a loud gasp from several women and a few men, then at the opposite end of the room a light glowed softly, growing in intensity until we could see the small, twelve-piece orchestra. The music started and immediately swelled. Standing by himself in a puddle of light was a man with an easy smile. "'I get no kick from champagne'…"

Doc's mother got out of her chair. "Oh, Sam. I love that song."

Spence walked quickly to Bella, whispered something to her, and led her onto the dance floor. They were followed by Sam and Beatrice. Mack even corralled Carrie and led her to the dance floor when Doc turned to me. "Did you enjoy the dinner?"

The music was magic. My breasts chafed against my clothing. My body pulsed in time to the hypnotic rhythm. My head was as fuzzy as if I had my hair shortened to a buzz cut. It was all I could do to keep from running my hand inside his jacket and across his chest so I could feel his heart beat against my palm. I wanted to feel his warmth, burning through me. I wanted to—

Oh, no. I was in heat.

It only happened once a year, and for me there was little regularity. But it was enough to kill a girl. With the swiftness of a fourteen-year-old boy, my sexuality turned hyperactive. I was attracted to tall, dominant males—and especially the good looking ones.

To say my body became sensitive to the touch put it mildly. I could feel it when a man looked at me. Knowing I was in trouble, I grabbed a glass of water and took a long drink.

What was I going to do? With a man as attentive and good looking as Doc sitting by me, I was in deep trouble. Just to be brutally honest, he could be the one in trouble. Left to my natural inclination, he *would* be.

The band started playing "The Very Thought of You" with Dave singing in his slightly gravelly voice.

"Come on." Doc pulled me from my chair. I was tempted to wrap my arms around his neck right there next to the table, but I contained myself until we reached the dance floor.

When he put his arm around me with his hand on the small of my back, I slipped so close my breasts pressed against him. Then I glided my left hand up his arm and fitted my right palm against his. He tugged me even closer until my head nestled in the hollow of his shoulder.

Finally I could take a full breath. Apparently he could, too, because he took a deep breath, then after holding it a moment, blew the air out in a rush which tickled the back of my neck.

He put his lips against my forehead and drew another deep breath. I knew he smelled the new fragrance I'd maxed out one of my cards for.

We moved together as if we were one, but I'm not sure my feet grazed the floor. His fiery touch made my body heat shoot higher. How would I ever pull away from this man who made me feel like so much sugar in a warming pan, slowly melting and changing until I was just a puddle of caramel?

By the dazed look on Bella's face, I could tell she had a great time, too. When the band took a break, she was so disappointed she looked like a little girl who'd lost her favorite doll. As it started again, she zoned out to a space where I couldn't reach her, not to wave or smile or even acknowledge I existed.

Doc and I'd danced together several times then Sam cut in. Although I hated to, I couldn't make a fuss when Doc had already taken his mother in his arms, spinning her across the floor. I was extremely leery of dancing with Doc's father, especially in my current state.

Being in heat did strange things to a girl. Parts of my body swelled enough at times that just walking could occasionally be a stimulating affair. So dancing with a man who had mature good looks and sex appeal, like Sam, could be a dangerous proposition.

If I made a pass at Doc's father, it would certainly kill any further relationship between Doc and me. I knew staying as far away as possible from the good looking older man was the best course. But with him standing in the middle of the dance floor, holding out his hand to me, what could I do without looking like an absolute idiot?

Dredging up any bit of resistance I had lurking in my body—and it had to be in the corners of my little toes because everyplace else was filled with hot longing—I stepped into his arms. Luckily, the music switched to a western swing with a tempo fast enough that I wasn't expected to snuggle close to him, as much as I was tempted. He kept me at arm's length as we two-stepped around the room. The length of his legs made it hard for me to keep up with him and soon, I was breathing hard beneath my newly designed heavy-duty undergarment—the offspring of a boa constrictor who mated with Satan.

That's when I started thinking of my total body girdle as a chastity belt. Getting into the garment had been like trying to shove toothpaste back into the tube. First I had to stand with my feet crossed to get the thing started. Then as it stretched a bit and I gained strength, I hauled it farther and farther up, until finally, after blowing out every ounce of air in my lungs, I'd edged it up, over my stomach to my breasts.

To get out of it, I would need the Jaws-of-Life.

Just the idea of trying to pry it off with a man looking on cooled my libido—at least a little. Especially a man as old as Sam. If he tried to help, and had a heart attack from the exertion, no one in Doc's family would ever forgive me.

I almost laughed out loud at the meandering of my mind. As if Doc could forgive me for having his father help me take off my underwear even if he *didn't* die trying?

Finally the music stopped and the floor cleared. The orchestra took an intermission. Time to go home? I looked around for Bella, but she'd disappeared, and so had Spence.

I fled back to the table and grabbed my glass of

water. After a long drink, I noticed Mack had taken the seat next to me where Bella had been. "Can I have the next dance?"

Before I could answer, Drew leaned over his shoulder. "I've got you for the one after that."

"But I'm first," Mack said, sticking his jaw out.

"No." Relief poured through me as Doc sat in his chair, sliding his arm along the back of my chair.

"No?" Mack bristled with Drew backing him all the way. "What do you mean no? And who are you to say? We're aren't asking—"

"I said *no!*" Doc didn't yell, threaten or get out of his chair, but apparently the intensity of his voice made an impression. "She's going to dance with me from now on. Only me. Then I'm going to drive her home."

Who says? I wanted to ask, as I normally would have if anyone played caveman around me, but I was in no shape. In fact, I looked forward to having him drive me home. I only hoped I could make it all the way to my apartment. I just hated backseat sex.

As the music started again, he took me onto the dance floor. I used steel control to keep from kissing him. From tugging his shirt from his trousers so I could run my hands over his back, his chest. I wanted his flesh under my palms. I wanted our bodies pressed together so there was nothing between us.

I wanted to ravage and be ravaged—like the animal I was.

There was something about his touch—even on that dance floor—that I couldn't get enough of. I don't know what it was, maybe just the wolf hormones coursing through me, but I wanted more. Much more. And not just the sexual part.

With a scowl at Doc, Drew and Mack each grabbed a girl and dragged her onto the dance floor. Anytime I looked up, one or both of them were looking in our direction. What was it with these guys? Trying to piss off their big brother or what?

After a while, one song started running into the next. We didn't stop dancing for the rest of the night. And no matter the tempo, Doc kept me close to him, snuggled in and loving it. The only thing that might have been better was to put those offices to the use I'd warned Bella about the night of the Halloween party.

Then Bella stormed into the room—her face blazing, her jaw set and her brows shoved so close together it was hard to tell where one stopped and the other began. She was practically running, and the spark in her eyes made me wonder what Spence had done. Had he grabbed another woman out there in the moonlight or done something equally as heinous? I didn't know, but I knew I was going to find out.

She marched onto the dance floor, took my arm—making me feel like a school girl caught smoking in the bathroom—and without a word to Doc or anyone, pulled me into the night.

****

Bella stopped next to Jazzy's Z4 and, without releasing her twin, held out her hand. The anger boiling through her made her sound sterner than she intended. "Give me the keys. I'm driving."

The look Jazzy flashed was typical. Her smug, I-don't-care-if-it-cripples-the-governor-I'll-do-what-I-want half smile and the lowered eyelids made Bella want to fight. Thank goodness, Jazzy only went into heat once a year.

Why hadn't she remembered? And why hadn't Jazzy said something? It wasn't as if she hadn't realized much earlier what was going on.

Taking her sweet time, Jazzy opened her tiny bag and pulled out the keys, which she held up and let swing between her fingers. "It's my car. I think I should drive."

"Where? Someplace you can go after innocent bystanders? No, thanks." With a quick move, Bella snatched the keys from her sister's hand and pushed the remote to unlock the doors. "Get in."

Jazzy shrugged, turned and strolled to the passenger door, a deliberate sway to her walk.

They had to get home. Now. Bella would decide then what to do.

Once inside the car, she started the engine. "Buckle up."

The belt snapped immediately, followed by the sound of Jazzy's sigh, which was anything but quiet. "Okay, Bella, I'm in heat. I haven't lost my mind."

Slamming the car into gear, Bella pushed the gas pedal so hard the tires squealed. "Why didn't you tell me?"

"That I'm in heat? Why bother, when you already know everything, Doctor." Clearly finished with the conversation, Jazzy turned away to look out the window.

"You always have some kind of warning. I know you do." Her stomach tensed, the anger roiled higher. First Spence, now Jazzy. What was it with the people around her?

"Maybe I didn't want to." Jazzy tipped her head to one side then glanced at her sister. "Maybe I like surprises."

Bella gritted her teeth to keep from screaming. "Maybe you do, but I don't. Not this kind, at least."

Jazzy turned back to the window again then mumbled something.

"What did you say?" Bella shot a sharp glance at her as she stopped at the end of the zoo's private road before steering onto the highway.

"I said maybe you should have been an animal psychiatrist. You think you know *everything* about every creature. If your shingle said you were a shrink, you could prove to the world that you know how their bodies and their minds work."

It was all Bella could do not to snap back at her sister. But a fight wouldn't make her feel better. After what Spence had said, nothing would.

When several minutes had passed, Jazzy opened the console and pulled out her planner. Flicking on a small overhead light, she studied the pages intently before glancing up. "Where are we going this time?"

Home was the obvious answer, but something told Bella there was more. Something she'd overlooked. "What do you mean?"

"I mean—" Jazzy paused dramatically, as if the night hadn't been stressful enough—"we're coming to an eclipse. Have you chosen a place to hide out?"

"You're going to be in heat *during* a blood moon phase?" Bella almost missed their exit as she tried to accept what her sister said. Blood Moon Wildness—as they'd nicknamed it while they were in their teens—was the only time Jazzy couldn't keep herself from going wild. But to have a BMW while she was in heat had never happened before. It could spell disaster. "No wonder you're so…so…"

"So what?" Jazzy was all sweetness. Way too innocent for it to be real.

"So blatant. So out there. So sexual." What she needed was a chastity belt that would fit a wolf.

Jazzy stroked one red nail along her jaw, then tucked it between her teeth. "Yeah," she breathed.

"Stop it!" Bella all but shouted.

With a small smile, Jazzy lowered her chin as she focused on Bella. "Stop what?"

The rigidness had moved from Bella's stomach to her jaw, making it difficult to speak. "I know how your mind works. I know what you *think* you want to do."

"Do you?" Jazzy lifted an eyebrow.

"I've been through it enough times. I should." Bella turned onto the street to their apartment.

"And how are you going to handle it this time?"

"I'm going to keep you busy tonight. Packing."

****

Waves of helplessness crashed over Chase as Bella towed Jazzy away from him. Grabbing the back of a chair, he gripped it to keep from running after her. It wasn't as if he couldn't have held onto her, wrenched her away from her sister. But the look on Bella's face was one he'd seldom seen, and when he did, he knew it meant something. He had enough respect for his colleague to let them both go—but later he would ask her what set her tail on fire.

Shaking his head, he found his way back to the table where his brothers and parents soon gathered. Sam gazed at him for a moment, then asked, "Ready to head home, son?"

Chase nodded then shrugged. Why go home? Why

stay?

Why did he suddenly feel so empty?

During the long ride home in the back of the Hummer, he tried to keep his mind off Jazzy.

The evening was darker than most, even with the moon practically at its fullest. Heavy clouds surrounded it, throwing them into darkness as they drove through the night. Toward home.

How was it that a place meant to be filled with welcome and warmth, even with his entire family nearby, just looked bleak? Maybe he needed to have a decorator in to give his quarters whatever it was missing—add a fireplace, some quilts.

He had to stop. He sounded like a girl, whining.

Maybe Spence could help him hire someone.

The long weekend stretched before him, and he was stuck in that colorless shell of a house. No, he wouldn't stay there. He'd head for the lab and do some work, something good, even if only for future generations.

The thought of work gave him a measure of relief. At least while working, he couldn't think about Jazzy. The way she'd danced with him had been almost more than he could handle. She'd snuggled into his arms as if she'd found home, her body moving against his as if she belonged exactly there.

Could they make a go of a relationship? Not a short term one, but one like his parents' that would last forever? He shoved down the need to laugh. Him, make a relationship work? Not if his past was any indicator.

But there was something…different about Jazzy. Something he couldn't quite put his finger on.

Chase stayed in the car while Sam got out, circling

it to open Beatrice's door. She glanced over her shoulder at her grown sons. "I baked apple dumplings today. Would you boys like to come in for a bite?"

"We'll be there in just a moment, Mom," Spence answered with a nod. He turned to Chase. "All right, big brother. Time for coffee and a cold shower."

Chapter Four

Chase glared at Spence. "What are you talking about?"

"I'm talking about Jazzy." Spence's voice was easy, as if he hadn't heard Chase's tone. "Yeah, she was nice. Yeah, she could have been some fun. But she's gone now, and you have a life to live."

"It's not as if she lives on another planet. I'll see her again."

Light jabbed Chase's eyes as Spence opened his door. "Then stop acting like she's gone forever and come on."

Getting out of the car, Chase walked shoulder to shoulder with his brother until the idiot again opened his mouth. "Besides, I have a feeling Jazzy's a wild one."

Knowing their mother was nearby, Chase couldn't bloody his brother. At least not immediately. "Why would you say a thing like that?"

"Didn't you see the way the men all wanted to dance with her?" Spence shrugged as he opened the front door. "She had some kind of vibes going out, and they were picked up by every guy in the place."

Heat seared his skin. Who did Spence think he was to speak of Jazzy that way? Chase spoke through gritted teeth. "Those damned brothers of ours, and probably the rest of those men, don't have sense enough to pour piss out of a boot before they put it on, much less act like well brought up human beings. How's that Jazzy's fault?"

As if he hadn't heard, Spence strode into the house.

"Get in here, son, and shut the door." Sam motioned to Chase from the kitchen.

"I've got coffee on," Beatrice added as Chase walked through the door, then patted Sam's shoulder. "Decaffeinated—so your father will be able to sleep tonight."

Sam grimaced then grinned at Chase. "I hate unleaded, but I do like a good night's sleep."

Spence came out of the bathroom with his jacket over his shoulder and his sleeves rolled up. "With apple dumplings swimming in ice cream, you'll never even taste the coffee, Dad."

Chase took off his jacket and laid it across the back of a chair, then accepted the dessert and coffee from his mother. Moving to the kitchen bar, he set his plate on the counter and slid onto a stool.

Cutting into the flaky crust, he took the first bite. Tart apple combined with cinnamon for mouthwatering sweetness. As he sipped from the steaming mug, he finally relaxed the muscles tensing his shoulders. But try as he might, he couldn't get the image of Jazzy out of his mind.

****

I lay across the couch as Bella rushed around the apartment, pulling out suitcases. Did she really think leaving town would make the incredible heat sizzling through my body go away? It was as if I'd traded in my blood for an infusion of caramel macchiato—hot, sweet and topped with creamy lusciousness. It made my toes sweat and gave the rest of me an interesting tingle. Well, I had news for my big sis. I didn't want to lose it.

"Are you going to pack? Or would you rather buy all new clothes while we're away?" Bella's words sounded like yips from a small dog.

"Are you going to tell me where we're going?" Just to irritate her, I picked up an emery board and smoothed a tiny nick on the nail of my right index finger. "I can't pack if I don't know—"

"Snowstorm!" Bella tossed a handful of underwear into her bag. "We're going to the spa at Snowstorm. It's the ski resort with the highest elevation in Colorado, so there's sure to be snow, even if they have to manufacture it. You can ski until you're too exhausted to do anything else. And we'll have healthy meals, massages, facials, anything that'll make us feel..."

"Human?" When she hesitated, I couldn't keep from tossing out a word guaranteed to make her feel guilty. Sometimes it was as if my problems were harder on Bella than on me.

But this time Bella didn't care. "Human...normal... Call it what you want, but we're going to be gone until *you* are back. Now pack, because we're leaving tomorrow."

A few hours later, we were on our way to Denver. The flight was uneventful—all right, it was *boring*. As usual, the airport teemed with people. As if she were afraid I'd escape, Bella glued herself to my side while we shoved our way through the swarm of travelers. At the first rental desk, she made arrangements for a car.

Her entire body shivered by the time we got to the courtesy van, which would take us to pick up the car.

"You shouldn't have packed your coat." I gave her

a sweet smile.

She practically snarled as she climbed inside. "And wrestle it the entire time we were on that plane?"

"At least you wouldn't be cold now." I shook my hair back from my face—a gesture she hates—and shrugged.

The fact that I wasn't cold simply because I was in heat infuriated her. It was as if she could forgive the fact that often, I didn't have human skin, teeth and senses but instead had a pelt and fangs, but couldn't forgive the fact that the animal hormones raging through my system kept me well warmed.

And I couldn't help reminding her of it.

When we'd gone through the line and filled out the papers, I was ready to move. Too much sitting always made me hyper. "I'll drive," I said, holding out my hand for the keys.

Bella gave me a hard look. "I'll drive. No telling where you'd take us, given the chance."

We waited near a glass wall as a young man brought our vehicle. A new Hummer H3, pure white. "Did you get white for camouflage? So we can hide in the snow?"

"I leased the Hummer because I wanted to be sure we'd have four-wheel drive and wouldn't get stuck in the snow. The rental company chose the color."

She set the course on the Global Positioning System and pulled out of the lot. Thank God for GPS, because normally Bella can't find her way around the Metroplex, much less through a different state filled with mountains. And snow.

Once we were on the highway, through Denver and heading west, we picked up some speed. The road signs flashed past faster and faster. Hit with a deep yearning to feel the fresh wind on my face, I rolled down the window.

The temperature had cooled considerably since we'd exited the plane. My ears numbed almost immediately, but who cared? I had air in my face and flowing through my hair. Exhilarating freedom filled me, spiking my spirits. I was almost as free as if I were flying.

"No." Bella's gruff bark plummeted me back to earth.

Jerking around, I glared at her. "Why—"

Before I could finish my question, she'd rolled up my window and turned on the child locks.

I couldn't believe my sister. Usually very malleable, since she'd realized I was under the effect of a Blood Moon *and* in heat, she'd turned into a real dictator.

It was difficult to blame her for being so worried since I'd never before gone through both afflictions at the same time. All I'd experienced was one malady at a time, and that was bad enough!

Reaching in my bag, I pulled out my planner, which showed the lunar phases. I hadn't read it wrong. We were coming to the time when the moon's influence over me would be strongest—the phase of an eclipse.

Being filled with Blood Moon energy was tantamount to putting too much helium in a balloon. The pressure grew more and more as we drove that day, making me want to jet into the sky, zoom along the ground, ricochet around a room, anything to expend some of it. My laugh grew loud, my ideas outlandish and my words something like a machine gun set on rapid fire.

By the time we arrived at Snowstorm, I could barely sit still. While Bella checked us in, I strolled—if you can call speed walking on well-packed snow a stroll—around the grounds. We'd been there before, back when I was a teen, but the spa had changed immensely. From the looks of things, mainly the rich and famous spent time there these days.

A heated pool and Jacuzzi steamed outside, and there was another, warmer, glass enclosed pool nearby. A gigantic greenhouse, built in the shape of a Victorian mansion and filled with plants, sat at the edge of the property. New buildings had sprouted everywhere, but they all looked as though they'd been there since about the time the mountains were born. Nothing new, garish or shiny about them.

At the back of the lodge where we'd be staying were the ski slopes. We could literally walk out the backdoor, put on skis and whiz off for the day.

Getting back when we were finished was almost that easy. A chairlift to the top of the mountain, and from there it was simple to ski back to the lodge. Or if a skier was too tired or inexperienced to take the more difficult slopes from the top, a shuttle could bring them.

I waited in the car when Bella got back patting my foot in annoyance by the time she started it. "Did they have our reservation?"

"Yes." When I shifted into blasting-words-mode, why did she speak in slo-mo?

"Full living room? Two bedrooms? Shower or tub?" Rat-a-tat tat.

"Full living room, big screen TV, shower and Jacuzzi tub. But I asked for a one bedroom, two queens." I could have climbed Mount Everest in the time it took her to finish.

"One? One bedroom?" I screeched. "That's ridiculous! Why would you ask for one bedroom? You knew I'd want time alone."

Not only were her words slow, so was her smile and the light that shifted to brighten her eyes. "Of course I knew you'd want privacy, and that's exactly why I got one bedroom. To protect you from…that."

Anger exploded in my chest, leaving a prickle of something on my skin. Sweat or bristle, I wasn't sure. "Who do you think you are? My keeper? My trainer? Did you bring a leash and a muzzle, too?"

Somewhere in a detached part of my mind, I noticed the sun drifting toward the western horizon, turning the snow a delicate shade of apricot while the sky darkened from blue to purple. In just minutes, the apricot would become a dramatic shade of peach, then flame to burnt orange while the sky would shift to indigo.

That's about the time my private chorus began to hum. Inaudible to anyone but me, it sounded as if the Mormon Tabernacle Choir gathered around me, singing a chord. In a moment, a single member of the bass section would slide into discord. In the balance of the music, it wasn't much, but it would be enough to raise my hackles.

Literally.

Bella put the car in park.

"Let's get unloaded. Fast." I shoved open the door and rushed to the back to grab our bags. Not bothering to wait for her, I snatched the suitcases, slammed the door with a hipshot and headed for the entrance.

Bella hurried to catch up. "Let me take something."

"Just get the doors." I marched on, trying to expend a bit of my scorching energy.

Bella scurried ahead, barely getting the door open before I swung through.

I gave the lobby a swift glance. Opulence everywhere—crystal chandeliers, golden oak floors, plush furniture, fireplaces and lots of brass. "Which floor?"

"This one. Room 111."

I gave a growl of acceptance, low and deep. One, one, one. The only one. I was alone. Oh, there'd been others. My maternal grandmother, for instance. And probably her grandmother. But for now, I was the only. Lost in a world of snow.

And growing very, very hungry.

By the time we were in the room, the fur was shoving its way through my skin. Knowing how horrified Bella became during my transformations, I excused myself as if I were going to the bathroom, which was off the bedroom. As I walked into the room, I saw my salvation. A door to the outside world.

Hoping Bella wouldn't enter anytime soon, I luxuriated in my change. Strength turned my muscles to steel. No longer did the energy surging through me hurt as if I were an overfilled beach ball. Now it belonged inside me. It made me powerful.

Before I had no choice but to drop to all fours, I opened that door then let the effect of the rising moon take me.

Exhilarated, I raised my face in adulation. With a long howl for Bella, I bounded into the night.

****

Make Me Howl

Darkness encompassed me. As if the night were made of rich satin, I savored that absence of light...until something started making a horrific noise. Very heavy and slightly off balance, my head was as hard to lift as if someone had filled it with quicksilver.

The noise came again, someone hammering in the next room. I opened one eye. Through a red haze, I realized I wasn't at home. After a moment I remembered where I was. And why.

I glanced at the other bed in the room. Empty. And Bella, the good little nun, had even made it. When the knocking grew louder, I yanked back the sheet and lunged to my feet. Just in time I saw my nakedness. Ripping the sheet from the mattress, I tucked it around me, stormed out of the bedroom to the living room, ready to give Bella a piece of my mind for not keeping things quiet.

No Bella. And with the kitchen adjacent, I could easily see it was empty, too. Even the coffee pot was empty.

Again, someone knocked. I gritted my teeth to keep from screaming and jerked the door open.

There in the hallway stood a woman, about fifty years old, judging by her hair color, with very red eyes and a soggy tissue. "I'm sorry to bother you, but I'm looking for my Bijou."

"Your what?" I briefly wondered if this was a joke, but another glance at the woman, shaped like an Easter egg with legs, and I knew she was deadly serious.

"My Bijou. She's a Maltese." I must have looked blank, because she kept explaining. "A dog, about this tall, all white. My husband says she looks like a dust mop without a handle."

As she talked, her voice tightened, rising so high, I thought *she* was going to howl. Tears filled her eyes then poured down her cheeks. "I can't find her anywhere."

Unnecessarily, I looked at my feet and behind me. "No Bijous in here."

The woman nodded then sucked a tear-filled breath. "No, I know. But your sister said you were out late last night, and I thought maybe you'd seen her then."

A heavy weight settled in my stomach. I tried to remember, but drew a blank. Had I seen the pooch? I could only hope I hadn't, because what a wolf could do to a squeaky lap dog wasn't pretty.

I swallowed hard as I shook my head. "N-not that I remember. But you might check outside, behind the spa. Maybe she slipped on a steep slope and couldn't get back."

Her face brightened. "Good idea. I looked out front, but didn't think about the slopes, since I don't use them."

With a quick pat on my bare shoulder, she rushed away. I shut the door and headed for the shower. When I was finished and wrapped in two towels, one for my hair and one for my body, I wandered back to the bedroom to dig through my suitcase for something to wear.

I was certain Bella had unpacked the night before—as usual—but I hated unpacking and repacking after just a few days. When I'd found the jeans and sweater I wanted, I slipped into my underwear then put on my clothes. Facing the mirror, I quickly wove my hair into a French braid.

Bella walked into the condo with a man, wearing a tool belt, following her. She gave me a long glance. After a moment, she pointed at the door to the outside. "Right there is where I want the deadbolt. And I'll take the key."

Without even glancing at me, the man nodded, handed her the key and went to work. I wondered what she'd said to keep him from at least looking my way then remembered where we were. At a spa, filled with women year around, most of whom were rich and famous, he'd probably had to learn how to focus and stay on task no matter what.

Sitting on Bella's perfect bed, I pulled on my shoes. Just to be sisterly, I messed up the quilt a little when I stood.

The workman swung the door open to do something to the outside. Bella folded her arms to ward off the icy air coming in, but I stepped closer. I couldn't get enough of the frigid temperatures.

Picking up an electric tool, the man turned it on and shoved it against the door to cut a perfectly round hole. The warm smell of sawdust filled the air as the high whine of the tool hurt my ears. Thankfully, it didn't last long. Turning it off, he laid it aside and had just reached for the lock when a scream pierced the solitude.

The workman startled, looking around to see if Bella or I had shrieked. But the screech had come from outside. I dodged past him and out the door.

Only a few feet away, the Easter egg woman knelt in the snow. And in front of her was a puddle of frozen blood where it had melted into the snow. Just the right size to be from a little dog.

A mountain of guilt filled me, making my body so heavy, my muscles couldn't carry me. With an evil glance, Bella rushed past. But what could I do? Tell the woman I'd probably done that to her Bijou? Apologize for something I didn't remember?

Bella helped the woman to her feet and back into the lodge. I trailed along, wishing I knew what to say. Helplessness rode me. I wished I could break something, get angry, do anything to ward off this underlying weakness.

As they passed me, I heard the woman sob, "If only she'd had puppies, I'd have something to remember her by."

Careful not to bang into the workman, Bella glanced back at me when she took the woman into the building. "Come inside. We have a class."

Who cares? I wanted to roar, but thought better of it. "What kind of class?"

She stared at me for a moment before answering. "They can't start our spa treatments until tomorrow, so I booked us for knitting classes today."

"Knitting?" I yelped. If I'd tried for a year, I could think of *nothing* more boring than knitting. Old ladies and people without a life knit. "No way."

She pulled several tissues from a box and handed them to the woman while she glared at me. "And why not?"

"I don't think I'm old enough to knit. You have to be a hundred and fifty, or at least act like it, don't you?"

That drew a small smile from Bijou's owner, but a deeper frown from Bella.

"Everyone knits these days. I planned to make Bijou a maternity sweater as soon as I knew she was pregnant. I spent a fortune, and sh-she was part of a test group, taking a new drug, Clomovidine, because she was having so much trouble." The woman hiccoughed as the tears flowed. "Oh, how rude. I didn't even introduce myself. I'm Jayne Lafferty, from South Bend."

Bella had to dig deep to find a smile. "I'm Bella Cannis and this is my sister, Jazzy."

"It's nice to meet you." Jayne blew her nose then looked at me again. "As I was saying, *everyone* knits these days. Even famous people knit—Julia Robins and Camera Ditzedge. Even Rooster Crowe knits."

I was careful to keep from smiling while she mispronounced the names. If I smiled even a little, I'd laugh myself into a coma. Rooster Crowe?

Bella glanced at her watch. "Are you going to be okay, Jayne?"

With a long sniff, Jayne nodded. "Yes, I think so."

"Well, don't give up hope. You don't know that blood belonged to Bijou. It could have been a wild animal or something." Bella tried to comfort both Jayne and me.

Jayne looked thoughtful for a few moments. "You're right. Maybe someone will find her and bring her home. I'm going to keep looking for my baby so I'll have to miss that spinning class. Are you taking it?"

Bella nodded. "We both are."

Jayne swiped at her eyes one more time then tossed the tissues in the trash. "I'll have to wait for the next one. I couldn't concentrate with Bijou lost in the cold."

Bella told the workman we were leaving then tugged me out the door. "We don't want to be late for our spinning class."

"You mean spinning, as on stationary bikes?" I could only hope.

"No." Bella's smile just kept growing more evil. "I mean as in yarn. First you have a basic knitting class then we'll spin."

"Just like a spider," I murmured under my breath.

Bella gave me a pointed glance. "Exactly."

The knitting class wasn't too hard after I learned the rhymes. *In through the front door, around the back, out through the window, and off jumps jack.* Easy. And to be honest, once I got started, the easy rhythm of stitching relaxed me. But I'd never admit that to Bella.

Next they taught us to purl, or tried to. It's like trying to pat your head, rub your stomach and dance the *Merengúe* at the same time, at least to me. Even the little poem didn't help. *Under the fence, catch the sheep, back we come, off we leap.* What sense did that make?

I knotted my perfect yarn into a snarled nest that looked as if it had been made by a bird on crack. After I threw my ball across the room twice, the instructor suggested that for the time being, I stick with the garter stitch—knitting only.

Then came spinning. I honestly thought I'd nap through it when they gave me a hand held spinner. But then I had a turn at the big spinning wheel, and I found bliss. In just a few minutes I was able to even out the speed of the wheel while I stranded exact amounts of wool between my fingers. I loved being in control!

I took to it so naturally, they stopped trying to make me take turns with the big wheel and let me work to my heart's content. By the end of class, I had a ball of near perfect yarn and blurry vision.

And I'd earned a small smile from Bella. "We don't have another class scheduled for a while. Why don't we get our coats, go outside and take a stroll?"

Back in our condo, she got her jacket, hat and gloves, then using her key, unlocked the outside door. We walked to the patch of bloody snow. Her face grew very serious. "Do you think you did it?"

Guilt filled me as I shrugged. "How do I know? I don't remember anything after I left the room last night until I heard Jayne pounding on the door this morning."

"Something Jayne said has been nagging at me." Bella kept her head down, but shot a glance at me. She didn't do secretive very well.

Figuring she was just trying to make me curious, I adopted a bored look then shrugged. "What?"

"About Bijou being in a test group, trying to get her pregnant." She took a breath and paused a moment. "I need to find out what it could do to you. You could be affected if that blood puddle is from Bijou, and you're the, uh, perpetrator."

I focused on the last word. "Perpetrator? Don't you mean executioner? Violator of the helpless? *Rabid wolf?*" Anger flaming through me caused my jaw to ache as though I were about to transform. All I needed was to morph right there in plain view of everyone. Bella would never survive the trauma.

Taking a cleansing breath, I bowed my head to ease the muscles tensing in my neck. "Sorry."

"No, it's my fault." Bella's eyes brimmed with sympathy. "I shouldn't have said it like that. It's just that I'm worried. About you. I don't know what effect Clomovidine would have on your body."

"On my…" I thought for a moment then shook my

head. "Why would drugs a dog that small was given have an effect on me?"

"Well, only if you ingested some of the dog's flesh. And because it's so new, just in the testing stages, I don't know how long it stays in the body. Since we don't know when Jayne gave Bijou the last dose, there's no way of knowing if it had been digested yet. Jazzy, I don't know what it might do to you."

I gulped a lungful of icy air, but it did little to cool the heat raging inside me. Damn dog. Damn BMW. And *damn* being in heat! "So what do we do?"

"First I have to find out what the effects will be." With a sudden movement, she turned and started back toward the lodge.

I ran along behind her. "How? Your books are at home. Can you find it online? Do they have that kind of information on the Internet?"

Her brow furrowed into what looked as if it could become a permanent frown. "Leave that to me."

****

I stayed on the slopes all the next day. Skiing off the lift that afternoon, I blinked hard when a snowflake hit me right in the eye. Most people wear goggles to keep that from happening, but it's too much like seeing the world through a window while someone else skis. Besides, who wants to ski in an artificially-colored world?

I edged to a stop at the head of the run, checked to be sure no beginners had wandered onto the expert slope then turned my skis downhill. No way was I going to traverse today. I had to drain some of the energy slamming through me, so I put my skis together, aimed the tips at the bottom and took off on a deadman's-run.

At first the going was fast and smooth with the air freezing my nose and ears and chilling my lungs. Then I came to a field of moguls—those exciting miniature mountains planted in the middle of a run to give inexperienced or occasional skiers fits. Although most people believe the easiest and safest way to navigate moguls is to curl around each one, I like to go over the top. It's a rough ride, but the revenge I get from taking a bit off the height is exhilarating.

By the time I'd made it through that mine field, my heart pounded like a timpani. So naturally, I tucked my poles under my arms, flexed my knees and made some real speed.

In the middle of a growth of trees, used as a divider between adjacent runs, several young men were forging a trail. At the end, they cut onto the far slope, where they took a huge jump. Very few of them landed without taking a spill. I couldn't wait to get to the bottom and jump on a lift back to the top so I could try it.

I rarely skied the trees after some of the tragic accidents I'd read about over the years, but this trip, I was going to.

As I edged to a stop at the bottom, I caught a slightly familiar scent on the breeze, but when I turned to find the source, it disappeared. Unable to let it go, I looked the other way, sniffing the air as I did. I picked up the odor of cedar wood smoke, frying hamburgers, hot ski wax, a doobie bogarted by some boarder and the oil used to keep the lifts mobile, but I couldn't find that enticing original smell. Brightly clad skiers were everywhere, some dressed as if on an Arctic expedition and others in shirtsleeves, but I saw no one who looked familiar.

Forcing the lingering memory of the aroma from my mind, I got in line and back on the lift.

I tried to take my mind from the odor by remembering Bella's fright the evening before when she realized I might have attacked Jayne's little dog. She'd done everything but shovel up some of the bloody snow and take it for analysis. She'd borrowed a laptop and been on it and the phone for hours, trying to find out what might happen to me.

Later that night she'd finally given up. We went to the big room with several other women and sat in front of the fireplace. The staff manicurists were doing their thing for us and several other women when a beaming Jayne came in, carrying something wrapped in a cashmere throw. She'd grinned from ear to ear then set it free on the floor. The puff of white had four legs, curly white hair and looked like a miniature sheep.

But Jayne must have thought it looked like heaven, because she made a dramatic introduction. "This…is Bijou!"

At first Bella paled, then she sagged back in her chair—with relief, I suppose. Who knew my sis had been so worried?

"Wh-where was she?" Bella had asked as the little white fluff made a circuit of the room, sniffing at each person.

"You'll never believe it," Jayne answered with a flap of her hand as she took a seat across from us. "Somehow she got into that sweet greenhouse that looks like Grandma's home. She's so curious. And when the workers left, they didn't notice she was there."

The other women in the room murmured their congratulations, but it was all I could do not to nudge the little troublemaker with my newly painted toes.

The creature growled at me. Jayne had the audacity to say it was Bijou's way of telling me she liked me, but I knew better. It was simply one bitch, meeting another.

As the top of the mountain approached, I lifted the safety bar and exited the lift. Before I turned my skis downhill, I stopped to look across the countryside. Pine trees, blanketed with snow, crowned the mountains. I wished I'd taken time to pick up a camera before I started out that afternoon.

As I started down the slope, that elusive odor came to me on the wind. Briefly I closed my eyes, trying to catch enough of it to remember, but I had no luck.

Then I came to the tree path. A little limited at this new experience, I did a quick turn and skied up a small rise in the first cluster of pines. The going wasn't bad until I got to the steep decline. With such a narrow trail, there was little slowing once I was moving.

The thrill of danger flashed through me. I leaned into my skis, picking up more speed before I was forced in another direction.

I knew better than to let my speed get out of hand, but the sun drifted low and much of my human sense was going with it. I zoomed along until I almost flew. The challenge of possible death flashing through me acted like a drug. I wanted more.

A hazardous turn came out of nowhere, catching me off guard. The path made a sudden ninety-degree angle, but at the speed I was traveling, there was no time to navigate it. In front of me the world dropped away. Treacherous boulders loomed below.

At the last possible second before I crashed over the precipice, something dark flew at me, knocking me off my skis. I hit the ground prone, skidding in an uncontrolled spiral until I finally stopped. Snow piled up around me. My arms were fully extended, stretching down slope, my legs up. My face was buried as if I were having an icy facial.

It took me a moment to realize what had happened. The buzz still jolted through me. I wanted to do it again, if I could only get my muscles to synchronize.

When I could finally lift my head, the white stuff blinded me, but the familiar odor was back, stronger than ever.

Before I could clear my eyes, I recognized the scent.

Doc.

Even filled with snow, my mouth went dry. It *couldn't* be him. We'd left him back in Texas. Knowing what I did to unsuspecting men when I went into heat, Bella had intentionally kept our destination a secret to keep him from following us.

I took another deep breath, which had me melting with desire from the inside out. Even as highly developed as my olfactory senses were—especially at that time—I still had to see him to believe it. I scrubbed at my eyes.

There he was; deep-ocean eyes filled with concern as he knelt next to me. I watched his mouth move as he spoke, but the choir had started humming again. I couldn't hear anything except the pounding of my heart above the harmony.

His hands spoke volumes as he brushed away the snow. While he helped me sit, I struggled to force air into my lungs.

Then he kissed me. Or maybe I kissed him, I'm not exactly sure. But we came together in an almost violent embrace, his hand tangled in my hair, my tongue tangled in his mouth.

Thankfully, I wore only a sweater with my ski pants, not layers of ski suit, underwear, a coat and wool.

We were alone, deep in the woods.

And the chairlifts had stopped for the night.

Chapter Five

I've never before thought of something cold, white and icy as sensual, but that late afternoon, I found out differently. Almost before I knew it, we were turning the white stuff into slush. In a tiny corner of my mind, I hoped Doc was as impervious to the cold temperatures as I. I'm not sure I could have stopped even if I'd seen him turning blue.

Thankfully, azure wasn't his color that day. His heat seared me like a brand wherever he touched. And in turn, I wanted to caress every part of him. Taste him all over.

There wasn't time for tender lovemaking. Purpling shadows lengthened, stealing our time even as we came together. In sheer moments the full moon would rise, and I'd be lost.

With the intensity of my arousal—and the fact that he was sex-on-the-hoof—it was next to impossible for me to stay in control. But I had to remain human. The last thing I wanted was for Doc to realize I was a werewolf. We moved together in a natural rhythm, that single thought thrumming in the back of my mind—*he can't know. He can't find out. If he does, he'll lock me up in his lab.*

Under most circumstances that might be a kinky thought, but knowing I'd just be an object for study, and any prodding done would only be to further science, I wanted none of it.

In a lab anyway.

He arched away from me, sucking his breath through clenched teeth as the edge of the full moon peeked over the horizon. I couldn't let him finish without me. No way I'd survive the maelstrom if I were left unfulfilled.

Unable to stop, I took command of the situation. I rose over him to touch and taste and feel even more of him as I moved. Very quickly the explosion building inside me became too much to contain. As his climax overtook him, mine detonated, nearly wrenching a howl from my throat.

Exhausted, I collapsed on his chest. After a moment, I could lift my head. The cold bit along my breast and stomach as I cast a quick glance at the sky. As much as I hated to, I had to get away from him. In mere seconds I'd go animal. Roughly I shoved all thoughts of afterglow away. I had to escape. Now.

The moon rose higher on the horizon. Inside me, stirrings reinforced the fact that I was about to morph.

Just as I was ready to slip down slope behind a tree, he rose and caught me by the wrist. "Wait."

Bristles stung as they charged my skin, ready to break through. My jaw ached as I fought to hold back its lengthening. My heart took on a slower, heavier rhythm. I glanced at the sky. Any moment now the moon would be free of the horizon, shining fully upon us.

Even my mind was shifting to the animal side where there was no refinement. I could only think of one way to escape. When a howl in the distance caused him to glance away, I gave him a light nudge.

He slipped on the slick footing, and I sprinted for safety.

****

At the knock on the door, Bella shot a glance at Jazzy, sleeping like a baby—a naked baby. Though she'd already slept five hours, even the loud thumping didn't disturb her. No telling where she'd been the night before. Or what she'd done.

When Jazzy had come in from the night, she'd told Bella a bizarre story about Doc rescuing her from certain death, then the two of them making love in the frozen woods until moonrise.

Having just spoken to him the day before, Bella knew he was in Texas. And Jazzy thought she'd made it with him yesterday evening? Her imagination—or wishful thinking—had to have been affected. It just made Bella wonder what, or who, Jazzy had been doing.

Bella threw the corner of Jazzy's abandoned sheet over her then pulled the bedroom door closed behind her. She wasn't worried about her exhausted sister being disturbed, but whoever was at the door might be if they saw her in her present state.

Hoping it was the double T breakfast she'd ordered—tea and toast—Bella tossed open the door. And the world dropped out from under her. Instead of the woman with the cloth covered table she'd expected, Doc and Spencer filled her doorway.

She blinked once, unable to believe they were actually there. "What are you doing here?"

Doc smiled warmly as he gazed past her, into the suite. "It sounded as if you had an emergency with Clomovidine, so I took a couple of days off to help."

She angled back so he could walk into the room, but stepped in the way when Spencer tried to follow.

Amusement brightened Spencer's eyes, but his mouth remained in a flat line. "Going to leave me in the hall?"

She hiked her chin, not willing for him to see in her face the thrill he'd sent spinning through her. "That's what I normally do with a cur."

"A cur?" His chuckle dropped low, coming from deep in his chest, as if meant only for the two of them. "A dog with a questionable heritage?"

"A dog with a questionable heritage *who should be muzzled*," she corrected.

Folding his arms, he leaned one shoulder against the door frame. "Now that's not a nice thing to call a guy." He lifted one eyebrow to give her what he obviously thought was a sexy look.

He was right.

She mercilessly smothered the pleasure warming her body. "About as nice as what you said about my sister that night."

He shouted with laughter then caught himself. "Yeah, but your sister—"

"Bella?"

At Jazzy's raspy voice, calling from the bedroom, all three of them paused. Bella held her breath, hoping her sister was talking in her sleep or going to ask a question, anything except come into the room. Her stomach dropped to the floor when the knob turned on the bedroom door.

"Bella?" Jazzy repeated as the door started to slowly open.

Please let her be dressed. Please let her be

dressed, Bella pleaded as the door swung wider.

"Did I hear room servi—" Jazzy stopped mid-word when she saw the men in the room. Thankfully, she'd taken time to wrap the sheet around her and tucked in the ends so it looked like a wrinkled strapless gown with a long side slit. A very long slit.

Her hair curled and tangled down her back, looking as if she'd been in a low-flying tornado, or as if she'd romped all night. She didn't have a bit of makeup on her face. Leave it to her to be beautiful, even before her morning shower.

Her eyes sparked, and with a haughty smile, she lifted the sheet so she wouldn't step on it and made an entrance like Miss America on the runway. The only thing missing was the boatload of roses.

Stopping in front of Doc, she gazed at him for a full ten seconds before she spoke. "You're here."

He stared at her, as stunned as if he'd just been smacked with a baseball bat. "Your sister sounded as if she needed some help, so I came to the rescue."

Jazzy flicked a glance at the doorway. "And you left your white charger in the hall?"

"Something like that." Doc took a step, turning his back to Spencer and Bella, and even though Bella couldn't see their faces, she could hear his words. "Why don't you get dressed and we'll…go out to breakfast?"

The intimacy of Doc's tone caused Bella's cheeks to burn. Jazzy's condition had him by the throat. In moments, as soon as Spencer got close enough, he'd be after her, too.

Bella's heart thudded so hard, she could barely draw a breath. She had to stop this before it got out of hand. But how? Jazzy certainly wasn't trying to get Doc out of there, and Spencer's only interest seemed to be getting in.

Spencer straightened, taking a step toward his brother. Jazzy murmured something. Bella couldn't understand the words, but the tone was obvious. Doc's deep chuckle sounded as if they'd just had sex, were getting ready to—or both. Electricity practically crackled in the air. At any moment now, the storm would break.

Why did things like this happen to them? Jazzy being in heat was unfair to everyone. Bella thought about the trouble she'd taken. The careful plans and arrangements she made so these men—and any other unsuspecting idiots—wouldn't know where they had gone. Her anger mounted with each breath she took, searing everything inside her until she wanted to spit.

"Out!"

Everyone froze. Surprise filled their faces as if they'd never before heard her screech. Well, maybe they hadn't, but she'd certainly spoken loudly to all of them. At least once.

"I said, get out." She tempered her tone this time, hoping their astonishment at hearing her squawk would quickly wear off and they'd actually move.

Jazzy was first to recover. With a gasp, she opened her mouth to speak, but Bella preempted her. "You. In the shower. Now."

When Jazzy started to argue, Bella allowed the anger sizzling through her to show on her face, then pointed toward the bedroom. With a shrug, Jazzy obeyed.

Clinging to the tone she'd used, Bella turned on the

men. "Where are you staying?"

Doc looked as if he didn't speak or understand English. She focused on Spencer. "Where?"

"Down the road a few miles in a condo."

"Then go to it." She set her jaw, clenched her fists and stomped one foot. "*Go.*"

As the men walked away, Spencer glanced back over his shoulder. Trouble was, Bella didn't know if he looked back hoping for one more glimpse of heat enhanced Jazzy.

Or her.

****

Chase stopped in the hallway and took a long breath. The building was full of enticing aromas. Sweet smelling cleansers, creams, potions and women filled the place, but the one fragrance that filled his head while locking his heels to the floor was Jazzy.

Her spiciness practically wafted through the air. All he had to do was remember the evening before, with the sky purpling and Jazzy heating up the snow all around them, and her scent filled him. Made him ache with wanting her.

He'd never known anyone like her. Never. Not even when he'd traveled to foreign countries.

And now that he'd found her, he wasn't about to walk away. He took a step toward her door, but Spencer grabbed him, his grip hard. "We're leaving, bro."

Chase kept his voice low to keep a wayward bystander from calling security, but he didn't try to hide the frustration. "What do you think you're doing?"

A frown creased Spencer's normally placid face. "Taking you out of here."

"Taking…me?" Chase arched his brow. He was a

long way from ready to leave.

"Yes, I'm taking you *before* you do something you'll regret."

"What? You think Jazzy will call security to keep me out?" He smirked, knowing she'd welcome him with that special grin curving her lips. "Or the cops?"

Spencer dropped his voice so low Chase had to strain to hear it. "No. But I'd bet the ranch her sister would."

"That's what you're here for. To distract her."

Spencer snorted and, using his shoulder, turned Chase toward the exit again. "Right. Beautiful Bella can hardly talk to me without wanting to smack me. What makes you think I can keep her from calling security?" Chase shook his head, irritation with his brother crowding his gut like so much gravel. He had to see Jazzy again. Now. Had to touch her. Be with her.

But that damned sister of hers—

He stopped himself mid-thought. Bella wasn't "that damned sister." She was his friend and coworker. And Jazzy was…

This time, when Spencer grabbed his arm, he let himself be led away.

****

I stepped out of the shower and glanced around the steam filled bathroom. After being in there all that time, I figured I'd drained every drop of hot water from the entire spa—hot tub and all. The bathroom was so heavy with fog it looked like a lost world sequence in an old TV show. After using every towel in the place, I opened the door to go into the bedroom. Bella waited just on the other side.

I quirked a one-sided smile at her. "Standing

guard?"

She glared at me as if I'd come out doing a bump and grind. "What else can I do?"

I opened my mouth to answer, but she cut me off. "From the time we got here, you haven't even tried to fight this thing. You walked into the room and disappeared out the backdoor before I could even get inside. You went skiing yesterday morning and you didn't come in all night long.

"When you finally came in this morning, you were talking about having made love with my coworker, who should have been hundreds of miles away. Then he shows up. Now I can't tell if you're delusional, imaginative or if your spores actually drew him this far."

"I don't know either."

Her startled look at my admission almost made me laugh. Almost. "What?"

"I said, I don't know if I'm delusional or not." I took a breath as I tried to clear my head. "I clearly remember going skiing yesterday morning. I skied on the Rocky Raccoon slope when I heard some boys cheering and laughing. They made a run through the trees and it looked like a great one, so I decided to try it."

"Jazzy." Her tone held a lethal combo of shock, scold *and* disappointment. "You know how dangerous that can be. When you found yourself wanting to do something that risky, it should have been a red flag. Why didn't you come back to the condo right then?"

"'Should have' isn't any fun." I shrugged. "Anyway I went back to the bottom, and that's when things started to get toggled."

"Toggled?" she interrupted.

"Yes, toggled. You know. Weird. Right place, wrong head." I struggled to explain. "Anyway, I caught a familiar scent while I was at the bottom, but I couldn't get enough of it to recognize. So I got on the lift and went to the top of the mountain. It was a double black slope called Booger Bear. It was great, Bella. Tons of moguls."

"I hate moguls," Bella murmured.

"I know. I love them. I went right over them from top to top. Whap! Whap! Whap!"

Unsmiling, she lifted an eyebrow. "Go on about getting…toggled."

I thought for a moment. "I caught the scent again when I got off the lift, but it still wasn't enough to recognize. Anyway, I finally found the path into the trees. It was wonderful, Bella. Faster than the regular slope with loose snow and very narrow. No room to maneuver. Like riding a rocket through space. My heart pounding a million times a minute."

The memory of that thrill was almost as exciting as living it. I closed my eyes and hurtled down the hill again, just a hair's breadth from disaster.

"Go on." By the sound of her voice, the second hand experience wasn't as exhilarating as being there.

"I didn't realize there was a ninety degree hairpin at the end. And if you don't make the turn, there's a drop onto a pile of boulders." I couldn't let her know how close I'd come. "Just when I thought I was going to have to either lie down or grow wings, something dark hit me from the side. Doc."

Her voice grew soft, almost gentle. "Jazzy, there's no way Doc could have gotten here that quickly. There were no flights out of Dallas until this morning, and he couldn't drive that fast." She shook her head. "The time is just too short."

"It looked like Doc. And smelled like him, too." I tried to make her understand. "It was *his* odor. There's no mistaking one for another."

"Are you even sure you had sex?" Her voice was hushed as if she wasn't sure she wanted to ask.

Sure I'd had sex? What kind of question was that? "What do you mean?"

"I mean in the shower." She swallowed hard, took a breath and continued. "Did you…find evidence of having sex?"

I almost laughed when I realized her question. "I don't know. I wasn't looking for verification. So either I had sex or I had the female equivalent of a wet dream. Or maybe he used a condom."

Her voice dropped to a whisper. "If he wasn't actually a wolf."

Now that startled me. I couldn't begin to embrace that. "No. Way."

"That's one of the reasons I've tried so hard to keep you locked up at night. There's no telling what might happen with you in heat during the phase of a full blood moon." She tipped her head to one side. "If you got pregnant right now, would they be babies or cubs?"

Yanking my towel tighter, I started pacing. I could hardly bear to stay in the room with her talk of me getting pregnant. And for my sister to worry about the species of my offspring. Unbelievable.

I wanted to just throw on some clothes and go out to work off the frustration, energizing my muscles. But that was exactly what I couldn't do. I had to stay there.

Locked up. Immobile.

I glanced around, trying to think of a way through this. Bella must have seen my look of desperation. "Get dressed. We're going to take advantage of this spa while it's still daylight."

Standing, she checked the backdoor to see that it was still locked then went into the living room to wait while I dressed. "Put on your running clothes and don't bother with makeup," she called through the door.

Tossing my towel aside, I shuffled through my suitcase, pulled out the requested clothes and yanked them on. Then I took the towel off my head and ran a comb through my hair. In record time I opened the bedroom door and gave her a smile. "Done. What's first?"

She hung up the phone. "First, we're going to the sauna."

"I get it," I said as we headed out the door. "You're going to roast the devil out of me."

After the sauna, we had massages. The dig-deep-until-you-cry kind. By the time we were finished, I didn't know if I'd ever be able to marshal my muscles so I could walk again.

Next we went for a mud bath. Talk about a throwback to childhood. The mud squishes between your toes and oozes all around you, except this smelled clean, where the stuff from kid-dom usually smelled like a swamp.

"You know, I have a vivid memory of being in a mud puddle at Grandma's house. Do you remember?" I asked as I settled in.

"Of course, I remember. We were on our way to Sunday school and wearing our pink Easter dresses."

She gingerly eased into the expensive mud. "I just knew you were going to get in big trouble."

"Yeah. You stood there begging me to get out—"

"And you were trying to make me mad enough to get in and smack you."

"And I got punished for the mud on me *and* you."

"You should have been. You threw it on me."

I took a tiny ball of mud and tossed it in her direction. "But I didn't tell you to stand where I could."

"And now these people make real money, letting adults get into gigantic puddles." She shook her towel shrouded head. "You were way ahead of your time."

"Oh, yeah, that's me. Ahead of my time." Moving in the warm muck was slow going. Even a shrug took time and concentration. "You know who likes mud more than kids? Pigs."

Bella giggled. "Wow, they could put some animal in hog heaven in here."

I couldn't help getting serious. "I just wish there was a way to get a handle on *my* animal life."

Raising one knee, she wrapped her arms around it. "I've never seen a study on the lives of werewolves, but Doc might have one. He's got a ton of research in his lab."

"It's probably all about killing werewolves." I leaned toward her. "He wants to wipe us out."

"It's the gene he wants to wipe out," she corrected.

"Which will result in removing werewolves from the face of the earth." My voice rose a little higher than I intended. But I was upset. Didn't Bella understand? This man I found myself attracted to hated my kind enough to dedicate his life to getting rid of us. "Look, Bella. I know this week is a rough one. But it's not like this all the time. Usually I like being a werewolf. I like having the ability at my fingertips, to use whenever I please. The strength, power, speed, cunning…it's wonderful."

"But you will admit to a downside." It wasn't a question.

"Okay, there's a downside, but it's outweighed by the good. Most of the time, I like my life."

"Yeah," Bella mocked. "And everyone around has the pleasure of spending time with a wolf."

The attendant came in and introduced herself as Mary. She gave us an easy smile as she checked the equipment. "Have you seen one of our wolves on the slopes? How lucky! Usually there's nothing to worry about with the wild animals around here as long as it's daytime. Just don't wander too far out by yourself after dark."

We nodded like a pair of bobble heads in the back of a redneck sedan as she checked her watch. "About ten more minutes and it'll be time for you to get out."

"What's next on the agenda?" I asked Bella, but the attendant thought I spoke to her.

Mary lifted her clipboard. "Let's see. Next you're going to the salon. First a deep pore vacuum, an exfoliating facial, and then a session with Line Arrester."

"Line Arrester?" That didn't sound good.

"Yes. It's one of our consultants who's trained in assessing you to determine what your next step should be—Botox, Restylane, hyaluronic acid filler, fat transfer or Thermage."

Could any of that be good? "Consultants do the actual work?"

Her mirth sounded plastic, as if she'd been trained in laughter. "No. We have doctors, plastic surgeons, on staff for that."

"Oh." I tried to put some enthusiasm in my words. "Good."

Bella shot a look at me as the woman left the room. "No way, I'm letting anyone get near my face with a needle."

I shook my head. "Me, either. But for future reference it might not hurt to at least meet with the Wrinkle Sheriff."

"Line Arrester," Bella corrected me.

"Whatever."

After we left the "sty," we showered then redressed in our own clothes. Mary took us to another part of the spa. I was more than a little wary—until they started my facial massage. Talk about heaven! The technician said it was to help break up the grime in the pores, but I'm sure it was to get me addicted. And it worked.

I knew when the sun drifted near the west horizon because, on cue, the choir started to hum and my energy level increased, which stimulated my muscles. I had a real problem sitting still.

When we went into the exfoliating session, I was tense as a clothes rack. The technician kept telling me to relax, but she might as well have been talking to a steel rod. I just couldn't do it.

By the time we got to the Wrinkle Sheriff, I couldn't even sit.

She was a blonde with a long face and a bottom so wide she emitted a beeping sound when she backed up. She took an instant dislike to me.

I was in the chair just long enough for her to focus

her lighted magnifying glass over my face. Almost immediately the energy inside me built to explosion proportions. I jumped out of the chair.

"I really can't do a proper assessment without making an examination." She had a definite whine to her tone.

But I couldn't do it.

"Just sit down. I'm not going to do anything but look. It *can't* hurt you."

But I can hurt you, I wanted to snap. Maybe I should have. "Sorry. I'm just a little…" Shy? Not even a complete idiot would believe that. I don't like to be touched? Like she'd believe that after I'd spent the entire day being touched by these people. "The light hurts my eyes." I hated lying…when the lie was so obvious.

"Well, f—" She caught herself just before blurting the entire word, which I'm positive was part of her every day vocabulary.

It made me angry, but that didn't surprise me. The choir hummed louder, their harmony growing closer. Pressure built inside me.

Good thing she was actually the Line Arrester, because if she'd had sheriff status, she'd have detained me for sure. And the night might have been better for everyone involved if she had.

Instead, I pretended to have a real aversion to foul language and huffed out of the room. I tried for an exit into the coming twilight, but Bella caught me at the door. "We're going back to the room." Having her hand on my wrist, I was trapped. She all but dragged me back to the condo.

With only moments to spare, she hauled me into

the bedroom, made a quick circuit, looking for anything dangerous then locked me in.

I stood in the middle of the room for a long time, fighting the coming change. As much as it hurt me, I can honestly say I worked at staying human that night. Tried to hold back the fur, deny the muscles, keep my body erect.

I paced the room. How could I stop the change? Maybe if I kept my mind occupied, it wouldn't happen. I grabbed a book from a nearby shelf, but found I couldn't read. The words were just nonsense, so I slung it against the wall.

I looked for something else to focus on. A pastoral painting—which had lost all color—caught my attention. But in the brush strokes, I found hidden pictures of wolves stalking their prey, dying animals, bleeding humans and dens of pups.

When the metamorphosis took me, it was painful but welcome—like intense pain just before one passes out. Or dies.

The next thing I remember about that night—and I'm still unsure if it was reality or a dream—was the silvery light of the moon, falling on pristine snow. Moments before the eclipse, the rest of the world was black. The trees were black. Mountains were black. Clouds scudding across a pewter sky were black.

I was so alone…and lost. My one soul mate for eternity hadn't found me and I ached for him. I lifted my chin and wailed my loneliness. Where could he be? When would he come? I hated being isolated.

The pain was almost more than I could bear.

As Earth's shadow edged over the moon, I saw him, creeping toward me. At first, I thought my mind had created him, playing in the shadows of the blood moon. Then he bounded over the snow, and at last, streaked to my side. My heart lightened, making me want to tease and nip and run. We played and romped until I could no longer stand it.

I attacked him.

Chapter Six

Two weeks later, having survived both being in heat and the BMW phase, which I always remember as the cycle-from-hell, I was back at work. I hadn't seen Doc again while we were at the spa, so I figured his brother dragged him away—not unlike the way my sister dragged me.

Having accepted an appointment with Beatrice to help with her cruise wardrobe, I drove to the Holliday home. I grabbed my tote, stepped from the Z and tried to keep my jaw from dropping. If the Holliday house was a wagon wheel, as Beatrice had described it, the wagon must be a Rolls Royce.

The estate was beautiful. From where I stood, I could barely tell there were other houses connected to it.

Straightening my shoulders, I moved up the brick walk to the door. I pressed the doorbell, and the chimes played, *Embrace Me... my sweet embraceable you.*

In moments, Beatrice opened the door and ushered me into a very comfortable room with a country kitchen, opening off one side. A fireplace stood in the corner of the great room. The furniture was expensive and overstuffed. The floors, golden oak, edged by the same rock as had been used on the outside of the house and the fireplace. I opened my mouth to tell Mrs. Holliday how lovely her home was, when Billie

Holiday sang, *you and you alone bring out the gypsy in me.*

"Do you play that song just to match your doorbell tones?"

Beatrice moved to a control panel and turned down the music. "That's one of Sam's new toys. He connected the sound system to the door chimes, so whatever we have playing, the bell picks up the first few notes." She shrugged. "I know it's silly, but it keeps him busy and out of trouble."

I stood in the midst of understated opulence; the study of which I'd made certain was part of my undergrad degree. "He must do well with it."

She chuckled as she shook her head. "He only does it for his amusement."

Then you must get a real kick as you haul your bucks to the bank. I kept my thoughts deep inside me. If I didn't know her son, I'd wonder if the family didn't have a Lycan connection.

While it's not universally known, being part of a family with a werewolf, while aggravating and sometimes horrifying, tends to bring certain good things—maybe it's the cosmos making up for it. My own father had struggled to make a living for his family until I was born. Then things smoothed into place quite nicely.

"Is he a veterinarian like Chase?" I asked. If so, he had to be vet to the stars to afford a home like this.

"Oh, no, dear. Sam's a geologist. Spence works in the family business with him."

The brother who'd irritated Bella so. "Is he a geologist, too?"

"No, he has a degree in finance. His father thought

he was too valuable to let work for someone else, so he hired him."

I nodded as I strolled to a wall of family pictures. "What a beautiful arrangement."

"That picture is Drew and Mack when they were babies." Pride for her family rose in her voice. "I think the only major they've declared so far in college is girls. Or partying. It's hard to tell which."

She took me to the bedroom, where she pointed out Sam's closet, then led me into her closet, designed to make any woman—even Oprah—jealous. Bright light filled the room, reaching into every corner. In the center of the room was an island in which she kept sweaters, lingerie, stockings and other things she didn't want to hang. Skirts, each one on a separate wooden skirt hanger, all hung on half racks as did shirts and blouses. Daytime dresses were on one side of the closet and evening dresses on another. The shoes were on shoe-sized shelves and boots on boot sized.

I couldn't hide my delight. "I could live in here! In fact, this would be the perfect design for a store."

Beatrice laughed. "My husband says if the bottom ever falls out of our business, he's going to throw open the doors and put me to work, selling my stock."

She led me through another door to an identical closet, holding her spring/summer wardrobe. "Feel free to go through my things."

I pulled my laptop from my bag, set it on the island and opened the cruise wear template, which I'd designed early on in my career. "Where is the cruise going?"

"We leave from Miami on December first, go through the Panama Canal, then up the coast to San

Francisco."

I filled in the blank. "How long will you be gone?"

"Three weeks or so. There is laundry service on the ship, but I'd rather not use it if I don't have to. You never know if you'll get your things back or someone else's."

"I understand." I glanced around, but didn't see any luggage stored there. "I assume you have plenty of luggage."

"I'll have one of the boys get it out of storage so you can see it. We'll just have to purchase more, if necessary." She glanced around the room as if checking for something she might have forgotten. "I'll leave you alone to get to work."

I filled in quantities of what she owned. Later I'd do a printout, listing suggestions for her. Luckily, they were leaving from a warm weather port, and during most of their trip, it would be warm. But San Francisco in January would require a few winter clothes. And often the nicer, private cruise lines throw an impromptu last night party, so we'd have to be prepared for that.

I started a separate page for Sam. His closet, while not as large and well organized as Beatrice's, was still impressive. Over the years, I'd learned to take a measure of a man from his closet. Sam was quite a guy. He liked his clothes nice, expensive and understated.

What I liked best about him, though, was his work clothes. They were stained, his boots had steel toes, and on one shelf, he had a hardhat. He hadn't just inherited the business. He'd worked and, from the look of his boots, worked hard to build it.

After saving their profiles, I packed my computer and went back into the bedroom, where an entire collection of Louis Vuitton luggage had been lined up next to the bed. It looked like a double set.

When I left the bedroom, Beatrice came out of the kitchen. "I made coffee. I hope you'll have some."

"I'd love some." I moved closer to the fireplace, where I stared at the flickering of the fire. Easy warmth moved through me, as if I were home. As if I could kick off my shoes, put up my feet and be at ease—unusual for me. Usually, my Lycanthrope stayed foremost in my mind, constantly reminding me I couldn't relax. I might say or do something to reveal my secret.

I drew a full breath, a prelude to a yawn, when I noticed Doc's scent tingeing the air. Spinning, I found him, lazed against the doorway into the kitchen. Delight spurted through me, but I forced a frown. "What are you doing?" As if he didn't have every right to be there.

His smile, slow in coming, started first at his eyes, then quirked his lips in a crooked smile that shot through me. To my core. "Enjoying the view."

I tried to keep his ambition in life—to eradicate werewolves—in the front of my mind. Hoping to irritate him, I smiled sweetly. "Did you get called for luggage detail?"

"No." He gazed at me as if he were a starving man and I were a mountain of ice cream. "My brothers took care of that. I saw your Z and didn't want to miss…seeing you again."

I tried to swallow, but the grit in his voice as he spoke those words kept that from happening. I wanted to breathe, but my heart slammed so hard against my lungs, there was no room for air. I wasn't even sure I could walk until I found myself gliding toward him. And him toward me.

"Jazzy, here's your—" Beatrice stopped mid-word. "Why, Chase! I didn't know you'd come in."

He stopped just before he touched me, but I still felt him, and it made me want to howl.

Swiftly, he moved to his mother's side, taking the small tray with two coffee cups on it from her. "Let me help you, Mom."

"Thank you," she answered. "I'll get another cup."

He set the tray on a small table in the midst of a conversation area next to the fireplace. Beatrice came back into the room with the third cup and handed us each one. "Oh, I should have asked, Jazzy. Do you take cream or sugar?"

"No. I like it black." I usually joked about liking my coffee like my men—strong and bitter—but I couldn't find the humor.

Amusement sparked in Doc's eyes. "Somehow I thought you would."

Beatrice shot Doc a glance, then returned her gaze to me. "Any idea how much I'll need to add to my wardrobe for the trip, Jazzy? I suppose I'll need to schedule time for shopping."

I took a sip as I thought about the classical pieces in her closet. "You have a complete wardrobe, Beatrice. I think you'll want to add a few items that reflect the latest styles, but it won't take too much time."

"Where do you usually take your clients?" she asked.

"I never take them shopping. I arrange for a few shops to deliver an assortment of pieces to my office. Then I'll set up an appointment with you to try them, see if you like them. I'll also take care of having alterations done then I'll have them folded and ready to pack in your bags when they're delivered to your door."

"Sounds like a very personalized service," Doc murmured.

"It is. And the women who use my services return to me year after year. I make a busy woman's life manageable. And a woman of taste, a woman of style."

"Do many people find this a career calling?" he asked.

"Very few." I tossed my hair behind my shoulders. Was he trying to piss me off? "When I first started, my sister said I was just trying to find a way to call my shopping vice a job."

Beatrice smiled, unaware of the vibes bouncing around the room. "What did you say, dear?"

I shouldn't have said it, I know. But self-righteous people give me a pain. "I told her it was better than sticking my hand up elephant rears."

I stared right at Doc as I said it, and was surprised when he laughed so hard he almost fell out of his chair.

Realizing I probably should have held my tongue, I glanced at Beatrice and, again, was shocked to see her grinning, too. "I would imagine that the basic requirement of taste and style in combination with business savvy isn't easy to manage. A kind of left-brain, right-brain way of life."

"Exactly." I finished my coffee and set down the cup. "I'd better be going."

"All right." Beatrice shot her son a pointed look. "*I'll* walk you out, dear."

Doc shrugged. "Guess I'll clean up the dishes."

As we walked out the door, Beatrice thanked me for making the trip out. "I'd like to ask you one more thing. Please don't feel you have to answer me right now, but would you consider flying to Miami with us? We'd love to have you as our guest at the bon voyage party."

I checked my calendar and found it clear. "I'd love to."

****

Busy as I am that time of year, the days flashed past. Before I knew it, I had to set aside clothing charts, appointment calendars and mall trips to dress for the bon voyage party. Naturally, I'd taken time to do a little shopping for myself and found a heart-of-the-ocean blue gown covered with Swarovski crystals with a plunging neckline. The wrap was a generous shrug with a single button closure.

I met the Hollidays at the airport, and I have to say, the vision of that family of men in their tuxedoes was wonderful. With his good looks, Chase held my attention and made me feel tingly inside, but I did my best to hide it.

Beatrice didn't look too shabby in her flowing evening gown, if I do say so myself. We flew to Miami in their private jet, the interior of which was absolutely beautiful by anyone's taste. The main seating area looked like someone's living room. A leather couch sat on one side surrounded by several matching or contrasting chairs. Just behind the conversation group was a pair of overstuffed chaise lounges. It looked as if pleasure was the main reason for the jet.

A limo met us at the airport, sent by the cruise company, which made me wonder just how expensive a trip this would be for the older couple. Happily, I didn't get the sense it that it would cause a strain on their budget or that they even had a budget.

I'd been to the ocean many times, but each time I'm near it, the scent of salt air surprises me. As Chase helped me out of the limo, I drew several deep breaths while mentally keeping my fingers crossed that I wouldn't make myself dizzy.

After we boarded the ship, the purser led us to the suite that would be Sam and Beatrice's home for the next three weeks. I'd had a few worries about whether the couple would get claustrophobic.

After we looked around the small, well appointed sitting room, Beatrice glanced at me. "Jazzy, why don't you come with me to find the kitchen?"

"It's called a galley, Mom." Doc's younger brother, Drew, corrected her as he sidled to the wet bar and opened a bottle of champagne. "If you're going on a cruise, you ought to at least talk like it."

His mother flashed him a sharp look. "Take it easy over there. We have a long evening ahead."

"Yeah. Don't embarrass the family tonight," Mack said as he trailed after Drew.

Beatrice shook her head, but with a sigh turned and led the way to the very small kitchen where she glanced around at the small fridge, microwave and two-burner stove. "Well, I guess they don't expect me to cook."

"I hope not."

We moved into the bedroom after that. The bed had a heavy satin comforter, the green-blue color of ocean water, a pair of upholstered chairs and his and her dressers. Even the closets were fair sized. The drapes matched the bedspread fabric exactly.

While I checked out the bathroom—complete with a tub and separate shower, Beatrice opened the drapes and revealed a balcony with a pair of lounge chairs.

Oh, yeah. I could get used to living there in a hurry.

Beatrice checked her watch. "Well, I guess we'd better go to the party. If I don't feed those two monsters, Mack and Drew, they'll drink too much, and I'll be angry at them the entire trip. And vacation anger is hard on a woman."

I tried to hide the smile pulling at my mouth. "We certainly don't want that."

"No. *They* don't want that. Because if I spend my entire trip planning their punishment, they'll be very sorry."

We went back to the living room, where Chase handed us each a flute of champagne, then stayed near me. After taking a sip, Beatrice set hers down. "Let's go to the party."

Chase's hand warmed the small of my back as we made our way to the ballroom, which looked as elegant as any restaurant I'd ever been in. Individual tables were covered with heavy white cloths, crystal vases held fresh flowers and the place settings were heavy silver. The room made me think of pictures I'd seen of expensive ships people traveled before flying was popular.

After taking my seat, I removed my shrug. I turned to Doc, who sat beside me. His gaze was all but aflame. I sat a little straighter and quirked a smile. "Hungry?" I murmured, leaning toward him a bit.

He swallowed, loosened his tie and collar button, then nodded, his gaze never leaving mine. His voice sounded rough. Hoarse. "Yeah."

"Let's get our food before the crowd at the buffet tables gets overwhelming." Beatrice pushed back her chair then gave me a smile. "Come on, Jazzy. You must be famished."

As we got up, the three Holliday sons jumped from their chairs. Those boys were nothing if not well mannered.

The ship had provided a seafood buffet. I chose lobster and clarified butter. A chef prepared Cesar salad nearby, so when he'd finished, I piled a second plate high with it.

Back at the table, the waiters served champagne. The frown on Beatrice's face looked as though it might become permanent, until Sam leaned over to whisper something to her.

With a shrug, she nodded at him, then lifted her brows and smiled. I couldn't be sure what Sam told her, but it seemed to do the trick. Her mood lightened for the rest of the evening.

The orchestra started tuning up and soon music to dine by filled the air.

"I hope you boys will get along okay while we're gone." Beatrice put a grilled shrimp in her mouth and chewed for a few moments. "You do have finals coming up."

Mack shrugged. "Yeah, same as this time last year. Not a problem."

But Drew wasn't as casual about it. "If I don't do well on them, I'm not going back second semester."

Beatrice drew a breath to answer him, but Sam spoke first. "If you're having problems, hire a tutor. There's no reason for you not to do well—unless you aren't putting your time in studying."

Mack stared at his plate. "Yeah. But I'm so busy, especially in the fraternity. There's—"

"You're at school to get an education. Not to be in a fraternity. If being in that organization is interfering, you can stop being a member. As of now." The severity of Sam's tone made me very glad I'd finished school.

Mack held up both hands. "No. No. I think I'll do okay. It's just hard."

"Life is hard. Get used to it." Sam glanced at me then produced a slight smile before focusing once more on Mack. "We'll let it drop for now."

"Good." The heartfelt word escaped on a sigh, earning Mack a chuckle from the rest of the table, even his father.

"As soon as your mother and I get home, I want an account from both of you. You'd better be diligent."

When we'd finished eating, and our table had been cleared by the staff, the lights dimmed as the orchestra started playing dance music. Their repertoire was spectacular. They played beautiful tunes from the Twenties all the way up to today.

Mack and Drew noticed several young women on the other size of the room and left us in a hurry. I didn't expect to see them, except maybe at a distance, for the rest of the evening.

I wasn't thinking about the boys, though. My mind was consumed with Doc. As he drew me into his arms on the dance floor, he slid his hand inside my dress to rest directly on my waist. The intimacy of his touch in the midst of all those people had me melting against him.

He bent his neck to put his mouth next to my ear. His lips brushed the sensitive spot as he said, "You're beautiful tonight."

I could have nestled right there, my head in the

hollow of his shoulder, and been content for life—or at least the next several hours. But the music changed and Sam cut in.

"Are you having a good time?" the older man asked.

I nodded. "Very much!"

"I hope you don't let our two youngest sons scare you away. They're kind of spoiled, but they come from good stock. They'll turn out all right."

I smiled up at him. "They don't scare me, sir."

He chuckled at my answer. "I can see that. But please, don't call me sir. Makes me feel like I'm a hundred and fifty years old. And I won't be that old until my birthday."

Surprised at his sense of humor, I laughed louder than the joke warranted, but he didn't seem to mind. When the song was over, Sam escorted me back to Doc.

The orchestra announced it would take a short break. Doc put his hand along my shoulder. "Want to go out on the deck for some fresh air?" His gaze warmed me all over.

"Let me get my shrug." I practically gasped the words.

While I slipped it on, Doc told his parents where we were going, and asked if they'd like to go, too.

"No thanks, son. But I saw your brothers sneak out a little while ago. If you find them doing gainers into the ocean, yank 'em up short. Would you?"

Doc chuckled and nodded, then with his hand on the small of my back, walked with me to the door.

The deck was dimly lit, intentionally I'm sure to give it a romantic atmosphere. And it worked for me. We walked a little way along the deck until we saw the partial moon, making a path across the water.

We found a secluded corner, and Doc was about to take me into his arms when his brothers and a pair of blondes made a noisy return. By the way the brothers argued, I knew they'd had too much to drink. One of the girls lifted something that didn't smell like a cigarette and took a puff.

Doc stopped them. "Back inside, guys."

Mack snarled at him. "Why do you think you—"

"I said inside."

****

Stepping onto the Hollidays' private jet the next morning for the trip home, I glanced around for a seat. Before I could claim the couch, Mack and Drew hurtled past me and crashed on it.

I chose a comfortable chair that looked as if it might turn into a recliner if I knew the combination. Not that I'd try to sleep. I still buzzed with the evening's energy.

I'd no more than buckled and settled in when Doc came out of the cabin. After he removed his tuxedo jacket, he sat next to me. Laying the jacket across the arm of an adjacent chair, he loosened his tie and buckled up.

"How old are your brothers?" I asked, keeping my voice soft.

"Old enough to know better than to act like they did tonight." He scowled and shook his head. "If I'd been that wild at their age, Dad would have... Well, at least they aren't driving."

I nodded, as much in sympathy as agreement. "True."

The jet taxied onto the runway, then lifted off the

ground so smoothly, it was hard to tell we were moving.

As we rose in the air, I leaned forward to see the brilliant colors of the sunrise. "Don't you love this time of morning?"

Doc shook his head, a half smile on his face. "I'm usually asleep about now."

"So am I. But when I'm not, I love seeing the sun come up."

The rising sun moved behind us as the pilot angled the plane toward home, so I picked up my overnight case, went to the restroom and changed.

I didn't sleep the entire trip, but the time passed much quicker going home than it had going out. Before I knew it, we were at the airport and I was being dropped at my car.

"I'd be happy to follow you home." With Doc's hair sexily mussed, his five o'clock shadow, wrinkled bow tie and open collar, he looked so hot I could hardly keep my hands off him. How could I tell him no?

Something within me took a step back, letting me see the emerging pattern. The last time I'd seen him, when I'd been at his parents' house the first time, I'd had a coming-home reaction when his scent reached me. He'd been in the forefront of my mind for the past few weeks. I hadn't even noticed another good looking man, and normally I have hot guy radar. I'd chatted with almost no one but him on our flight to Miami then danced almost only with him at the party.

My heart thudded slowly as awareness gripped me. The predator in me had chosen him as my mate. Although I knew it could happen, I thought I'd evolved enough from the primitive wolf to control that sort of thing. No, I *knew* I had. *I would control it.*

No matter what, I would choose my husband when I fell in love. I wouldn't be bound by the he's-the-alpha-male-who-can-best-take-care-of-me instinct.

Even if it killed me.

"I'll be fine." Snatching my bag, I fished out the keys and was in my car before he could do more than blink.

Driving home, I scolded myself. What was I doing, thinking I'd chosen a mate?

Being in heat *during* the Blood Moon Wildness was too much for my system. On top of that, I'd taken this job with Hollidays, while gearing up for the holiday season at the mall had exhausted my system. And that's all there was to it.

Besides, I was a human first. *Then* a werewolf. Even if it were true I'd chosen him to mate—and I was certain it wasn't—I could control it. Like a recovering alcoholic controls the longing for a drink. I would be the one in charge of my emotions, not some animal side of me, passed down from ancestors who'd lived in caves.

He would never know.

As I walked into our apartment, I met Bella, awake, dressed and drinking coffee in our kitchen. "Why are you up already? Did your date for last night fall through?"

"I canceled it." She took a sip then set her cup in its saucer with a shrug. "I wasn't really excited about a blind date."

"So what excuse did you give him?"

"I had to work." She looked a bit sheepish then rushed on. "Doc had a process running in the lab, and I wanted to keep an eye on it for him."

"Your poor date," I snarked. "That's about as lame an excuse as I've ever heard."

"He sounded almost relieved when I called him." She gave me a weak smile. "So, did all the boys go to Miami to see their parents off?"

"You should have come with us. There was plenty of room on their jet, like Beatrice told you." I decided to quit skirting the issue. "Spencer decided at the last minute not to go."

"He did?" Her face brightened momentarily then dimmed as another thought hit. "Did he have a date?"

I shook my head. "I don't suppose he called you?"

She shifted her gaze away from me. "No." Her tone dulled.

I tried to wait her out, but she didn't continue.

Bella had always enjoyed making me sit up and beg when I wanted to know something. Rather than play the same tired game, I changed the subject. "So what kind of process was Doc running?"

She tossed her empty yogurt container in the trash. "A research project, still trying to get isolation."

"You didn't do anything?"

"Like what?"

"Destroy it, maybe?"

She lifted an eyebrow as she went into veterinarian mode. "Do you know how unprofessional of me it would be to sabotage his work? Even if I don't necessarily agree—"

"Agree?" I interrupted, my hackles rising. "He's trying to eradicate my species, and you're too professional to do anything?"

She rolled her eyes. "It's not like he's trying to end

your life. He's only isolating the Syzygia Gene. Big difference."

"He's trying to isolate it so he can eradicate it." Frustrated at Bella's blank look, I lifted my voice. *"Kill it*. He wants to wipe what and who I am from the face of the earth. A werewolf is who I am." Making a breakneck decision, I nodded sharply. "I'm going to fulfill my pledge. Starting tomorrow."

"Your pledge?" Horror crept over her face. "You mean the one you signed at the dedication? You're going..."

Her voice faded to nothing, so I finished the sentence for her. "Start helping Doc in his lab."

****

Surprise jolted through Chase and was quickly followed by sharp pleasure when Jazzy walked into his lab early Tuesday morning. His mouth went dry just seeing her. "How did I get lucky enough to see you this morning? Did Bella have car trouble?"

Jazzy's smile was pure magic as it broadened, lighting up her face. As she shook her head, her hair flipped over her shoulders to curl around her breasts. He tried hard to swallow as he forced his gaze back to her face. "I've come to learn my job. Fulfill my volunteer commitment."

Had her voice always had that smoky quality? It made him want to pull her close, her lips near his ear, so he wouldn't miss a syllable. He tried to draw a breath, but found the air thick. Uncooperative. Clearing his throat, he tried again to inhale.

Job? Who could work when she was there? Within his reach? "Great. Then why don't you put on a lab coat and come he—"

"Clean recovery cages," Bella all but shouted.

Momentarily confused, he glanced around at the woman. Where had she come from?

Jazzy took a step toward him, a slight frown marring her face. "I'd really rather help in your lab."

He forced his gaze from Jazzy to focus on her twin. "I *was* goin—"

"No. The cages are where she'll be the most help. I'll get the supplies." With a forceful nod, she turned on her heel and left the room.

Damn. Unable to argue with Bella, especially now that she'd left, he gritted his teeth to keep from yelling after her. Besides, she was right. The recovery cages had been neglected. But why did Jazzy have to do it? Frustrated, he jammed his fingers through his hair then shaking his head, forced a smile. "When you've finished, I can at least give you a tour of the lab. Why don't you let me buy you a cup of coffee before you get started?"

Leaving the clinic, he walked with her across the compound to the canteen. Inside, he grabbed a pair of white mugs and moved to the steaming coffee urn. He filled their cups, handed one to Jazzy and led her to a small table, where he took a chair adjacent to her.

Bella rushed into the room, her face stormy. She took a moment to focus on them before marching to the cups kept for employees and snatching one for herself. After filling it, she claimed the chair directly across from Jazzy.

Concern at Bella's attitude ate at Chase's gut, but Jazzy just set her cup down, a manufactured look of surprise on her face. "What are you doing, Bella? You had your two cups before we left the house."

Bella lifted her shoulders, her shrug insolent. "Maybe I needed an extra one to get me started." Tilting her head, she stared at Jazzy with a half smile.

"That's unusual." Jazzy sipped from her mug then flicked Bella a hard glance. After a moment she raised her hands to massage her temples.

The smile, still on Bella's lips, left her gaze. "One of your headaches, Jazzy?"

Jazzy stopped all pretense of smiling. "A tiny one, but it'll pass."

"Maybe you should go home *before* it gets worse." Bella's hard tone sounded almost like a threat.

Chase straightened in his chair as concern changed to alarm. He enjoyed a girl fight as much as any guy, but not now. And not between these two.

"I think once everybody goes about her own business, it'll get much better." With a determined smile, Jazzy picked up her cup and took another drink.

"Mind if I join you beautiful ladies?" Norman Briderson's laugh reminded Chase of fingernails on a blackboard. "And you, Doc Holliday?"

Chase forgot his worry about the twins as his gut tensed at Norman's presence. "We don't mind, Norman. But we were about to go to work."

"Well, maybe I could just take care of this pretty lady. She doesn't work here." Norman leaned close to Jazzy, the oil on his hair all but dripping and running down his face.

Anger flashed, but Chase clenched his jaw to keep it contained. This was no time to act like a Neanderthal, but he *wasn't* letting Norman anywhere near Jazzy—especially if he wasn't around.

Before he could speak, Jazzy answered, "I do

today."

If possible, Norman's cheesy smile grew broader. "That's great. What job will you be doing? Maybe I can give you a hand."

Smile sweetening, Jazzy blinked innocently. "I'm cleaning recovery cages."

Norman's mouth dropped open as a look of horror spread across his face. "Recovery cages? That's, like, the worst job in the park."

Jazzy fired a lightning glance at Bella then zeroed in on Norman. "And you offered to help me. Aren't you the sweetest man?"

"I… I …" Norman looked like a fish out of water, his mouth opening and closing as he gasped for his last breath. "You know, I just remembered I have to see about the giraffes' feed mixture. They're looking a little, uh, pudgy. But if I get finished, I'll come find you. Maybe lunch?"

Jazzy's gaze lingered on Bella this time. "I doubt I'll have much appetite by then."

After Norman left, Chase didn't try to contain his laughter. "I shouldn't have worried about you, Jazzy. You know how to handle him."

She gazed back at him, her face softening. Suddenly all he wanted was to pull her into his arms. Then as if remembering Bella, she blinked hard. "I'm about out of patience with that man. The next time he bothers me might just be the last."

Unsure about her meaning, Chase swallowed his libido along with the last of his coffee, gathered the others' cups and took them to the counter. Then walking abreast, they headed back across the parking lot. He glanced left, then right, and with a blink of the eye he'd reverted to high school mentality. *Five boobs in a row. And four of them too beautiful to be believed.*

But before the fantasy could burgeon, Bella touched his arm. "I'll just take Jazzy and get her started then I'll be right back."

He nodded, wishing he had time to help Jazzy at her task. It was dirty, hot and smelly, and could discourage the most determined volunteer. Too bad Bella had demanded Jazzy do it. This would probably finish Jazzy off as far as the zoo was concerned. And if she did nothing else, she made for great scenery.

As he turned to walk into the lab, Bella said, "All right, the cages are out here. Come on."

Jazzy's answer sounded a little like a snarl.

****

Determined to show Bella I could withstand any nasty job she forced on me, I cleaned all her damned cages. I didn't even take a lunch break since Doc and Bella were out at the zoo's far acres, seeing about some animal or other. I just grabbed a sammy at the canteen, inhaled it on my way back to the cages, and got busy again. When at long last I'd finished every enclosure in the room, I went back to the first one.

Using a machine made for the job, I fogged the cages to get any bacteria that might have escaped. Or were they viruses? Whatever, I went after it like I knew what I was doing.

And when I finished that interminable day, I looked like an old flag on a still day. My neck was stiff, my back sore, and all my nails except one had broken. Bella would definitely pay for that.

Bella and Doc were in surgery. Again. Obviously trying to find an animal to stick in the recover cages that I'd just finished cleaning to within an inch of my life.

I glanced around the room, wishing for something to kick or throw or bite, but I failed to find anything. Nothing there would give me the satisfaction I sorely needed, so I'd do the next best thing while I waited for Bella to finish.

I'd go for a run. A wolfed-out run.

Knowing better than to go wild before leaving the clinic, even with night falling, I took a swift walk to the area beyond the compound. Once there, I knelt behind a tree and thought about what Bella had done to me that day.

I gathered my lingering anger into a fiery orb. Within moments, I'd begun to change. Energy, the human portion of which I'd used up during my cleaning enslavement, flowed through me. My muscles lost their soreness as I grew strong. I was ready to clear my mind!

Funny how things change when I'm in the wild. The heat, building in my muscles, seems to sterilize even the meanest problems. Irritations level out. Prejudices disappear. Niggling worries turn into nothing.

The world becomes a place with only a few basic choices. Food. Water. Survival—and the survival of my kind.

I moved into an open area, where many fairly docile species were allowed to commingle. Lowering my head, I ran flat out until the bottoms of my feet burned with the pounding. Most of the animals ignored me, with only an occasional cow rolling her eyes in case I were to go into feeding mode.

Make Me Howl

As I ran, the country grew rougher. Drainage ditches crisscrossed, making it difficult to maintain my speed, so I slowed some, my breathing deep and full.

That's when I smelled blood on the wind, fresh and hot. Surprised, and not a little curious, I followed the odor into heavy brush. I took my time, not wanting to happen onto a feeding animal that might think I was there to fight for his kill.

The scent in the air grew heavy. Lowering my belly to the ground, I crept along until I came to the scene of the devastation. A dead buffalo calf, torn up almost beyond recognition. A hungry predator wouldn't do that kind of damage, and it wouldn't leave most of the animal uneaten. Dread filling me, I moved closer until I found the first clear print made by the attacking animal.

Wolf.

Curious, I sniffed the print. It smelled like a wolf, but there was more. Something that upset me so, the hair bristled along my spine.

Glancing at the sky, I confirmed what I feared.

The moon was full.

Chapter Seven

Turning, I ran as hard as I could to get back to the compound. Only a newly turned werewolf would do that kind of damage for no reason, and they were probably the most dangerous creatures walking the earth. They had nothing to relate to. No one had taught them to contain themselves. To hold back.

They were a threat to everyone around them.

And in my experience, they usually had to be destroyed like a rabid dog.

By the time I got back to where I'd started my run, my lungs ached. I didn't have time to cool down. I morphed, threw on my clothes, and rushed to find Bella, standing at our car.

Unfortunately, Doc was kicked back next to her against the vehicle.

I slowed to a walk. My heartbeat had dropped, but sweat dampened my face.

Doc's eyes widened when he saw me. Bella straightened, alarm creasing her face. "What's wrong, Jazzy?"

It's next to impossible to carry on two conversations at once—one telepathically and one orally—but I did it that day. "When I heard you had an emergency surgery, I decided to go for a run."

You've got a terrible problem here, Bell, I shouted in my mind.

What is it? What's wrong?

"You went for a run in a wild animal park?" Doc interrupted our mental dialogue. "That's dangerous."

I gave him a weak smile. "Not nearly as much for me as for a baby buffalo that some predator decided was dinner."

I continued to Bella. *He tore it completely up. I couldn't tell if he'd eaten any of it. It was a werewolf.*

Doc frowned, concern filling his gaze. "That shouldn't happen. We try to keep the animals separated so it doesn't, and we feed the lions and wolves so they don't feel a need to hunt."

Bella grasped my arm. "How awful for you. It's a good thing he was full of buffalo and didn't decide to taste you for dessert." *What makes you think it was a werewolf?*

I nodded, as if agreeing that I didn't want to be part of a meal. *Because when I sniffed his paw print, I smelled the human part of him. And aftershave.*

Bella frowned sharply as if she was ready to argue with me, but changed her focus to Doc. "We'd better call someone to take care of the mess before the scent makes every carnivore in the place go on the prowl."

With a nod, Doc took off for the clinic with Bella right behind. I had no choice but to follow. By the time Bella and I got there, Doc was talking on the park's inner-communication system and I only caught the tail of his conversation. "Find Tony and some of the guys. Take the second truck and follow us there. I want to survey the site before anything is moved."

His nod finished their talk. He turned to Bella and me. "I need you to show me where the carcass is, Jazzy. And Bella, if you don't mind some overtime, I could use your help in assessing the situation."

Bella nodded as I wondered if I could get back to the same place while riding in a truck. I hadn't followed roads on my run. I'd followed animal trails, which often were little more than tunnels through the grass and brush.

Maybe I could leave a window down and follow my nose.

We walked into the night, made bright by the fat moon. I could taste the strangeness on the wind. Actions took on a dream-like, slo-mo quality.

"Let's take the tiger truck," Doc said, his voice hushed. "If the killer animal is still around, we'll sedate him and move him back to the clinic."

"Is the gun in the truck?" Bella asked.

"Yes, but I'd better get extra darts."

While Doc headed back to the clinic, Bella caught my arm. "Jazzy, that's not a full moon."

I lifted my gaze to the sky and my heart dropped to the ground. The moon *was* barely lopsided, as if someone had shaved a bit off one side.

"It's a waxing moon." Fear filled her face as she gripped my arm harder. "Oh, Jazzy. You know what that means."

I knew. It meant we had a werewolf on our hands who'd been filled with uncontrolled anger before he'd been bitten, giving the Lycan contagion deeper control. He'd be affected all three days of the full moon. The night of waxing, the night of the full moon and the night of waning.

And unless he was caught, we'd have three nights of terror.

I had to force myself to breathe. I gripped Bella's

hand until we heard Doc coming, then we climbed into the truck. I sat by the door and rolled the window down a little. By the time he'd stowed the sedative and buckled his seatbelt, I had some control of the fear rocketing through me.

"You said it was a buffalo calf that was killed?" he asked as he started the engine and shifted into gear.

"Yes. I'm not sure I can get back there in a truck, though. I didn't exactly stay on the roads."

"Just do the best you can. I imagine the animals will help us."

The scent of blood would frighten some of them, while many of the others would lust for a taste.

With a shrug, I nodded. What else could I do? As we started down the road, another vehicle pulled in behind us.

We drove in silence, except when I had to tell him which direction to go. It took longer than it had getting there on foot, but finally we reached the correct enclosure. I could tell by the sharp odor of blood. Entrails, lying exposed to the wind, scented the air as well.

"Veer to the right up ahead." My voice seemed abnormally loud after the silence in the truck. I wondered what Bella was thinking. And Doc? Was he worried that one of "his" animals had done this? And would have to be put down? Or was he afraid that a wild wolf had happened into the park again?

Maybe the one that had treed Norman Briderson on Halloween?

We found the spot and stopped the truck just short of the gore. The vehicle following us pulled around to another side to add their lights to ours. With the brightness, it was almost like day. The blood had coagulated into a dark, thick syrup. The animal's body parts, including its insides, were strewn as if a bomb had been placed inside. Its head, still intact, lay to one side, eyes staring at nothing.

Doc pulled out a camera and took several pictures while Bella jotted notes on a clipboard she removed from behind the seat. The men who'd come in the other truck waited, as I did, with nothing to do. From the look on their faces, this wasn't the first time they'd seen this kind of problem.

Boredom settled in until my brain turned to cement. Why was this taking so long? I considered yanking Bella's clipboard from her hands and writing, *One animal shredded another. There was blood. Guts. One less buffalo. The end.*

But knowing Bella, she'd start again at the very beginning, and write even more slowly, just to irritate me.

Bella walked over to Doc, murmured something I couldn't hear then strolled around the circumference of the area and knelt next to the head. Doc followed, got on one knee next to her, and shot several pictures.

What could they be looking at? The buffalo's head couldn't look more normal if it had died of a heart attack—or maybe tedium—and been stuffed and hung on the wall. Even the place where the neck separated from the body was smooth. It wasn't a jagged tear, but almost a razor cut. Or a very sharp claw.

****

Bella placed the clipboard behind the seat then patted Jazzy's leg to wake her. How could she have fallen asleep practically in the middle of the devastation? It had been all Bella could do to keep from sobbing when she saw what had happened to the baby buffalo. The poor calf's mother had to be wondering what had happened to her baby. Why her udder ached from being overfull.

Jazzy awoke slowly, her hair curling around her shoulders when she sat up and all but snuggled against Doc as he slid into the seat beside her.

"Sorry that took so long. I'll bet you're exhausted after cleaning those cages and your run." He shot Bella a glance that sent a thread of guilt through her. "You won't have to do that job again."

"I am pretty tired." Jazzy put that raspy just-made-love tone into her voice that men found so enticing.

Chase lowered his chin and gazed into her eyes as if they were the only two in the truck. "We'll find something else for you to do next time."

"I'm really interested in your research. That's why I volunteered in the first place."

Bella stifled a gasp at her sister's audacious lie. The only thing Jazzy was interested in was destroying his research.

Chase started the truck and turned it toward the compound. "I could use some good help in the lab. Next time you're here, I'll put you to work."

Jazzy tossed Bella a look of triumph, which Bella pointedly ignored by turning her face to the window for the remainder of their ride.

When they finally reached the parking area, they climbed out of the truck. Chase nodded his thanks to Bella then put his hand on Jazzy's arm, sliding it to her hand. "Thank you for what you did today. Finding that buffalo as soon as you did potentially saved us a lot of trouble."

"She's a real asset around here, isn't she, Doc?" Norman Briderson said, coming out of the darkness.

Chase frowned, anger kindling in his gaze. "Why are you still here, Norman? I thought you never worked overtime."

"Well, once in a while, I don't have a choice but to stay late. And this was one of those nights." Norman laughed then gave Bella a look that filled her with nausea. "Did you all have some excitement that kept you late?"

"Not excitement. A dead buffalo calf, killed by a wolf."

Norman lifted a brow. "Maybe it's the same one I located the night of the Halloween party."

Bella almost laughed at Norman's take on being treed by a wolf.

Chase didn't answer for a moment. "From the damage done to the calf, I doubt it. This wolf was heavier and meaner than the one that had you hiding on top of your car."

"Hey, I wasn't hiding. I was—" Norman took a long breath. Giving himself time to think of an excuse for being on the automobile's roof. "—getting out of its way. I didn't want to hurt it."

"Right." Reaching into the truck, Chase picked up the camera and gun then turned to Bella. "Why don't you let me take care of your notes so you can get your sister home? She's had a long day."

"All right. If you're sure you don't need me—"

"I'm just going to put these things away and head home myself. I'll see you tomorrow. Late."

Bella nodded then with a glance at Jazzy, headed

for their car. It had been a long night, but had the likelihood of getting much longer. They had a lot to talk about.

Without even discussing it, Bella knew Jazzy would want her to drive. She had too much on her mind to pay attention to traffic. They were silent until they reached the highway. Deciding to dive in, Bella took a deep breath. "So…any idea who the neophyte is?"

Jazzy shook her head. "It would be nice if they were considerate enough to wear a pentagram on their palm, like in that stupid old movie, but unfortunately, it's not that easy."

"Sometimes the phyter doesn't even know he is one, does he?" she asked, using the term their grandmother had coined years ago.

"No." Jazzy sat quiet for so long, Bella wondered if she would continue. "And it would have to be here in the zoo for Doc to see."

Bella didn't follow the logic. "What difference does that make?"

"He already hates werewolves enough to dedicate his life to wiping out the gene." The breath Jazzy took was so thick, it sounded as if she were about to burst into tears. "Now that this has happened, if he comes to the realization that it's a Lycan who did it, he'll want to hunt us down one by one. Probably lobby congress for a season on Lycans so everyone can come after us."

"Oh, Jazzy, I don't think—"

"People don't know the difference between a werewolf who was born with the gene and one who became one as the result of an attack. All they know is that a killer wolf is a killer wolf, and there's no place for them in this world."

"You don't know Chase is like that." Bella kept her gaze on the road, but reached out to touch Jazzy's arm. Then it hit her. "You really care about him, don't you?"

"No. I don't care about him." Jazzy shifted, crossed her legs then uncrossed them. "He's... What I mean is, I'm not ever... Oh!" She grumbled the last words then turned to stare out the window, obviously finished with the conversation.

"You're a Montague and he's a Capulet?"

Jazzy shot Bella an amused look. "It's more like he's ice. And I'm fire. There's no place where we can coexist. I'd either melt him or he'd put me out. Permanently."

Bella understood her frustration. It was kind of like having a family that meant everything to you, and caring for a man who had a special disregard for one of them.

She struggled to push Spencer from her mind, but the harder she tried, the more she thought about him. Hazel eyes and a sardonic sense of humor had drawn her to him in the first place. Just the memory of him had her gripping the steering wheel hard enough to leave fingerprints. But it was his I'm-all-business demeanor that gave her lucid dreams at night, because she knew it was only a shell he wore to hide the man he truly was. A man who could set her ablaze with only a glance and burst into flame himself.

But his opinion of her sister had ruined any relationship they might have had. Because her family—her sister—meant everything to her. There was no way she could live without Jazzy in her life. And no way she'd ask her to spend time with a man who said the things he had about her.

Besides, she hadn't seen him except once or twice by accident, since the ski resort. And those times had been awkward, at best. That he'd wanted her had been obvious to even the most casual eye. Even Norman had looked at Spencer, who was looking at her, and advised them to, *Get a room.*

Because of his magnetism, it had been impossible to tear herself away. But she'd had to do it. Succumbing would mean losing Jazzy. And she could never do that.

But not a day went by that she didn't think of him. Wonder where he was and who he was doing, because a man like him wouldn't go very long without another woman moving into his life.

After a ride that had taken forever, they finally reached the apartment complex. By the time she'd parked the car, she was so exhausted, she had to drag herself to their door. But there was more to do.

Inside, she secured the deadbolt, set the alarm and followed Jazzy to her bedroom.

"What now?" Jazzy asked, exhaustion evident in every line of her body.

"We've got to decide what to do about the…"

"The newly created monster?" Self-derision filled her voice. "He'll have to be destroyed."

"But first, he'll have to be found." Bella sat in the black wingback chair that complemented the comforter on Jazzy's bed. "I don't suppose you'll be able to—"

"Not unless he fails to shower. Then I might smell the blood on him, but so could you. And so could…"

Bella waited, but Jazzy didn't finish the sentence. *Doc.*

She finally continued. "But even the newest and most ignorant Lycan can still smell when he comes to himself. He might not know how he got that way, but he'll know he has to clean up to go into public."

"And after he's showered, there's nothing you can do?"

"Not until he turns again." Jazzy sighed. "Looks like I'll have to be at the park tomorrow night at moonrise."

"Won't that be dangerous for you? Chase said this wolf was bigger, heavier than you when you treed Norman. He might turn on you and—"

"We'll have to hope that my experience will outweigh his anger." She sniffed then gave Bella a lopsided smile. "Or that he'll get hit by a car and save us all a lot of trouble."

Bella shook her head at Jazzy's macabre sense of humor. Even after being with her every day of their lives, she'd never be able to understand her entire life. And she was as close to a werewolf as one could be without going animal herself.

****

Early the next day, I canceled my appointments. No way I could spend hours with four rich women, helping them choose holiday wardrobes, then be sharp enough that night to track a *phyter*. I needed to be prepared.

How do you prepare for a wolf hunt? the tiny voice in the back of my mind demanded.

"I don't know." Yanking off my clothes, I threw them on the floor. Then I walked over them on my way to the shower. I needed to be well rested, but the nervous energy in me was going to make it hard to sleep. I needed a hot shower and something warm to drink.

After that, I'd do whatever was necessary.

When I was out of the shower, I dried my hair and dug in my drawer until I found my most comfortable pajamas—which were my only pajamas since I normally slept nude. Wrapping myself in a soft robe made of t-shirt material, I padded to the kitchen for a cup of instant cocoa.

But Bella awaited me with a steaming pot of the real thing. "I thought you might like some of this."

"What's up, sis?" I asked, slipping into one of the kitchen chairs while she poured a mug of chocolate love, topped it with whipped cream and set it in front of me. "Afraid that neophyte's going to take a hunk out of me tomorrow night?"

"Of course not," she answered. After pouring herself a cup, she sat in the chair across from me and held the mug between her hands as if trying to warm them. "I just wish this weren't happening. And that you didn't have to…"

She couldn't finish the sentence, but I knew what she meant. She wished I didn't have to hunt down one of my own kind.

"Now you see how important Chase's research is."

Her words hit me like a slap in the face. "This isn't a werewolf born because of a gene, Bella. It's an aberration. A monstrous creation that should never have happened."

"But where did he come from?" Her tone was gentle, but her meaning wasn't.

"Probably the result of another creature just like him."

"There had to be a starting point. A true Lycan who lost control and attacked a man in anger. And left him alive."

I wanted to rage at her, but what she said was true. Somewhere out there was a true werewolf who'd done this thing to the world. Grudgingly, I nodded.

She lifted her eyebrows. "And if there's one who would do that, there could be more."

I glared at her for a long time, but she didn't take back the comment. Didn't leave the table, as I knew she wanted to do. She just waited for me to answer.

I finally nodded. But only once.

"And if Chase gets rid of that gene, then it can't happen again—once the last generation of werewolves are gone."

I hated it when my sister made sense. She sipped her cocoa.

"That's wiping out an entire people because one or two of them might cause a problem. They tried that with the American Indians, remember?"

In her surprise at my comparison, she set her mug down with a thump. Hot chocolate splashed on the table.

"They even tried to kill off the buffalo in order to wipe out the Indians' food supply. And they gave them blankets infected with small pox. All because they wanted the Indians' lands, and the Indians fought back."

"But these werewolves aren't fighting back. They just kill anything they can."

"Dammit! It's wrong to wipe out any group, just because one or two cause trouble." I took a long breath as I fought to stay in control. "Take care of the specific problem, not the entire group."

Bella went to the sink for a sponge to clean up her

spill, then carried her cup back and dumped the contents. "I'm not sure what to think, Jazzy. But I am sure about one thing. We have to take care of *this* specific problem tomorrow night, and he'll be even stronger than he was tonight. If we don't stop him then, by the next night, he might be unstoppable." She came around the table to give me a hug.

"On that, big sister, we agree." I finished my drink, then went to my room and crawled into bed, immediately dropping into a deep sleep. But my slumber didn't last long. Dark dreams that made no sense kept waking me. After a very long night, I dreamed of a pack of salivating dogs, hunting down an injured wolf. I was the wolf.

I was trapped in a box canyon with no place to go. The dogs individually kept snapping, trying to get at me. Then three rushed at once, knocking me onto my back. And just as one went for my throat, I awoke.

It was daylight, and I was exhausted. I got up and went to the bathroom, and just as I wandered back, a tap came on my bedroom door.

"Jazzy? Are you up?" The door opened and Bella leaned in. "I thought I heard you moving around. I fixed breakfast, if you want some."

I didn't try to hide the grin tugging at my mouth. Bella rarely apologized verbally, but breakfast was a great way to show it. "Sounds good. What are we having?"

"Waffles and ham."

I pretended to consider for a moment. "All right. I'll be right there."

I found my robe where it had fallen on the floor and put it on. Then I tossed my comforter up over the pillows and headed for the kitchen.

I tried to keep my mind off the coming evening by paying bills, reading or watching television, but I couldn't concentrate. Heaviness weighed my belly. Dread? I wasn't sure.

Bella called the zoo and told them she'd be in, but she'd be later than she'd expected.

I had my computer on my lap, filtering through emails, when the doorbell rang that afternoon. My heart jumped as Doc flashed to my mind, but as if she could read my thoughts, Bella shook her head. "That's for me." She put down the book she'd been reading, grabbed her wallet and went to the door.

Curious, I followed. A young man in a bright orange uniform stood there with an insulated pizza carrier in his hand. "You order a My Pie?"

Without mentioning it to me, Bella had sent out for my favorite pizza. Because of the calorie and fat content, she rarely agreed to it, but apparently she thought today was special.

She pulled a bill from her purse, folded it and handed it to the kid. "Keep the change."

The bill disappeared into his pocket. He unzipped the bag and shoved a flat box at her. Then he muttered, "Thank-you-call-us-again-for-a-meal-to-make-you-smile," and was gone as if he were afraid she'd realized how big a tip she'd given him and ask for it back.

She carried the box to the table while I pulled a pair of diet sodas from the fridge. We sat across from each other. I popped my can's top while Bella opened the box lid.

The escaping steam was laden with the fantastic odor of spicy meats, rich tomato sauce and has-to-be-delicious crust. No surprise, she'd ordered my favorite—a super supreme. The one where they used every ingredient in the restaurant and three kinds of cheese on a crispy thin crust. I drew another appreciative breath. "'A sigh from My Pie,'" I quoted, putting as much gratitude as possible in my voice.

Glancing up, I caught her watching me with a worried look.

I don't believe in dancing around an issue, so I said, "Are you thinking this might be my last meal?"

"N-no," she stumbled over the word while she tried to put conviction behind it.

"Then why cook breakfast *and* order my favorite pizza?" I reached for the biggest piece in the box and pulled it out, stringing all three cheeses behind it.

"Because we had time." Her face looked pinched, but she shrugged and took a piece of the pie. "Usually we're in too big a hurry to have more than a quick salad."

"Right." I closed my eyes while I chewed so I could concentrate on the melding flavors. This was too good to rush. I had to take my time and enjoy every satisfying mouthful.

By the time we'd finished, I knew the sun drifted toward the horizon. Occasionally I can feel it when the full moon is getting ready to rise, and this was going to be one of those evenings. Not because of anything atmospheric or astrological, but because I had attuned myself to the natural.

"We'd better get ready to go."

Bella looked as if she wanted to argue, but after a moment, she changed her mind. "Let me clean this up then I'll be ready."

Oh, yeah. She was afraid for me, all right. I just hoped she had the sense to stay out of harm's way. I didn't want to have to worry about her while I stalked a killer.

We were quiet as we drove to the park. She didn't turn on the radio to NPR—her favorite station—and I couldn't think of anything to talk about. All I could do was concentrate on the night ahead.

If I found him, would I be able to control the beast? I snorted as I wondered if Doc used silver bullets in his gun.

Bella shot a glance at me. "What?"

I shrugged then gave her a half grin. "I was just imagining Doc and his pistol full of silver, out on a hunt."

"Cut the guy some slack." She turned onto the zoo's entrance road. "He's studied your sub-species long enough to know silver bullets came from some guy's imagination."

"Or the Lone Ranger."

Her chuckle was forced, but I appreciated her trying. We were quiet the rest of the way to the employees' parking lot. By the time Bella stopped the car, Doc was there to open my door. His gaze held mine. He didn't glance around or let his attention wander. It was as if I were the only thing in the world that could possibly interest him. "I wondered if you were coming today."

I all but forgot Bella—the person I'd been aware of since I was in the womb—was with us. I wanted to forget everything in the world existed—even ignore the fact that a mad werewolf would soon be on the prowl—and simply be with Doc.

But I couldn't. And he couldn't either.

As we walked to the clinic, he stayed beside me. Never touching, but constantly enveloping me in his nearness.

The sun hovered on the horizon. It wouldn't be long before moonrise. The werewolf's strength would hit him full on, and the human part of him wouldn't know what was happening. If any of his mind remained as he morphed, he'd probably think he had flashback to a bad trip, or had accidentally ingested PCP or some other hallucinatory drug.

But most likely, he wouldn't have any lucid moments at all. He'd simply turn into a mindless being who craved the taste of blood and killed for the sport. It wouldn't matter if the victim was animal or human, male or female.

"What about our wolves?" Bella asked, clearly speaking to Doc.

"They've been moved to the enclosure where we're keeping them under observation."

Bella nodded as if she'd expected him to say that. "If the wolf who killed the calf was one of ours, we'll know it."

I went with them into the clinic, found a tall stool and watched as Bella logged into the computer. She pulled up a screen that brought a view of the wolves' enclosure, but there was nothing unusual going on. Just a pack of canines, lying around.

I let my gaze wander a few feet away, where it met and held Doc's for a few moments. I knew I'd have trouble tonight, making myself leave his company.

Was it the full moon that made me feel this connection to him? I hoped not, but I couldn't worry about that then, even though it would take everything I had to tear myself away from him. I could only hope Bella would help me. She knew what had to be done, so I planned to depend on her when the time came…until the door opened and Doc's brother, Spencer, walked in.

Bella stopped what she was doing and stared at him for a moment as her face paled. I'd never been able to get her to tell me exactly what he'd done to upset her the night of the dance, but I wouldn't forgive him for it—at least until Bella did. I offered, however, to tear a hole in him—literally—if she wanted. "What is this? Old home week?"

Spencer barely glanced my way then turned back to Bella. "Hello."

Bella's brow puckered as her eyes flashed. Her mouth flattened, her anger with Spencer darkening her face. Leave it to her—she wasn't about to sugarcoat her words. "What are you doing here?"

Spencer crossed the room and stopped in front of her. "I want to talk to you." His tone was intimate, but if they'd even spoken besides at the dedication dinner and at the spa, I didn't know anything about it.

I shot a questioning look at Doc, but he lifted his brows and shook his head. He was in the dark on this, too.

The look on Bella's face gradually softened. "Do you want to go outside where we can—"

"No!" Spencer encircled her wrists with his hands, but he grasped her as gently as if he'd put his arms around her. "Doc told me about the buffalo calf last night. Stay where it's safe tonight, Bella. They still aren't sure what did that damage, so whatever you do, don't go out."

Bella swallowed hard, opened her mouth then closed it. I'd never before seen her at a loss for words, but she was tonight.

This was going to be interesting.

Too bad I couldn't stay and watch. I slid off my stool. "Well, I'd better get going."

Before my sister could respond, Doc crossed to me. "Spencer's suggestion is a good one for all of us. You were lucky you weren't attacked last night. Stay inside where you're safe."

"I just came in to say hello. I have an appointment in a little while." I glanced at my watch, then back to his face. My mind went blank when I saw the intensity in his gaze. It took me a moment to remember what I'd been saying. "I'll be back to pick up Bella in a little while."

Doc stared at me for a moment as if testing for truth then slowly nodded. "I'll walk you to your car."

I should have known better than to go into the clinic. If I'd never gone inside, I wouldn't have to resort to subterfuge now. Irritated that I had to go to such trouble, I stalked out to the parking lot with Doc right behind me.

When I got to the car, Doc reached for the door. But rather than open it for me, he moved close. I was trapped within the circle of his arms, his face mere inches from mine. Oxygen left the atmosphere.

"I imagine Spencer would be happy to drive Bella home if you don't want to come all the way back out here."

With the lack of oxygen to my brain, it took a moment to grasp the meaning of his words. "Don't even go there. My sister would sleep in the clinic before she'd accept a ride from your brother."

Doc lowered one eyebrow then crooked a smile that turned me to liquid. "Especially if Spencer were here to sl—"

"Don't finish that sentence. If Bella accidentally heard you or even knew you'd thought it, she'd be harder to deal with than whoever killed the calf last night." I sucked my bottom lip between my teeth and bit down hard as I realized what I'd said—whoever instead of whatever killed the calf. Maybe if I kept talking, he wouldn't pick up on my mistake.

"And Bella isn't easy to be around when she's pissed. I'd rather deal with a rabid viper than have to deal with my sister when she's angry. I've seen her..." I rattled on, trying to obscure my mistake with a gush of words.

He stopped the flood by kissing me.

As if struck by lightning, I flashed hot all over. Very slowly my arms wrapped themselves around his neck and my body leaned into his.

He slid his hands down my back to my bottom and held me against him. He was hard, tight, and almost more than I could bear to walk away from.

But he lifted his head in order to gasp a breath, and over his shoulder, I saw the moon.

A fat, white, perfectly round harbinger of death.

I dipped my head to stop his next kiss, resting my forehead on his chest.

"What's wrong?" he rasped in a voice so low, I barely heard him.

My brain spun, making it hard to form a logical thought. After a long moment, I remembered my faux appointment. I glanced up at him. "I-I'm going to be late."

He frowned as if trying to make sense of my words, then tightened his arms around me. "Can't you cancel?"

It was all I could do to force my head to shake side to side. I didn't want to leave the shelter of his embrace. I wanted to stay there with my heart next to his, where it belonged.

But someone out there was infected and would, without a doubt, attack. Tonight. And I had to be there to stop him.

I gave him a fast kiss then tearing myself out of his arms, got into the car. I started the engine and, with a wave, drove out of the lot. As I left, I glanced into the rearview mirror. He stood there, his hands on his hips.

Watching me drive away.

Chapter Eight

I didn't drive far. A picnic area near the compound stood empty, so I pulled in. After parking at the back behind a small outcropping of trees, I stepped out and quietly closed the door.

The moon had edged higher in the sky, gilding the world with a silvery highlight. It was nothing for me to morph that night. All I had to do was release.

And I did.

In no time I ran on all fours, free in the world of the untamed. I ran hard, heating my muscles as I ducked under low growing bushes and dodged clumps of tall grasses. I dipped into a small trench then back out again, delighted with my freedom. A giraffe rolled her eyes and maneuvered her calf behind her when she saw me running in their direction, but I veered away. Slowing to a trot, I topped a small rise.

Sitting on my haunches, I lifted my nose in the air and howled. I wasn't sure exactly where I was, but the wild in me didn't care.

As I drew a breath for another howl, I caught something on the wind. Another wolf, but something was wrong with the scent.

His underlying scent was man.

With a jolt, I realized I'd temporarily lost all memory of who I was and why I was on the hunt. I didn't remember shifting or the beginning of my run.

I moved from the hillock to the low ground then deeper into the tall grasses where I burrowed down, keeping my body on the ground.

He was coming. For a moment, I was in concert with him. I could hear his heart, beating too fast. Feel his breaths searing his lungs. Experience the tumult of his mind—swirling, angry, confused.

His fur practically brushed mine as he passed without realizing I was there. Heat wafted from him, as if he'd run for miles, searching for something. The musk of his scent was heavy with blood. Without actually seeing him, I knew his muzzle was covered with it. He'd already killed. And, if he wasn't stopped, he'd do it again.

Not wanting him to notice my movement, I slowly raised and, keeping low, crept through the underbrush after him.

When he was far enough ahead not to notice me, I increased my speed so I could keep his stench in my nostrils. We made a huge arc, looping past the area where the baby buffalo had died then turning toward the compound.

Navigating a drainage ditch, I lost his scent—which had to be a miracle in itself—but as I came out, I picked it up again. Instead of it coming from in front of me, it was beside me. I dropped prone then edged along the ground toward heavier brush. Now his scent came from behind

Fear stiffened my muscles as animal instinct hit. The hunted was now hunting me.

Finding a rabbit run through the extremely heavy lower brush, I shoved my way into it, my heart pounding in my chest. If this inexperienced animal, now on my trail, was a male the size and weight Doc had spoken of the night before, he'd never fit into the run. I could barely force my way inside.

The space tunneled through underbrush so dense, I couldn't see out. And nothing could see in. But I didn't stop.

I pushed and wiggled until I was safely inside. Even the tip of my tail couldn't show. I clamped down on my fright until I was able to quiet my breathing so I wouldn't be heard, and only hoped the rabbit hair, which lined the run, wouldn't tickle my nose enough to make me sneeze.

Before long, I heard the snuffling sound of his tracking. After what seemed like hours, he must have found the entrance, because I heard frantic scratching, digging, then at last, whining born of frustration.

Good. If I had any luck at all, he'd give up soon.

But I'd have to leave the rabbit hole and follow him once more.

Time slowed. I imagined him lying at the entrance, waiting for me like a cat for a mouse to come out of a hole. I couldn't turn around in order to look outside before emerging, which meant I'd have to leave tail first.

If he were still there, by the time I could see anything at all, I'd be in big trouble.

Instead of backing out, I decided to force my way farther into the tunnel. Sticks poked at my eyes while tiny branches scratched my hide, but I didn't care.

Anything was better than being exposed to were-baby, while blinded by the brush. After working for some time, I came to a break in the tunnel that, presumably, another wolf had made at some time trying to get a rabbit. Or maybe the werewolf had made it, trying to get to me tonight. Luckily he hadn't been able to force his way inside. At least I could see out.

Hanging low in the sky, drifting toward the horizon, was the moon.

I had to move. Now.

Shoving out of the hideaway, I opened my senses. The man's cleverness and ability to navigate in his new waters amazed me. I couldn't let the animal take me by surprise again.

When I could get no sense of him, I glanced again at the moon. It had dropped to balance on the horizon. In moments, it would be completely gone, and the neophyte would shift back to human.

On full alert, I started back toward my car. The last moments before he lost the moon could be the most powerful, and hardest, on a *phyter*. The last thing I wanted was to come upon him unaware.

As I reached the picnic grounds and my car, I heard a pain filled howl.

Then nothing.

The moon was gone.

I shifted, dressed then got into the car. After glancing at the clock, I saw hours had passed. I took my cell phone from the ashtray where I'd left it and saw I'd missed a couple of calls, so I listened to my messages.

As I thought, there was one from Bella. "Where are you, Jazzy? Probably hung up in that meeting. I'm going to catch a ride home, so don't bother coming back to the park for me. I'll talk to you tomorrow."

By the tone of her voice and what she didn't say, I knew someone stood nearby, probably listening.

She couldn't have contacted me mentally while I

was hairy and scary, but I might be able to reach her now, even with all those miles separating us. Especially if she was thinking about me.

Bella, can you hear me? I paused a moment. *Bella? You aren't asleep, are you?*

Bella's gasp crossed the miles to me, but her words were as soft as dried leaves whispering in the wind. *Jazzy! I was so worried about you. Are you all right?*

Her thoughts, so muted, made me wonder if she'd fallen asleep. *I'm fine. I can tell you all about it in the morning.*

All right, she answered. *If you're sure you're okay.*

She quickly spiraled away from me, making me think there was something tugging at her. Maybe she'd taken something for a migraine or a sleeping pill. Either would do it, but I couldn't imagine her letting herself be out of it when I was in such a dangerous situation and not home yet. She was usually such a worrier.

I started my car and put it in gear. Because of the late hour and the light traffic, I didn't look as closely as I should have for oncoming traffic. I pulled onto the highway right in front of a DPS trooper.

Naturally, he flipped on his lights, so I pulled to the shoulder.

The man talked on his radio for a moment, got out of his car with a flashlight and walked toward mine. I watched as his lights drenched him with color. First red, then blue.

I rolled down my window as he neared the car. "Good evening, ma'am."

Weariness made it difficult, but I forced a smile. "Good evening, officer."

"May I see your license and proof of insurance?"

I reached under the seat, where I'd stowed my purse, and pulled it out. Then I fished inside for my wallet. After finding it, I pulled out the requested cards.

He took them, lighting them with his flashlight. After reading each, he said, "Mind if I ask what you're doing out here, this time of night?"

"Going home. I was at a meeting that ran longer than expected."

He lifted both eyebrows. "Meeting?"

I gave him my haughtiest smile. "I'm a fashion consultant. As such, I must be available whenever my clients have time." I let my smile soften. "And sometimes that's not very…convenient for me."

"But it is for them, right?" He glanced around at the dark landscape as if imagining faraway houses. "Probably one of those country western people who're starting to buy up the place, huh?"

I gave him a light shrug. "I can't discuss the name of my clients. They like people to believe they're naturally fashion gifted."

He barked laughter then grew serious. "Well, be careful driving home. There've been some ritual type deaths in the area tonight. Mutilation of animals at the drive through zoo, that sort of thing. You wouldn't want to run into that."

I firmly shook my head. "No, sir. I would *not*."

"And check for oncoming traffic before you turn onto the road next time."

With a wave, he walked back to his car.

I checked the mirrors then pulled back onto the road.

The drive home was longer than the one out had been. I turned on music to keep myself awake, but it didn't help much. Finally, after what seemed like hours, I was on our street. But even the block before our garage was longer than usual. As I drove the final hundred yards, I almost dozed off three times, but at long last, was ready to turn in.

First, though, I had to wait for a car, pulling out. Who in their right mind went places at that time of night?

Besides me, that is.

Finally, I parked in my space then dragged myself to our apartment. Exhaustion fogged my brain. It took me quite a while to get the correct key for the door then fit it into the hole.

When I was at long last inside, I was disappointed that Bella wasn't waiting for me. It was hard to believe anything could have kept her away. Whatever she'd taken to help her sleep must have been powerful.

I went into the kitchen for a glass of water. Opening the dishwasher to load the glass, I found two wine glasses, side by side.

I hadn't had a glass of wine in several days.

If Bella had taken a sleep aid, she had no business drinking alcohol. But she knew that better than anyone. So it hadn't been a pill dragging her away from our mental conversation.

It must have been a man. Walking to her door, I eased it open, careful not to wake her. I took a long breath. It was redolent with the scent of a man…and sex.

Surprised there was someone she cared enough about to sleep with but hadn't even mentioned to me, I quietly closed the door.

Who could it be? The only one who'd caught her

attention in the last year was Spencer, and that relationship had crashed and burned almost as soon as it started.

So who?

My heart dropped as an answer came to mind. Could it be Doc?

After all, she worked with him every day, and a man who had so many good qualities would be difficult to resist. Besides, they had so much in common. It only made sense.

But it broke my heart.

Going into my room, I crashed on the bed, facedown, hoping for oblivion. But after several moments, I could still smell myself. Crawling back out, I tossed my clothes where I'd been lying and padded to the bathroom.

After the fastest shower in the record books, I staggered back to bed, scooped my clothes onto the floor, fell back in and slept like the dead.

After a few hours, the dreams started. Nonsensical dreams, as if I were caught in the mind of the new werewolf. We hurtled down a brush-filled tunnel, not unlike Alice's rabbit hole, when a distant noise disturbed me. The noise sounded again and again, lifting me through layers of sleep until I came to awareness.

The phone. Barely able to open my eyes, I fumbled for it, pushed the on button and rested it against my ear. The first time I tried to speak, I could only whisper, so I tried again. "Hello?"

"Jazzy? It's Bella. Are you awake?"

While she talked, I rolled to my side and drifted again toward sleep. I knew I had to answer, but since

I'd buried my mouth against my pillow, I just hummed.

"Jazzy! Wake up! Talk to me."

Her tone grated, yanking me to wakefulness. Not where I wanted to be, but Bella would have her way. Dammit. I lifted my head far enough to speak into the mouthpiece. "All right. I'm awake. What's so urgent?" Shoving myself upward, I stacked my pillows then relaxed against them while I straightened out my tangled bedclothes.

She dropped her voice to a whisper. "Did you see the wolf last night?"

I closed my eyes for a moment as the memory of what I'd experienced in the rabbit run returned. The night's fear sent my heart pounding. "Let's just say I made his acquaintance."

"And?"

"He's gotten a handle on his condition rather quickly, Bella. I tracked him over half of the zoo property, then he pulled a switch. And started hunting me."

"Oh, Jazzy. What if he'd hurt you? Why didn't you wake me when you came in?"

I started to tell her why, but decided against it. "It was a long night, and I needed a shower and sleep time. Sorry if you were worried."

I could almost see her shrug. "It's an older sister thing. I'll get over it."

I chuckled obligingly.

Then she turned serious. "We lost three more animals last night, and one was a full grown javelina."

"Da-amn." A full grown wild boar is dangerous. Definitely not an animal to be taken lightly. And this new creature had not only attacked but killed the hog.

Maybe I was lucky to have survived the night.

"Jazzy, we've got to do something."

We? I wanted to snap. *Maybe we could get you a fur coat and let you put your life on the line this time.*

If I said that to her, without a doubt I'd regret it. If it were possible, she'd be out there with me, hunting this creature down. But I wasn't exactly enthusiastic about putting my life on the line again. "What do you suggest?"

"I don't know. Maybe we need to bring Doc in on this."

I knew the truth of what she said, but didn't want to think of it. For a werewolf to have to take out another one was one thing, but for a werewolf hater to help in the kill was quite another.

Feeling as if sugar ants crawled over me, I kicked off my sheets and got out of bed. Why involve Doc? He'd only enjoy the killing, and use the neophyte as proof that his cause was justified.

My arms itched as the urge to smack something took over. Then the tingle climbed my neck to my face. Shoving my hair from my face, I glanced into the mirror, and saw why I'd been unable to open my eyes.

My face was red and swollen with welts. I glanced at my breasts, my belly, my thighs. Everything was covered with huge lumps that looked as if someone had shoved rocks under my skin.

I started chuckling into the phone at my predicament.

"What's so funny?" Bella asked, her crankiness coming to the fore at my laughter.

"I had to hide in a rabbit run last night to escape the wolf. Trouble is, that run must have been in the middle of a clump of sumac. Poison sumac."

She was quiet for a moment. "But we're allergic to poison sumac."

"You should see me." I snorted as I watched my reflection in the mirror. "I look like the Michelin Tire Man after a hundred miles of bad road."

"I'll be right there."

By the time she got to the apartment, the sugar ants had morphed to fire ants. My lips were big enough to make Angelina Jolie envious. My eyes were swollen so badly, I could barely see the door to walk out of it with her.

At the doctor's office, I got a steroid shot, a prescription for heavy duty itch relief and one for pain. I took the max prescribed while Bella changed the sheets on my bed and put the dirty ones into the wash with hot water and bleach.

When we were sure my room was clear of all sumac residue, I went back to bed and slept like the dead.

This time I didn't dream at all. Anytime I awoke, it was to take another pill and fall back into that deep sleep where no ants could reach me.

I didn't come fully awake again until late the next day. After checking the mirror to be sure my skin was well, I wrapped up in my robe and went in search of Bella.

I found her, still in our kitchen, dressed for work with a cup of coffee in her hand. I poured myself a cup and sat down opposite her. She glanced at my face, my neck then my arms. Relief brightened her face when she saw my allergic reaction had cleared. "You're looking better."

"Thanks. I feel better." Taking a long, hot drink, I leaned back in my chair to savor the bitter taste.

After a few moments of quiet, I remembered the waxing moon. And the *phyter* I should have stopped, but hadn't. I couldn't stand it that she wasn't telling me. "So what happened last night?"

She stared into her cup for a long time before she answered. Wolf got your tongue? I wondered, but wisely kept silent.

"It's not good," she began.

Exasperated at the way she danced around the subject, I snapped, "*What's* not good? Just tell me."

"Tony's in the hospital. The neophyte attacked him."

I straightened in my chair as I tried to get my mind around what she said. "You're kidding. An inexperienced werewolf attacked a man? That…that's ludicrous." Like all wild creatures, most werewolves were leery of men. Of what they could do.

And they should be.

"I'm not kidding, Jazzy."

"Can you be sure it was the werewolf that attacked him?" I grilled. "Who found him?"

"Doc did. He was trying to get to the clinic and collapsed."

"Was he torn up or just shaken up?"

"He was hurt, not just shaken up. But I'm not sure if he was badly bitten or not."

For a man to get the Lycan infection, he had to be deeply bitten in a fleshy part of the core. A nip on the hand, foot or lower leg usually wouldn't do it. "Where is he?"

"In St. Luke's." The hospital had been built

decades ago in downtown Dallas.

I knew I had to do something, but just what, I wasn't sure. Making a swift decision, I slammed my cup on the table. "I'll be dressed in five minutes. Don't leave without me."

She glanced at her watch then nodded. "Hurry."

I showered and threw on a casual jog suit. I didn't have time to dry my hair, so I drew it in to a short, sassy style. I grabbed my purse, shoved my travel makeup bag inside and skidded into the kitchen at just under five minutes. Barely. "What are you waiting for? Let's go."

Shaking her head, Bella led the way out the door and to the garage.

We got into the car and buckled up. "You know, Jazzy, some people put their makeup on *before* leaving the house."

I did a quick brush on with my eye shadow, shrugging as I smudged black eyeliner along my lash line. "But you're supposed to put it on in the car. Why else would they put so many mirrors in here?"

When Bella chuckled at my old joke, I knew she was worried. Usually she just shook her head or threw something at me. "At least this time, you aren't driving."

"I can if you want me to." I put away the liner and pulled out my mascara.

Now she shook her head, a half smile curving her lips. "No thanks."

I smirked at her as I finished my lashes and opened my foundation. Without spilling a drop, I sponged it on, set it with powder then finished up with a lip stain. Who wanted to be concerned about lip color when we possibly had a new werewolf to be worried about?

"How's that?" I asked. "I don't look like I've seen a ghost."

"You didn't look like you'd seen one yesterday, either. You looked like you'd been smacked around by someone."

"I felt as if I had been, too."

Bella flipped on her XM radio, and we drove the rest of the way to the zoo listening to her favorite jazz station. Maybe listening to music helped her forget her problems, but it just gave me more time to concentrate on mine.

I had a lot to do while "assisting" Doc in his lab that day. I had to pump him for information about Tony while I looked for ways to sabotage his research.

It was going to be a full day.

As we walked into the clinic, Doc's face brightened and a long, slow smile spread across his lips. "Hello, Jazzy."

I barely found enough oxygen to answer him. "Hi, Doc."

My face warmed as his gaze caressed each part of it. "I heard you had a bad bout with poison sumac, but you look…good."

"Thanks."

He looked at Bella then. "Good morning, Dr. B."

"Morning." Bella shrugged into her smock. "Anything going on this morning?"

"Just the usual."

"Well, I'll do recovery checkups this morning since I wasn't here yesterday."

Doc nodded. "And I'll put Jazzy to work in the lab."

It was all I could do not to grin triumphantly. Without even pushing, I got what I wanted.

I followed him into the adjacent room, where he handed me a clipboard and a pen. "I could use your help cataloguing some data, if you don't mind."

"After my last stint here, this will be a piece of cake," I joked, referring to cleaning the recovery cages.

He moved past a table covered with small machines and glass tubes. After a moment, he booted up a computer. "Was the sumac rash very painful?"

"Not if you don't find being pummeled by a street gang painful," I joked, then needing to learn as much as possible about the wolf attack, I sobered. "I hear one of your helpers was injured last night."

"Yeah. Tony had a run in with a crazy wolf. I'm thinking it's the same one that's been killing animals the two nights before that. I'm going to see Tony this evening at the hospital."

"Really? I didn't know you were good friends."

"We're not." He glanced at me over the top of the computer screen then walked around the table to stand near me. "I'm glad you came in today. I was afraid I'd have to come get you to help me."

I had no idea where he was going with the topic, so I didn't answer, but my nerves tightened as if I waited for the floor of the gallows to drop.

He leveled his gaze, concentrating as if trying to speak to me mentally, the way Bella does. Of course I heard nothing. After a very long moment, he drew a breath. "Just between the two of us, I think this wolf that attacked him might be truly insane. A werewolf."

I thought Bella and I had kept that idea just between us. Had my sister said something to tip him off? "What makes you think that?"

"The damage done to the buffalo calf first caught my attention. It didn't make sense for an animal to do that kind of damage. *Most* creatures won't kill except to eat. And nothing was eaten. So I knew we had some kind of predator killing for sport. The second night, when an animal of the same approximate weight with the same kind of tracks killed three animals for sport, especially one as dangerous as a full grown mama javelina, I was fairly sure."

Hell, the guy was too observant. I couldn't answer him. Couldn't think of a single thing to say that might change the direction of his logical mind.

"But I witnessed the attack last night. Or at least the very end of it. The wolf looked normal in every way. But it attacked a man, walking across the compound just far enough behind two others for them not to hear what was happening at first. Only a rabid animal will do something as fool hardy as attack a man like that. And when one of the men grabbed a gun from his truck and shot at it, it just turned and ran into the night." He lifted one shoulder in a half shrug. "He might not have hit a vital area, but I don't believe Lawrence missed completely. Not at that range."

My mouth went dry at his words. He knew a human couldn't kill a werewolf while in his animal state, which is why it wasn't affected by the shot. Practically proof it was a werewolf that had attacked Tony. I swallowed hard. "But why do you need me to go to the hospital with you?"

"Because I need to draw blood from Tony. It could be that he'll need an injection a week until the next full moon to kill the Syzygia infection."

"Veterinarians who practice medicine on humans are looking for trouble," I murmured softly, then raised my voice a notch. "You didn't answer my question. Why should I go with you?"

The long slow look returned. Maybe he weighed his words, but it honestly felt as if he'd read my mind. "I know, Jazzy."

"You..." My mind froze. I didn't know what to say. What to ask. How to lie.

"Yes. I finally added it all up." His eyes grew darker, more intense. His fingers tightened around mine, and for the first time I realized he touched me. His voice dropped to a whisper. "I know you're a werewolf."

Chapter Nine

I fought to draw a breath. My face must have been a study in horror. I'm sure my alarm glowed like a grand opening spotlight on a moonless night. I finally gathered my thoughts enough to speak. "You think I'm a what?" I was even able to make a whispery laughing sound.

"I know." He didn't try to argue with me. Just went on talking as if making the statement made it true. "I need you to be with me when I go to the hospital to talk to him. I think I can cure him, but I want him to know that if I can't, he can live a normal life. He'll just have to learn to stay in control. The way you have."

When my heart finally started beating again, it thudded against my chest wall so hard, it was painful. My knees grew weak as I realized what this meant. I pulled my hand away from his and crawled onto a nearby stool. "Would you get Bella? Please?"

Another pause. A stare. Then he went in search of Bella. Frantic, I tried to make my brain work. What could I do to change his mind? To make him think—no, force him to think—he was wrong?

I looked around at the data he'd collected. Rows of information, logged, duplicated, and backed up. Dammit, the man knew too much. Had too much knowledge for it to be easy to fool him.

Maybe I should just wipe him off the face of the

earth. My heart beat a little easier at the thought, then Bella came in and I knew she'd never let me. And in just a moment, Doc followed her, and just one look at him reminded me.

I couldn't do it, either.

My sister rushed to me as if she thought I was sick. Or breaking out in lumps again. "Are you okay?"

"No." I tried to think of a way to tell her my secret was out.

She looked me over, trying to assess the emergency. Since I wasn't retching or holding my head— "What is it? Do you need me to take you home?"

"I *wish* that would solve my problem."

Bella shifted her glance from me to Doc. "Do you know what she's talking about?"

I had a feeling he was trying for a casual stance, as if what he was about to say had little consequence. He leaned on one elbow and shrugged. Then he cleared his throat, shot a quick look at me then focused on Bella. "I just told Jazzy I know—" He took a long breath.

Right there my granny, my dad's mom, would have said, *In for a penny, in for a pound. Get about it, boy.* I held my breath instead.

"She carries the Syzygia genome."

Bella's mouth dropped open and her eyes all but popped out of her head. Very slowly her gaze migrated from Doc to me. He might have guessed she thought he was nuts, but I knew that look. It was her scramble-for-cover-we're-in-trouble goggle.

She blinked twice, shook her head slightly. "You think my sister carries what?"

"She's a werewolf," he simplified. Straightening,

he sighed, his shoulders sagging. "Don't pretend you don't know."

Bella drew her brows together, her gaze hardened as she readied to do battle. "What, exactly, put that notion in your head?" I'd never heard her speak to him with such a sharp tone.

"Observation." His tone softened in direct proportion to hers. "Remember, I was with her at the dedication dinner. I went nuts when you whisked her out of there, then I couldn't find her the next day. I put our pilot on standby and was ready to hire a private investigator. To find Jazzy."

Bella just stared at him, her face draining of color.

"I took off minutes after your call. I found her on the slopes. And again during the eclipse." His nostrils flared as he took a quick breath. "She belongs to me."

He couldn't have said anything that did better job of shaking me out of my stupor. Fury flamed through me, all but setting my hair on fire. "Belong? To you?" I roared my indignation as I leaped from the stool.

He moved closer, capturing me with his total attention. Cornered against the table, I had to climb over the top, knock him down or listen to him. I listened. "Yes. And I belong to you. We're mates."

I wanted to fight the truth of his statement. After all, I was a human first, not an animal. I carried the gene, but I wouldn't be controlled by it. As an independent woman of legal age, I didn't have to do what anyone or anything dictated.

Even if my body screamed for him while my heart could only beat in concert with his. Even if denying him meant dying or living a celibate life, and I wasn't sure which would be worse.

Rather than voice my indignation, I snorted with laughter. "Sorry, guy. If mating is what you're hanging your argument on, I've belonged to Perry Oliver since my senior year in high school."

Bella moved behind him where I could see her. She smiled, although it didn't reach her eyes, and nodded her encouragement.

Doc glowered at my mention of another man in my life. "You didn't mate for life, or you'd still be with him."

"And I didn't mate for life with you either." I put my palm against his chest and shoved. Unexpectedly, and a little disappointingly, he fell back a step back. "And now I'm leaving."

I grabbed Bella and we headed for the door. Just as I yanked it open, I glanced at him, and my heart stuttered. Maybe I shouldn't go. Maybe there was something to what he said.

****

When Jazzy hesitated at the door, her gaze, warm as a mesquite fire on a cold day, seared Chase. He stared after her, wondering how she could walk away from him. More than just wanting her, he had to have her near him. Without her, he couldn't go on.

But if she didn't share his urgency, maybe he'd been mistaken. Maybe she wasn't really a werewolf and it had been wishful thinking on his part. Or privation.

Anger roiling in his gut, he stormed around his lab, finding the things he needed. Putting them in a small, zippered bag, he tucked them into his jacket pocket, fished his truck keys out of another pocket and headed out the door.

He stalked to the parking lot, climbed into the

pickup and started the engine. After shifting into gear, he drove to the service road where he remembered to buckle his seatbelt. No use getting himself killed. He'd already made one mistake that day. He didn't want to make another.

The drive into Dallas took long enough that he'd calmed down by the time he got to the hospital. Lucky enough to find a spot in St. Luke's inadequate—and not a little dangerous after dark—parking lot, he locked the truck and walked inside. After a glance around, he spotted the information desk just past the gift shop, with a pair of older women manning it.

He gave the nearest one an easy smile. "I'm here to see Tony Vulasgo."

She nodded then read through the half glasses perched on her nose. "Mr. Vulasgo is on the tenth floor. Room 1032."

"Thank you." He turned to the row of elevators and pushed the up button. While he waited, he checked the list of floors. The fourth floor was maternity and newborns. Eight was for surgery and ICU. Ten was for psychiatric patients.

Psychiatric patients? Unable to stand still, Chase glanced around for the stairs, but the green light came on over one of the elevators. He stepped on with several other people, and when they'd all indicated the floor of their preference, the tenth hadn't been highlighted, so he pushed it.

Chase stayed on the elevator after everyone else exited, riding alone to the top floor. When he stepped out, he glanced around. It looked like every other hospital floor he'd ever been on. Pleasant colors. Clean smells. Closed doors. Absolutely no padded walls.

Maybe those were inside the rooms.

He checked for numbers and started up the hall. After turning down another hallway, he found the room. He knocked lightly then hesitated as he stepped into the darkened room. Near the bed, Tony sat in a chair turned toward the window. "Hello, Tony."

Chase checked the blinds to make sure they were closed. Tony could see nothing, but from the look in his eyes, he was so heavily sedated, he didn't know the difference.

Tony's lips moved as he whispered something. Unable to hear him, Chase crossed the room and knelt beside his chair. "What'd you say, Tone?"

Finally Tony turned his head toward Chase, but he still wasn't sure Tony knew he was in the room. In a voice almost too low to hear, Tony whispered painfully, "Mother Mary, full…"

A uniformed woman bustled into the room, giving Chase a professional grin. "We have a visitor, I see. Isn't that nice, Mr. Vee? We love to see friends, don't we?" She nodded to Chase as if they had a mutual secret.

Chase stood, glad his blood draw supplies were still in his pocket. "Hello."

"Would you like a chair? I can bring one from another room for you if you'd like."

"No, thank you. I can only stay a few minutes," Chase answered.

The nurse moved to Tony's side, took his blood pressure and, using an external monitor, his temperature.

The entire time she noted Tony's vitals, he kept murmuring the prayer.

"Well, I'll be back in a little while to put him in bed."

Chase nodded, but she'd bustled out of the room as fast as she came in, pulling the door closed behind her. He doubted that she'd seen him nod.

Pulling the bag out of his pocket, he unzipped it and pulled out the supplies. Working quickly, he strapped Tony's arm, cleaned the site with an alcohol swab and slid a needle into a vein. As the blood bubbled into the first tube, a dark feeling settled in his gut. By the time he'd drawn both vials his entire being was drenched in darkness.

As he finished, he once more swabbed Tony's arm, then held a dry pad over it to make sure the bleeding stopped so he wouldn't have to use a bandage.

Just as he tucked his bag of supplies back in his pocket, the door swung open again.

"I brought you that chair," the nurse announced, but instead of carrying the seat herself, she had a man behind her with it.

Chase fought the darkness as he searched for his normal voice. "You shouldn't have bothered. I'm just leaving."

The woman's face fell as if she'd hoped he'd stay. "Oh, well. It'll be here for you when you come back."

He nodded, a bubble of dark mirth stirring inside him. It looked as if he'd be back in a day or two in order to give Tony that injection to kill the Lycan infection. He'd sit on it then.

If this trip was any indication, he needed to have someone with him to stand guard. He definitely would need someone next time.

Maybe he could convince Jazzy.

****

Bella sat with Jazzy in front of the TV, watching a movie. But she hadn't paid much attention to what was playing. Her mind was occupied with Chase and his statement that he and Jazzy were mated. For life.

He'd spent too much time lately studying wolves. And werewolves. How long would it be before Jazzy could convince him she wasn't a Lycan? How hard would that be for her sister? Hopefully, not too hard. She'd had to deny her heritage practically since she'd first learned she could morph.

Well, not denying, maybe. Hiding was really a better word. A pastime encouraged by Bella and demanded by their parents. Only their maternal grandmother had nurtured Jazzy's animal side.

Thank God for Nana.

Jealousy niggled Bella as she glanced Jazzy's way. Had that been Chase's way of saying he loved her? Wanted her to be his? Had he, in essence, been proposing?

Or merely propositioning?

Chase was a perfect match for Jazzy, even if she knew better than to believe they'd mated. He was strong enough to keep up with her while not being overwhelmed by her personality. She couldn't run over him, no matter how hard she tried.

Perhaps marrying someone like him would dilute Jazzy's Lycan gene. Maybe, someday, in generations to come, the Syzygia strain would be completely eradicated from their family.

Bella looked forward to that day, although she wouldn't dare tell Jazzy. For some reason, her sister had convinced herself that being a werewolf was a good thing.

"Are you hungry yet?" Jazzy asked, her tone as demanding as it was irritating.

"Yeah, I am getting a little empty. Where do you want to—"

"Pete's Steak House and Bar."

Bella couldn't help curling her nose. "Jazzy, that place is so…"

"I'll buy," Jazzy answered.

"And it's kind of rough."

"Perfect." Jazzy nodded sharply, stood and went to her room. She came back almost immediately with her purse over her shoulder. "All I want is a steak. Rare. Not ambiance. Not candle light and magnolias. Not even to watch movie stars coming and going. And I don't want classical music while I eat. All I want is meat."

Shaking her head, Bella got up and found her purse. "And I'm stuck eating there, too. Yuck."

"You'll live. And next time, I'll let you decide where we're going."

Bella couldn't help smiling at her sister. "I think you said that last time."

Jazzy's eyes sparked as she grinned. "I did."

The ride to Pete's was fast and exciting. But not dangerous. Not with Jazzy behind the wheel. It might feel as if she took chances when she drove, but she knew what she was doing. Bella knew she was as safe with her sister as any driver she'd ever ridden with.

As they pulled into the graveled parking lot, Bella thanked the heavens above that she hadn't changed into good shoes. The old joggers she wore had enough miles on them that she couldn't hurt them, no matter how sharp the gravel they'd have to navigate on their way inside. As long as she didn't break an ankle, she'd be fine.

Jazzy stopped the car, unbuckled and jumped out before Bella could much more than unbuckle. Without hesitating, she took off for the restaurant with Bella in her wake. They circled past everything from farm trucks to brand new Cadillacs, and were finally inside, where the mouthwatering aroma of smoked meat greeted them.

The wood floor hadn't been varnished or waxed in so many years, they walked on bare wood. On the walls were antique and rusted farm and kitchen implements. And there were about two acres of tables, most of which were filled.

Once seated, Bella picked up the menu and started reading through the salads.

Jazzy took Bella's menu and closed it. "We're having steak."

Gritting her teeth to keep from saying anything, Bella reached past Jazzy and picked the menu up again.

"I said we're having steak." Jazzy reached for the menu, but Bella held on tight.

"You can have anything you want," Bella answered without looking at her.

"This meal was my idea, so we're having—"

"Mind if we join you?"

Startled by the voice she'd heard so often lately in her dreams, Bella glanced up to find Spencer and Chase standing nearby. Spencer grinned at them.

"No," Jazzy answered with a flippant shrug. "Please. Sit."

Doc took a chair, angled it toward Jazzy, and sat.

Spencer, dressed in a casual jacket and jeans, pulled out the other chair, but waited as he watched her.

She stared hard at him. Why should she let him sit near her? After his attitude toward Jazzy, she shouldn't speak to him. Ever again.

But a glance at Jazzy, her head so near Chase's as they murmured together after she'd just been angry enough with him to squash him like a bug, gave Bella a second thought. Why should she hold so tightly to her anger? For the safety of what's been for so long? The comfort?

She had to either let him sit or make him stand there and watch all evening like a medieval man servant. And as enjoyable as having her own personal come-when-I-beckon-slave sounded, she couldn't do it. After making him stand a moment longer, she grudgingly nodded.

He sat near her. Too near. "Have you ordered?" His tone was as smoky as the air around them.

"Not yet. I think I'm having the steak salad. What do you like to eat here?"

Spencer chuckled. "I have what most sane people have at a steak house. A steak."

"And ordering a salad at a steak house means I'm not sane?" Bella tipped her head as she silently dared him to answer.

He shrugged. "At least it has steak in it, so maybe you aren't too far gone."

A waitress, casually dressed in jeans and a pink t-shirt that said, *Pete's Texas Steak House—50 Years of Damn Good Food* stopped by their table with a pad in her hands. "You ready to order?"

"Steak salad for me," Bella answered before

someone could try to order for her.

The other three at the table groaned, then Jazzy cleared her throat. "I want the rib- eye, rare. Forget her salad and give her a steak."

"Leave my order as I gave it to you." Bella instructed the waitress.

"I want a rare rib-eye, too," Chase said. "And I really think you'd enjoy the steak more than the salad, Bella."

"No. But thank you," she answered, not a little irritated.

Spencer nodded. "Make it three rare rib-eyes. Actually, make it—"

"No!" Bella kept her voice even as she grabbed Spencer's hand in a tight grip. "I don't want my order changed. I. Want. My. Salad."

He lifted an eyebrow. "I was going to say, make it medium rare."

Heat flashed through her entire body. Why hadn't she kept quiet? She loosened her hold on his hand. "Sorry."

"And forget her salad. Give her a steak."

The waitress chuckled. "Want anything to drink? Or just water?"

The three steak eaters ordered beer. Bella wanted water, but after her trouble ordering the salad, decided against it. "I'll take a beer, too."

"I'll be right back with your drinks."

Jazzy spoke to Chase in a low tone, making Bella wonder if she was threatening him if he mentioned being mates again. She probably whispered so she wouldn't have witnesses.

"Looks like you're stuck with me as a dinner

partner." Spencer put his hand on the back of her chair.

"Think they'd notice if we moved to a different table?"

"Maybe they'd notice—" he answered seriously, then softened the words with a slight grin—"when they left to go home, found they had an extra car and needed someone to drive it for them."

She watched his mouth. As he spoke, the corners of his lips had a way of quirking, as if he were making fun of himself. Or his words.

She'd just taken a sip of her beer when the waitress came back with a heavy tray. With an expert maneuver, she kicked out a stand next to their table, set down the tray and started unloading. In front of Jazzy, Chase and Spencer, she set platters of steaming steak, running with red juices, and a mound of French fries. In front of Bella she set a huge white bowl of salad greens, with a rib-eye steak, running with red juices, sitting on top. The waitress grinned conspiratorially. "I thought this might satisfy everyone."

With a groan, Bella couldn't help but agree. It looked, and smelled, like heaven.

"I can take it back for the normal steak salad, if you'd rather." The woman widened her eyes as she waited for Bella's answer.

"This will be fine." Bella picked up her fork and steak knife and cut into the meat. Spearing a bite, she put it into her mouth then closed her eyes in order to enjoy the flavors from the blend of spices and mesquite smoke.

Now that was good.

No one spoke while they tore into their steaks, forgetting all about the French fries and lettuce.

Bella was the first to set her knife and fork aside and lean back in her chair. Next time, maybe she would order just a rib-eye. In just a few moments, Jazzy had finished off her steak, and was quickly followed by Chase and, finally, by Spencer.

Chase put his arm along the back of Jazzy's chair and whispered something to her. At her nod, he looked at Bella. "Would you mind giving Spencer a ride home? Jazzy and I…"

He didn't finish the sentence, but Bella fully understood. They wanted to be together. And alone.

"But I don't have my car," Bella gently teased.

"You can drive mine." Jazzy reached into her purse then tossed her keys across the table to Bella. "Thanks."

"You're welcome."

The words were barely out of her mouth when Chase stood, grabbed the check with one hand and Jazzy with the other and headed for the exit. "I'll take care of this."

At least Spencer looked a little embarrassed when they had gone. "If you don't want to drive all the way to my house, I can call a cab."

Her heart sped up. "I don't mind driving you, but you'll have to give me directions. I have no idea where you live."

"Does the term *BFE* mean anything to you?" he asked, his tone dry.

"Yes, but I can't imagine a dazzling urbanite like you living there."

"You'll find dazzling urbanites in every chink and pothole in Texas." He lowered one eyebrow then stopped her heart with the world's sexiest smile.

She took a moment to remember how to breathe.

"Well, if you're ready."

He stood and held her chair as she got up. When they reached the exit, he opened the door for her and when they reached Jazzy's car, he took her keys and unlocked it then opened the door for her again.

She watched him as he circled to get into the passenger's seat, amazed at what she'd discovered. He was the rarest of men. Good looking with impeccable manners.

And sexy as they come.

Starting the car, she slowly drove to the edge of the parking lot then shot him a glance. "Which way?"

In the small confines of the Z, it shouldn't have surprised her when he caught and held her gaze. But it did. For some reason, men were often intimidated by a woman in her position. After a long moment, he tipped his head to the right without breaking their connection. "East."

The ride took forever—and was over much too soon. Once they were away from the city lights, the quarter moon's glow drenched the landscape. Too bad they couldn't go on, riding forever with the radio playing softly in the background.

When they finally reached his home, so close to his other family members' homes, she knew herself for a traitor. No matter what this man had said about her sister, she couldn't hate him. She pulled to a stop in his driveway.

"Would you like to come in for a nightcap?"

Tell him you've got to get home, her mind instructed. "I'd love to."

His nod and slight wink kept her in her seat as he got out.

What am I doing? I'm vulnerable enough as it is. If I go into his house, I could really fall under his spell. I'll tell him I'm leaving as soon as he opens my door.

But when the door opened, he took her hand and every thought and protest evaporated. He helped her out and led her up the brick sidewalk to his door, made of leaded glass.

She waited while he unlocked, then held it for her. The small entryway had oaken floors, a rug of dusty earth tones and a bench that looked as if it were made from smoothed, varnished branches from a tree. Southwestern art, quilts and hand-carved wooden bowls with inlays of turquoise filled the living room. With just the flick of a switch, a fire blazed in his fireplace.

"Well, that saves you from having to carry out ashes."

"Big brother said it was cheating to have a fire without having to do the work. But I figure living in Texas, I should take a little extra advantage of the nearby gas wells." His chuckle came from low in his chest. "And it leaves time for more enjoyable things."

He disappeared into the kitchen, and in just a moment, returned with two glasses of wine. "I hope you like Burgundy."

Surprised, she nodded. "I do, but how did you know? Most women I know prefer white zin."

He responded with a roll of his eyes. "Please. Might as well drink RC Soda."

She took the glass he held out to her then glanced at the curved sofa.

"Let's sit by the fire." He tossed a pair of cushions from a built-in wood box to the floor then pulled her down so she sat in front of him, her back to his chest.

The fire was warm, but the real heat in the room came from him. His breath stirred the hair at her nape, tickling ever so slightly. She wanted to let herself go. Lean into him. But she knew if she did, if she relaxed even a bit, she'd belong to him, whether he realized it or not.

Remembering the Burgundy, she lifted the glass and took a long sip. From the corner of her eye, she saw he drank, too. When he set his glass on the floor, he leaned into her.

She glanced over her shoulder. His bottom lip was moist, and without stopping to think, she licked it with the tip of her tongue.

His gaze kindled. As if he could no longer be restrained, he pulled her into the circle of his arms, covering her mouth with his. His tongue stroked hers, and without breaking the kiss, he captured her glass and set it down.

Her heart thrilled in her chest, beating double time and causing her head to swim. As he deepened the kiss, she pulled him with her to the floor, where she could at last wrap both arms around him. Press her chest into his. Feel the weight of him as he cocked his knee across her thighs.

Lifting his head, he breathed an obscenity. Admiring the way the fire gilded a small scar that ran down his cheek, she traced it with her index finger. "I like it here, by the fire." She dropped her hand to his chest, where she unbuttoned the top button on his shirt, then the next. She ran a finger down the exposed skin. "Where would you like to go?"

Humor sparked in his eyes when he realized what she'd done. "To my bedroom."

She unbuttoned the next pair of buttons then lifted her head to kiss his neck, just below his ear. "Is there a fireplace in your bedroom?" She pulled his shirttail from his jeans then reached for the buttons closing his fly.

His "uh-huh" sounded a lot like a groan, but sent an electric charge through her.

She slid her hands inside his jeans. "And can you make it burn as easily as you did this one?"

He gasped as she touched him then kissed her again. With gentle fingers, he pulled her sweater over her head and off her arms. Just a flick of his fingers, and he unlatched her bra and pushed it aside, exposing her breasts. He held her gaze as he bent low over her, then closing his eyes, covered her nipple, gently sucking it into his mouth.

Pleasure pulsed through her, making her short of breath and ready to beg for more. She slid her fingers into his hair, hoping to hold him there.

But rather than obey her silent request, he raised his head and gazed at her, his eyes at half mast. Slowly he lowered the zipper on her jeans then pushed them, along with her panties, down her thighs. His touch had a fiery gentleness she'd never before known.

She tried to think, tried to remember something, anything, before she lost herself completely. What had they been talking about? The bedroom? The fire? There was something…

With a swift move, he tossed her jeans away and moved over her, fitting himself to her. She wrapped her legs around his and lifted her hips to meet him. As he entered her, she gasped a long, slow breath.

They moved together in a primal rhythm, her mind

catching fire. How had she survived her entire life without him? So many years wasted. So many nights empty.

This man, whom she'd hated so fiercely, morphed in her heart.

He moved against her, as if trying to put himself so far inside she could never remove him from her soul. If she could speak, if she could think, she'd tell him he was already there. She'd never, no matter what, be able to erase him from her heart. Or her mind.

He came with a final thrust, and lifting his head he arched his back and voiced a cry that wrenched her heart and sounded very nearly like a howl.

Following immediately behind him, she did the same.

Chapter Ten

I readjusted my seat atop one of the stools Doc had in his lab, but I couldn't get comfortable with my butt on that cold metal disc. Why were aluminum seats ever invented? And why would anyone with a living, feeling backside allow one of the cold monsters in a place where they might have to sit?

So unwanted visitors wouldn't hang around? Or so when a coworker took a break, they'd remember to go back to work when the "in pain" signals hit the brain?

Doc flicked on a light, not unlike ones I'd seen used in old black and whites for interrogating bad guys. Then he reached in his pocket, pulled out a small bag, which he unzipped and removed two vials of blood.

"Ew." I wrinkled my nose. "Did you have that in your pocket at dinner?"

"Of course not. Something might have happened to it in my pocket." He shook his head then warmed me with a quick glance. "I might have gotten attacked by a woman gone wild."

"Right." I watched for a few moments while he tinkered with his machines, then I heard something mewling in the distance. "What's that?"

"Day old wolf pups. Lost their mother, so we're hand raising them. Sounds like they're hungry."

Butt aching on the now warm stool, I asked, "What happened to their mother?"

"Werewolf attack." He gazed at me for a moment, blanking my mind for all intents and purposes then he refocused on his work. "Funny thing is, he broke her neck, but it was as if he realized she was about to whelp and didn't tear her apart like he did the other animals. We delivered them right after she died."

"Oh, the poor babies." I used a soft tone, just short of wheedling. "Would it be okay if I helped with their feeding?"

"Since we didn't have another mother who could feed them, they're being raised by humans." He gave me one of his delicious half smiles. "I think you'll qualify."

"At least most of the time," I murmured as I slid off the stool. "Which way do I go?"

"Just let me get this started and I'll show you."

After a few agonizingly boring moments, he finally started one of his toys humming, clipped a timer on his pocket then turned to me. "Ready?"

Can a wolf bite? I wanted to snap, but decided against it. "Yeah."

I followed him to the nursery, where four baby wolves huddled together in a bed of straw. He filled a bottle with warmed milk, handed it and one of the pups to me.

I held the baby close. "Were they all in the same litter?"

"Yeah. This was her first pregnancy, but I think she would have been a great mother."

Guilt rose in my throat. "Poor babies." I shoved the nipple in the baby's mouth, and was glad to find feeding a wolf cub was a lot like feeding a dog pup. Exactly, in fact.

I moved to a nearby rocker and sat down. "You keep rockers around for puppies?"

"It's really for the surrogate parent. We found that our volunteers—men and women—were rocking the animals, even if we gave them metal folding chairs. Even when we took out all the chairs. No matter if they had to stand or sit on the floor, they still swayed." He shrugged as he filled bottle and picked up another pup. "The humans raising the animals have a need to rock. And now some of our animals do, too."

When the pup he held slowed his nursing, he put it back in the straw and picked up the other crying baby. The last one was dead to the world. When the one I held wouldn't allow the nipple in his mouth anymore, I set him down. "Should we wake up that last one so he can eat?"

Doc laughed at the puppy in his arms who seemed to be trying to get the entire bottle in his mouth, then sobered at my words. "It's a female. You can wake her and try to feed her, but we're not having much luck with that one. I don't think she's interested in living."

"And she's the runt of the litter." I ran one finger down her head to her nape. I picked her up and she curled against me, snuggling as if she were cold. But it wasn't the least chilly in their nursery.

I took a fresh bottle, settled back in my chair and bumped the nipple against her lips. When she didn't respond, I gave her a gentle shake. "Wake up, darlin'. It's time to eat."

Doc checked the chart, lying close by. "She didn't take a measurable amount at the last feeding, either."

Grim determination hardened to a knot in my belly. I couldn't let this baby die. Pulling my feet onto the rocker's seat, I balanced the pup on my knees then tapped her on the head. After a thump or two, she lifted her muzzle and whined. "Good. You're awake."

Doc's timer beeped. "Okay, I've got to get back to the lab. If you need anything, come find me. I don't think anyone else is around."

I nodded as he walked away. I put the nipple to the baby's muzzle, but while she sniffed as if trying to see what wet her nose, she wouldn't open her mouth.

Poor thing. It wasn't her fault that a rogue werewolf killed her mother. She shouldn't have to die just because she hadn't been quite ready to be born.

Too bad they couldn't get one of the other wolves in the zoo to feed her. But unless she accepted the babies right away, another nursing mother would quite likely kill a strange baby.

If they could even get one of the older females to lie with her while they fed her, just so the scent would be right, it might help the baby eat. But no matter how old the female, she could easily kill a strange baby.

That's when it hit me. I was a female wolf. Well, werewolf. Why couldn't I morph and get her to eat?

Without weighing the pros and cons, I decided to try it. Taking the cub to an out of the way corner, I made her a nest of straw and propped the bottle beside her. Then holding all my anger at the unfairness of the baby losing its mother because one werewolf who needed to die, I slipped out of my clothes and morphed. I went quickly to the baby and sniffed around her face. When she caught my scent, she immediately whined her hunger.

Without an opposable thumb, however, it's not an easy task to get a bottle into a pup's mouth, no matter how wide she's holding it. But there's no halfway point. I'm either a werewolf or I'm not. I had to find a way.

After spinning three times, I curled around the baby. Then with my snout, I pushed the bottle her way. It took some time to get her to accept it, but finally, she latched on and suckled until her tummy was full.

When she'd finished, she had milk running out of the corner of her mouth and a fat belly. I quickly turned human again, redressed and took her back to sleep with the other pups.

I walked back into the lab, where Doc stood, staring at nothing. I'd never before seen him look as if he'd lost his best friend. "Are you all right?"

A bleak look on his face, he shook his head. "I was right. He's got the Lycan infection."

"Well, that's something Texas doesn't need. Two wild werewolves, tearing up the place."

"Tell me about it." His tone was grim. "I'm going to have to try the injection, and just hope it works."

"Take me home."

****

Chase turned at her whispered words. The look in her eyes—vulnerable strength—drew him. Unable to resist, he raised his hand to cup her cheek. Her tone held a promise that blasted the "this-has-all-been-for-nothing" feeling ramping in his brain. Sliding his fingers down her cheek, he glided his index finger along her bottom lip.

She sucked his finger into her mouth and tugged hard on it.

Visions of her naked in his arms flashed through his mind. He lifted her to a stool and kissed her, letting his hands drift down her arms. With little effort, he nudged her knees apart, edged as close to her as he could get and still remain dressed.

He throbbed against her, wanting to be inside her more than he wanted oxygen. But he couldn't make love to her in a sterile laboratory. The odors alone would probably be enough to kill the desire she had for him.

He lifted his head. "Let's go home."

Eyes glistening, she caught her breath and slowly nodded. He helped her from the stool and, keeping her close to his side, took her to his truck.

After tucking her inside, he circled the truck, yanked open the other door and climbed in with her. Without a word, he started the engine and dropped the gearshift into drive. Halfway down the zoo's entry, he buckled his seatbelt.

Trying to look casual, as if he drove with the safety of his seatbelt all the time, he stretched the strap across his shoulder and snapped it into place.

"I wondered if you were going to." Her voice was cloudy. Thick.

Why pretend? Why act as if he had anything on his mind besides getting her home. And naked. As the vision of her again took possession of his mind, he pushed harder on the gas pedal. Clearing his throat, he hoped his voice wouldn't break like a young teen's. "I had something on my mind."

He could feel the heat as her gaze kindled. "Where are we going?"

"Home." He fought the urge to clear the gravel gathering again in his throat.

Her chuckle came from somewhere deep in her

chest. "Yours or mine?"

Calculating quickly, he counted the miles to her house, then to his. "Mine. It's closer."

"You all live together, don't you? Won't your family be there?"

He couldn't help teasing her a little. "Why? Are you worried about what Mom will say?"

She shifted toward him, and laid her arm along the seatback. "You don't mind if she knows you're bringing women home to sleep in your bed?"

"No. Not women. Woman." Stopping at the highway, he took his attention from the road to give her a straight look. She had to see how serious he was.

"At a time?" Her tease was gentle. Loving.

"Ever." He should have cleared his throat again. Should have known that the word would emerge as a whisper. Would sound as if he needed her.

"Then she'll probably be really shocked if she notices." Her voice, too, was barely audible.

He laughed, trying to lighten the mood while he prayed that they could make it all the way home. "Well, that won't be until she comes to tuck me in."

"Which should be in, what? Another week when they get home from their trip?" Her laughter, as rough as his, filled him.

If he were clairvoyant, he'd see his future now. Mapped out with her and filled with a roller coaster ride of excitement for eternity.

At least, he hoped so.

He turned the radio to a station he knew played slow, sensual music. The music thrummed—not unlike certain parts of his body.

She slid as low in the seat as the seatbelt would let

her, closed her eyes and hummed along. She couldn't know what her body in that position did to him.

Like most guys in Texas, his first time had been in the bed of a pickup truck on a hot summer evening. But in the cold winter of his high school years, he'd found a way to make it with a girl, actually several girls, sitting in just that position.

Maybe Jazzy did know.

The closer they got to his house, the faster he drove. He had to get home before he couldn't hold out any longer, found a dark back road and grabbed her. He wanted her in his oversized bed. Lying under him. With him buried deep inside.

Finally they made it to the private road to his house. He turned off the radio and hoped his brothers wouldn't hear him drive past—if they happened to be home. Although it was rare, they had been known to visit late at night, especially when they wanted a game of pool and were too lazy to venture out very far. Hopefully, tonight they'd find their games someplace else.

****

I straightened in the seat as we turned onto the part of the road that circled the house. Although I'd visited the older Hollidays' part of the wagon wheel when I topped off and organized their cruise wardrobe, it looked different at night.

One thing was obvious—the landscaping had been done by professionals—very good professionals. The lighting, angled at the trees, sent odd shadows across the lawn. "I've been in your parents' house. Is this yours, next door?"

"No, this one's Spencer's," he answered as they

drove past. "The one on the other side of Mom and Dad is the guest house. Next to the guest house is Mack, then Drew. I'm between Drew and Spencer."

It surprised me to see the lights out at Spencer's and the driveway empty. He'd had plenty of time to drop Bella off and get home. Maybe he had a girlfriend Doc hadn't mentioned.

Doc opened his console and reached inside. His garage door opened as we pulled into the driveway, and we drove straight inside. Even before we were all the way in, he started closing the big door.

Killing the engine, he unbuckled and got out. I knew he'd open my door for me, but hey, my hands aren't just painted on! And I wanted to get inside to his bedroom without wasting time fooling with doors or mama-taught-southern-manners.

He tapped out a few numbers on a keypad next to the entry. When the electronic pad beeped back at him, he caught my hand and tugged me in the door.

We stepped into a kitchen that looked as if it had never been used for more than brewing coffee. I thought about asking if he ever cooked, but before I could formulate the words, he led me into the living room.

At least, I *think* that's what it was. It was the part of the elder Hollidays' house that had been the living room. It had a huge fireplace, like the parents', and I assume all the houses, had.

But had it been in a different location, I would never have guessed what it was originally designed to be. In front of the fireplace was a huge pool table and directly overhead a rectangular light asked, *Who's your Brew?* It looked like a beer ad. On the wall, off to one side, near the kitchen, hung the largest flat screen TV I'd ever seen, and clustered around it were five recliners, each with a TV tray, standing nearby. There was even a small refrigerator that looked as if it had been stolen from a dorm room. Or maybe a frat house.

I couldn't believe what I saw. How could a man with Doc's money live in a house, decorated as if he didn't have two nickels to jingle in his pocket?

Before I could ask, he pulled me into his arms. My breasts pressed hard against his chest as he slid his hands to my hips to pull me yet closer. Heart pounding, I struggled to remember how to breathe when he slid his tongue into my mouth.

I couldn't make myself wait a moment longer. I had to have him. Then. There. Completely naked or with just enough unzipped and pushed aside to get the job done, I wanted him hot and hard and deep within me.

Slipping my hands to his chest, I flattened my palms there, and sucked hard on his tongue. He growled, thrust his hips lightly against me, and broke the kiss. I thought he would pick me up and carry me to his bed, and if he didn't have time to take the dozen or so steps to get there, I thought we'd at least make use of one of the recliners.

Instead, he swallowed and took a breath. A long breath. A look of sheer determination came over his face as he stiffened his back and he took a step away from me. If he hadn't kept his hand on me, holding me in place, I'd have followed him just like a partner in a slow dance.

He nodded once then asked, "Want a beer?"

I was shocked he could stop like that—that he

didn't want me as badly as I did him. All I could do was gape.

He must have imagined I nodded, because he turned and walked away from me. Leaving me alone. And cold.

My entire body quaked with my need for him. I wasn't going to let him escape without fulfilling me. He *would* want me as badly as I wanted him. Even if I had to hurt him to make him do it.

Glancing around, I again focused on the pool table in front of the empty fire place. Too bad there wasn't a stimulating fire burning, but I'd have to use what was at hand.

And if my hand didn't work, I'd use my mouth.

I took off my blouse and draped it across the recliner, arranging it to make it look as if I'd tossed it there. I kicked off my shoes, first one, then the other, on my way across the room. Next came my jeans, and then my bra. After stripping off my thong, I slid on top of the table and lay down. Rolling to my side, I rested my head on my upturned fist.

The roughness of the felt against me was one of those pleasure/pain sensations, rubbing hot places on my skin. But when I got Doc on it with me, all I planned to feel was pleasure. The fragrance of cigar smoke drifted to me, making me smile as I envisioned him celebrating something or other with his brothers.

He came out of the kitchen with a beer in each hand, stopped dead and gaped at the shirt I'd left on the chair. Without moving, he followed the trail of my clothing with his gaze, stopping to stare at each article in turn. When he looked at my jeans for a few seconds, he took a few steps toward me until he found my bra.

I pushed to a sitting position, took aim and flipped my thong at him, slingshot fashion.

It landed perfectly, encircling the beer in his left hand and falling to hang from his wrist.

He stared at it for so long, I wondered if he recognized what it was. But when he lifted his face to look at me, I had no doubt. He watched me for a long moment, his face darkening as his eyes almost glowed.

I curled my legs under me as I waited for him to make a move—if my antics hadn't given him a stroke or heart attack.

Finally he moved toward me, his movements as fluid as a fox. Without a word, he handed me both beers, then scooped me off the table as if I weighed no more than a fluff of fur.

He carried me to his bedroom, and I knew why the rest of the house looked as it did. He'd spent all his time—and talent—making a sleeping space that a sex goddess would dream of. The colors were dark but bright, the fabrics rich and sensual. And the room smelled wonderful. Almost as if we were outside in the woods on a moonless summer night.

And in the corner a small fireplace blazed away. In front of the hearth was a rug, or it could have been a throw, that looked amazingly like ermine or mink. He carried me to it and, as gently as if he were helping a woman stand after a very long illness, he set me down.

My feet buried in the deep fur. It curled between my toes and tickled my ankles, wrenching a giggle from me.

While he yanked off his clothes and shoved on a condom, I sat down. The sensation of the long fur as it caressed the more tender parts of my body was amazing. It crept into hidden crevices, stimulating me to heights I'd never before known.

Then he was behind me, one firm thigh on each side of me, his chest at my back. He pushed me onto my belly and stroked the length of me, his hands firm yet gentle, his breath hot on my neck while the fur tickled my breasts, belly, thighs and everything in between.

Never having been the passive type, I could only take so much of the pleasure before I had to join in. In a single move, I turned, pushed him to his back and straddled him. Raising my body, I lowered myself over him, gasping as his length filled me.

Finally, I knew what I'd waited for all my life. I'd found what had always been missing. My heart swelled, along with other parts of me, as I started moving.

Putting his hands on my bottom, he levered to an almost sitting position and moved with me, stimulating me as no one ever had. How did he know the way to make me feel so alive? So much a part of him?

I'd never known a man who fit me so well, both physically and spiritually, in my life. How was he able to make me feel so cared for? So well loved? Realization that it could only come from long nights of practice on his part sparked a nip of jealousy, making me want to ruin any other woman's chances at love with him.

Our movements grew faster, more frenzied until I started to lose my mind. Not ready to let it end, he rolled me beneath him so he was in complete control. I curled my legs around his long muscular ones as he slowed the pace. This time, while I grew as excited as before, the depth of the feeling was somehow broader.

Deeper.

Richer.

As we neared climax, I felt my control slipping, my mind going. I wanted nothing but to lose myself completely, rush to the edge, fling myself off and during the climax become the true being I was inside. If I didn't hold myself back, I'd morph right there in his arms.

I could tell he neared the edge, too, as he moved over me. But just as I thought he would shout with triumph, he seemed to take a step away from me.

He rose to his knees with his hands on my shoulders, as if he held me back. With an extremely controlled movement, he took a long, quavering breath and, simply, finished.

His completion very subdued. Very disappointing. And I very nearly didn't climax at all.

I'd never been so disappointed in my life.

He made a sound that was close to a groan then, with a kiss, collapsed on the fur beside me.

What was that? I wanted to scream, but I couldn't find my voice.

Why, when I was about to have the most fantastic climax of my lifetime, had he backed off? Shut down?

Why had I been gypped?

But before I could find the energy to ask, my body shut down from the exhaustion of having to fight morphing while in the midst of wild lovemaking.

We moved to his bed, and after a very long, lonely time, I fell asleep and dreamed of a wolf and her mate, deep in the Texas woodlands.

I must have slept hard, because when I awoke, it was morning and I smelled coffee brewing in the kitchen and heard the shower running in the adjacent bathroom.

Not ready to force myself out from under his quilts, I snuggled down for a little time of twilight sleep and drifted in and out until I heard him shut off the shower. Knowing it was time to get moving, I sat up just as he opened the door and left the steamy bathroom with a towel wrapped around his waist.

He glanced at me then let his gaze slide slowly to my breasts. I could see in his face the internal battle with himself, so I pushed back the covers and got out of bed. Just as I reached for my clothes, which lay at the foot of the bed where he must have put them, I glanced in the mirror.

Down my left buttock there was a long scratch. Unable to believe what I saw, I touched it. The sting made me yelp in surprise.

"How did you do that?" he asked, his eyebrows high with concern.

"I don't know." I glared at my backside in the mirror. "I don't remember scratching myself there."

"Must have done it when you climbed on my pool table." Frowning, he shook his head. "I'm sorry. I should have had that rough place fixed." *For naked women climbing on top,* remained unspoken.

Why hadn't I felt it when it happened? I was stimulated and having a good time when I blazed my trail to the table, but I hadn't been *that* turned on. I should have felt the pain if I'd torn my flesh like that.

Unless somehow in the night, I'd somehow lost control, morphed and done it while I was out of my sane mind.

Fear cut a swath through me as the possibility

occurred to me. If that was what happened, why had it started? The other time had been at the Halloween party. But this time why wasn't it the same? When I'd lost control at the Halloween party, I'd awakened in a cage and naked, experiencing a nauseous headache wasn't unlike a hangover.

This time I woke up right where I'd fallen asleep. Naked, yes, but I'd been naked when I crashed. No headache. No nausea and no reason to believe I'd gone anywhere.

More than a little worried, I tried to calm myself as I turned to him. "Okay if I take a shower?" Not wanting him to see my concern and delve into my psyche to understand it—or whatever werewolf researchers do—I tried not to look him in the face.

"You bet. I left out clean towels for you." He watched me for a moment, as if wondering if I would invite him in to shower with me.

Not a chance. At least, not while I felt so uneasy. Vulnerable. I headed for his shower, wishing I had someone to talk to about it. Someone who knew werewolves and the changes that could happen.

Going into the bathroom, I closed and locked the door behind me. I turned on the shower and waited for the water to warm before getting in.

I went over it again and again in my mind. Why had this happened to me? Was it because I held back too much for too long? Or didn't hold back enough? If he were a born-in-the-flesh werewolf, I believed he'd started to morph and scratch me as he neared climax. Too bad that wasn't the case. It had to be something I was doing wrong.

If only Grandma Maleva were alive. She'd known

everything about werewolves. And she'd always been able to make me feel better about myself, even when I was a young teen and knew I was different from every other girl in the world.

In the shower, I let my hair out and washed it really well before drawing it in a bit. After I washed my injury, I finished up and stepped out onto a thick rug. It wasn't as cushy as the one by his fireplace, but it soaked up the water sluicing from my body. Taking a towel I found on the cabinet next to the sink, I blotted the water from my skin and dried my hair.

Maybe the previous evening's lovemaking had just been an off night for him—I hoped! Hoping to make him suffer just a little, I left my towel in the bathroom and walked naked into his bedroom, where I'd left my clothes. Too bad he'd left the room.

I quickly dressed, grabbed my purse and pulled out my comb and makeup. I slicked my hair back into a ponytail with an elastic band I found in the bottom then put on a little mascara and lipstick.

That was all I had time to do. I had to find someone—or something—that could give me some answers. I shoved my purse over my shoulder and left the bedroom, ready to ask him to take me home.

The dark fragrance of strong coffee stopped me. The pungent aroma filled my head and shoved everything else out of my mind. I had to have a cup. Or ten.

"Buy a girl a cup of coffee?" I asked, hoping it sounded teasing.

His eyes sparkled with unvoiced laughter. "Anything you want."

I waited as he grabbed a man-sized mug from the

cabinet and poured it full. "Cream or sugar?"

"Don't ruin it," I answered.

He gave me a half smile of appreciation and handed me the mug. I took a sip and sighed with enjoyment. A single sip made me feel human. By the time I'd finished the mug, I might feel like a woman again.

He walked to a bar stool and sat down, so I followed him. "Do you usually eat breakfast?" he asked then took a healthy drink from his mug.

"If someone else is cooking."

He almost choked on the coffee. After clearing his throat, he nodded in agreement. "Me, too. Exactly."

"So you won't be…?" I smiled as I left the sentence unfinished.

He snorted then shook his head. "Believe me, you wouldn't want me to. I can make toast, if you're really hungry."

"I'm hungry, but toast wouldn't satisfy me." Hearing the double entendre in my own words, I ignored them. "I mean, when I finished, I'd still be hungry."

The heat in his gaze, coupled with his slowly spreading smile was proof, indeed, that I'd made it worse.

"What I meant to say was I'm hungry for sausage and eggs. Or biscuits and gravy. Just toast wouldn't be enough."

"Uh-huh." The sexual-innuendo-induced grin remained. "And I know a great place, not too far from here. We'll stop on the way to take you home."

What I really wanted was to go home, so I could change clothes and really go home—to the house in the panhandle where Grandma Maleva had lived. Maybe there I could find the answers to the upset in my mind, which was starting to remind me of a killer bee attack in my head.

As we left his house, I thanked my lucky stars it was Saturday and I had no appointments set up for the weekend. Maybe I'd be able to go to Grandma's without having to change any appointments.

We stopped at a small, mom-and-pop restaurant called A Taste of Home. The tables were all antique oak with mismatched chairs, and on the windows were drapes that would have looked right in someone's home. The sign outside that blazed their name hadn't lied. If it weren't for the cash register and the waitresses, it would look exactly like someone's home, right down to the Christmas decorations.

A young girl, who looked barely old enough to work in the state of Texas, brought a pair of menus and a pot of coffee to our table. "Morning, Doc." The girl grinned at us.

"Good morning," he answered.

I turned my cup upright so she could fill it and opened the menu.

She filled my cup, then Doc's. After she'd taken the pot back to the warmer, she came back to our table to take our orders.

Hungry as I was, it didn't take me long to decide. I glanced up to see she was ready. "I want steak and eggs with biscuits and gravy on the side. Make the steak rare."

When she nodded, I turned my attention to Doc. On his face was a grin of admiration. "Make that two. And put a rush on it, Angel."

"As usual." The girl made a note on her pad and hurried away.

"Angel? Kind of familiar with that teenager, aren't you?" I teased.

He shrugged. "Her parents own A Taste of Home, and Angel's her name. She has a sister named Star."

"Angel and Star?" I lowered my voice, not wanting anyone to hear me and be offended. "Do they have any more siblings? Cloud? Or maybe Moon?"

He barked a short laugh. "Well, their mother's name is Luna."

"The moon goddess? What's their dad's name? Sol?"

"No. It's Alan."

"Too bad." I sipped my coffee, wishing for the burn of a strong fresh cup and I wasn't disappointed. "I really hope their food is as good as their coffee."

"I don't think you'll be disappointed." He took a drink from his cup then slid lower in his chair. "I'm really tired this morning."

As if his lovemaking, as subdued as it was toward the end, had exhausted him. I didn't believe it. "Why? Did my snoring keep you awake?"

"No. I slept like the dead." He lifted one eyebrow, sending a curl of desire through me. "I think it was what came before I fell asleep that wore me out."

I shook my head. "We weren't exactly swinging from the chandeliers, Doc."

"No, thank heaven." He slid his hand across the table and captured mine. "What we did was more fun."

I wasn't used to discussing sex the previous night at breakfast, so I glanced around, looking for a way to change the subject. "When are your parents due back?"

"I think they're supposed to be home next week."

I settled my gaze on the tinsel strewn tree near the door. "Where do you all celebrate Christmas?"

"It depends. Some years we fly to warmer climates. Some years we go skiing. But this year, since they'll just be back from that cruise for a few days, I doubt if Mom made reservations anywhere. We'll probably stay close to home." He tipped his head. "How about your family?"

"We always celebrate at Mom and Dad's." I shrugged. "Mom believes in tradition. Before, when her mother was alive, we went to Grandma's house."

"Kind of like *Little Red Riding Hood*?"

More like the big bad wolf, I almost quipped, but caught myself just in time.

Angel came back to our table with two identical plates of food then refilled our cups before leaving us to enjoy our breakfasts.

I cut my steak and was happy to find it as rare as I'd requested. I took a bite, and found the center still cool. Perfect! The biscuits were homemade with a lightly browned top and a golden, crunchy bottom. I broke a biscuit in half and put it on my plate and ladled gravy over it.

After eating for several long moments, I realized I must look like a starving refugee. But when I glanced up, I saw Doc working through the food on his plate as single-mindedly as I.

When we'd eaten every crumb of food on the table, we were both too full to move. "That was good," I groaned.

"I know," he echoed my pain. "I do this every time I come here—breakfast, lunch or dinner."

"If their food is this good for every meal, I'm surprised they haven't gotten rich and retired by now."

"A Taste of Home is a well kept secret." He rested his hands on his belly. "And I intend to keep it that way until I find a woman to cook for me at home."

"Maybe one of the daughters will take after their parents and you can marry her."

"Or maybe someone closer to my age can take lessons." He gave me a pointed look, which I returned.

"Better idea. You *learn*."

Chapter Eleven

His laughter echoed through the restaurant. He put down a hefty tip and picked up the ticket. We paid at the checkout then went back to his truck.

He drove me to my condo, and I directed him to pull up at the sidewalk. "Have a good weekend," I said as I got out of his truck.

He lowered one brow, looking serious. "You sound as if I'm not going to see you tonight."

I widened my eyes as I tried to look surprised, and just a little indignant. But rather than go into a just-because-we-slept-together rant, I shook my head. "I'm going out of town for a couple of days."

I could see by his face that he wanted to demand to know where I was going. Luckily, he was too smart to do something that stupid. "Uh, okay. Well, I'll call you."

I nodded, shot him a quick smile and hurried into our apartment building. Unlocking the door, I rushed inside and called out for Bella. No answer, and the house was dark.

For a moment I wondered if she'd made it home last night, then I remembered who she'd been with. Spencer.

She'd made it home.

I stepped into the kitchen and checked the message center, where we kept a calendar to let the other know about our lives, and where we left each other notes either scrawled on the blackboard with chalk—colored when I bought it, white when she did—or tacked to the cork.

She'd written me a note, telling me she was going out to the zoo to check on the newborn wolf pups.

If she'd waited, I could have told her they were fine. Even the runt had caught on and had started chowing down with the rest of them.

I erased her note and picked up fuchsia colored chalk. *Sis*, I wrote. *Going to Grandma's house. I've got to take care of something I've put off for too long. See you Monday.*

When she got home and read my note, she'd probably be a little put out with me. She'd loved Grandma Maleva as much as I did and enjoyed going "home" for a visit, even though Grandma wasn't there anymore. But this was one of those things I needed to do alone. Not even my twin could go with me.

Finding my favorite weekender, I tossed in my sweats, a pair of jeans and a couple of t-shirts. After adding my toothbrush, toothpaste and deodorant, just the necessities, I zipped it closed, grabbed my purse and took off.

As I pulled out of the parking lot, I didn't know whether to wish I didn't have to make this trip or that it was already over. But since wishing didn't make it so—at least it rarely did in my life—I forced myself to think of something else.

As I pulled onto the highway, I thought of the old couple who lived in the mother-in-law house there on Grandma's farm. Mr. and Mrs. Newkirk took care of things—mowing, keeping the houses clean and repaired, letting my parents know if anything happened they needed to know about—and in return had a place to live with a small space for a garden and a chicken coop. They'd been there since Grandpa got too old to do it all himself, and Grandma provided in her will for them to stay on until their deaths.

I couldn't help wondering if there was any way to get rid of the Newkirks for the weekend. Not that I'd be doing anything wrong or that I didn't want anyone else to see. I just didn't want to have to answer a lot of questions.

But then, the older couple rarely asked a lot of questions.

They'd lived on the farm for longer than I could remember, and usually didn't make their presence known except when they were needed. They weren't werewolves, but they had been gifted with a sense of knowing about that kind of thing. Or else Grandma Maleva and her offspring were super loud when they were having problems and the Newkirks couldn't help but hear.

It's several hours from our apartment to Grandma's farm, depending on the traffic through Dallas, and sometimes entire years went by when I didn't visit. And at the end of those years, I really didn't know why.

I wondered if the ponds were still stocked with blue gill and perch. And if the cane poles were still in the barn where Old Blue used to live. Were the pear trees still alive? Did Mr. Newkirk still keep honeybees?

I drove until I was bleary eyed, then stopped at a drive-in along the highway for a quick lunch and was back on the road again in record time. After traveling forever, I finally reached the small town of Winnie

Rose. My heartbeat sped up. I was getting close. Just a few more minutes and I'd be pulling into Grandma's graveled drive. I could hardly wait, but remembering the strict law enforcement in that small town, I kept my speed just under the limit.

I turned onto a blacktopped road, which for years had been dirt, and drove until I came to a fork in the road. Taking the right, I drove another mile and turned into Grandma's.

There in front of her house were two pine trees Granddad had planted, now taller than the roof. The enclosed porch looked as if it had new screen all around, and on it the metal rockers still sat at the ready.

Off to the side and a little behind was the Newkirk's house. As usual, I drove over to let them know I was there before I went to the big house.

As I pulled to a stop, the front door opened. Mr. Newkirk, who'd always looked as if he were about 150 years old, pulled on a hat as he stepped out to blink at me with cloudy eyes.

I got out of the car before he started across the lawn to me. "Hi, Mr. Newkirk. It's me, Jazzy."

"Well howdy, Jazzy." The old man smiled at me. "Long time no see."

When I got to his front step, he took my hand in his, which felt like a cool, leather glove. "How's Mrs. Newkirk?" I asked.

"Finer than a cow's hair split three ways. How's the family?" he asked.

"Everyone's fine." I gave him my business smile. "Well, I didn't come to bother you. I just wanted to get something done I've been putting off for too long."

Mr. Newkirk nodded as if he knew what I was

talking about. But he couldn't know. No one knew.

"Well, the key's still where it belongs." He took one of those breaths that old people breathe. The kind that take forever and make you worry that it's the last one coming. "When she finds out you're here, Mrs. Newkirk will want you to come for dinner. It'll be ready at seven. Don't make me come get you."

I grinned as I nodded my acceptance. Mrs. N was the best cook in the state of Texas. I never turned down an invitation to dinner with them.

With a quick hug, I turned and stepped off the porch and got in my car. I drove to the back of the house, where I went into the small, screened-in porch. High, in a corner far from the door, a nail had been hammered years before, and on that nail hung the key to the front door.

I knew it would be there. And the house would be clean, the sheets fresh, as if they'd known I was coming, because in some places in the world, things never change.

Standing on tiptoe, I retrieved the key and strode around to the front door. The screen door was unlatched, as usual, and in just a moment, I unlocked the door and stepped inside.

I closed my eyes and took a deep breath, then let it out on a long sigh. Grandma. The house had always had that sweet, powdery smell that reminded me of her. Or maybe she'd smelled like the house. I'm still not sure which way it was; I was just glad it was still true.

Walking through the dining room, I unlocked the backdoor, stepped onto the porch and put the key where it belonged. Then I went to my car to get my bag and purse, and out of habit, locked it up.

I took my things to Grandma's room and tossed them on the floor. We'd learned long ago that no matter where we stayed or how short the visit, Mrs. Newkirk always gave the room a deep cleaning as soon as we left. And since Mrs. N was probably on the uphill side of ninety—and looked as if she were years older—we slept and stayed in as few of the downstairs rooms as possible.

Grandma had bought sturdy blond furniture in the fifties, when it had been at its height in popularity. It was extremely good furniture, so when the style swung away from uber-light colors, she'd seen no reason to replace it. The double bed didn't have a chenille spread, which would have made the room feel as if you'd stepped back in time. Instead, it had the wedding ring quilt in shades of pink, blue and white that Grandma's mother had made for her the first year she'd been married. And it still looked almost new.

There was a dresser scarf and pictures of Bella and me, from the day we were born through most of our childhood. But nowhere did I see the journals.

I knew exactly what they looked like—leather bound notebooks with the year stenciled in gold on the front cover. We'd loved watching Grandma write in them when we were kids, and after watching her we'd both tried journaling.

I'd never been able to keep it up for more than a few days, but I think Bella was fairly regular for a while.

After stowing my things, I looked around. Where had Grandma kept her journals? I remembered seeing them lined up—muted shades of forest green, burgundy and navy blue. Once in a while, there'd be a burnished gold or tan, but for the most part the colors were somber. Dark.

I checked through the drawers in the dresser, chest of drawers and both bedside tables. Nothing. But I wasn't worried. There were four bedrooms upstairs. She could have stowed them in any room in the house, with the possible exception of the kitchen. And if Grandma had some reason she thought they belonged in the kitchen, she'd have put them there no matter what anyone said.

I checked the bookshelves in the living room, but no books of any kind there or in the dining room buffet.

With a glance at the mantel clock, I saw it was a quarter to seven. Only fifteen minutes before Mrs. N would have dinner ready.

I decided to wait until the next morning to search upstairs, and went to the bathroom to wash up.

As soon as I was finished, I put on my jacket, grabbed my purse and left the house by the backdoor. No need to lock up out in the boonies of Winnie Rose. At least not this early in the evening, and probably not later, either. But I would, because without locks, I'd never fall into a deep sleep.

I walked the distance to the caretakers' cottage. When I was almost there, I smelled a delicious aroma coming from their house. Lengthening my stride, I hurried to the porch, where I knocked on the door.

An eternity passed while I stood there, smelling heaven in the air. Finally, Mr. N opened the door and it was all I could do to keep from charging past him to the dining room table as I would have as a child.

Being an adult, at least in age, I forced myself to wait on the old man.

"You're just in time." His eyes sparkled as he smiled at me. "And just as pretty as ever."

Mrs. Newkirk stuck her head around the door, her thinning white hair curling every which way. "Well, Daddy, for heaven's sake. Let her come in. She looks like she's starving to death."

"Yes, come in. Come in." Mr. Newkirk took my jacket. "We're just now ready."

I walked with him to the table, where we both sat down while Mrs. N finished placing the bowls of vegetables.

When Mrs. N was seated, the couple insisted I serve myself before they would take any of the food. First they handed me the platter with roast beef on it—the delicious fragrance that had me nearly drooling as I walked to their house. Then there was a bowl of green beans, one of black-eyed peas and a green salad, dressed, as always, with Miracle Whip salad dressing.

We ate on the blue willow dishes Grandma Maleva had given them years before. As I ate, I marveled at how this elderly couple could raise and can their own vegetables year after year, with little help from anyone. They had no children or other relatives that we knew of.

And anytime we'd asked Grandma why they lived there and worked for her, she snapped at us so sharply, we quit asking.

"So why did you come down this time of year?" Mrs. N asked. I could see by her gaze she knew something was up.

Too bad I hadn't thought to bring them a Christmas present. At least it would have been an excuse. I shrugged, trying to make light of my life. "Oh, I just wanted to slow the pace a little, and I haven't been here in a while."

Mrs. N shot her husband a quick glance, then settled her gaze back on me. "You'd better clean up that plate if you think you're going to get dessert."

"Is it pineapple upside-down cake?" I asked, all but reverting to childhood by bouncing in my seat.

"What else could I fix with you here?" She grinned at me. "And before you ask, yes. There are cherries in all the pineapple o's."

We all laughed at the question Bella and I'd started asking as soon as we could talk, but as soon as the laughter ended, my eyes burned with tears. It was wonderful to be among people who loved me and accepted me, no matter what. People who, if I burdened them with the fact I was a werewolf, would love me just the same. Or perhaps even more.

In this place, my secrets didn't seem as dark or my problems as insurmountable.

My energy, which had lagged as I'd searched Grandma's downstairs, filled me again. I helped Mrs. Newkirk clear the table, then I dried the dishes as Mrs. N washed and Mr. N put them away.

"How's your sister?" Mrs. Newkirk asked. "And why didn't she come with you?"

"She didn't know I was coming," I answered. "Besides, she's so busy with the clinic at the zoo where she works. You know Bella. Classic over-achieving eldest child."

Mrs. N laughed. "Wait until she's married and has children. Her over-achieving days will be over."

Mr. N nodded in complete agreement with his wife.

I almost laughed at the notion that my super

professional sister would let anything, even a husband or family, keep her from advancing in her chosen career. But that would only hurt the elderly couple's feelings. And I'd never do anything to hurt them.

We chatted a little longer, then I said good night, but when I started for the door, Mr. Newkirk went with me.

Surprised at his actions, I tried to dissuade him. "I'll be just fine, Mr. N. You stay here with the missus."

His brows dipped low over his eyes in a frown. "Now you don't think I'm going to let you walk home alone in the dark, do you? I couldn't do that."

I knew the battle was lost before we'd ever started. "All right, but just to the back door. No need to come in."

He nodded in agreement. We walked a few steps then he said, "If you don't have plans for tomorrow, how about wetting a line with me in the morning?"

Suddenly I was excited I'd decided to come. It had been years since I'd taken time to fish. "In Grandma's pond? I'd love to."

"And I'll let you have dibs on the willow tree," he teased, his laugh sounding like dead leaves, rustling in the wind.

When we were kids, Bella and I fought for the position by the willow tree each time we fished. "Well, that's the best spot on the whole pond."

"Will you be over for breakfast? Mrs. N will make whatever you'd like."

"Please thank her, but tell her not to bother. I usually just have a cup of coffee."

He nodded. "All right then. I'll meet you at the

barn to pick out our poles about eleven o'clock."

"Good night." I gave him a swift hug, then opened the screen on the back porch and stepped inside.

He ambled back toward the cottage, strolling along as if it were the middle of the afternoon. I watched him as far as I could see him, hoping he wouldn't fall.

When I finally heard the slam of their door echo through the still night, I went into the house. Although I'd thought I might search some more, I was so tired, I decided to go straight to bed.

The next morning, I awoke filled with a burning energy to find those journals. I fixed a pot of coffee then took a quick bath in the claw-foot tub while it perked. Dressing quickly, I went back to the kitchen, poured myself a cup and took it with me upstairs.

There were three bedrooms on one side of the hallway and one huge bedroom on the other. I started in the big bedroom. When I opened the door, I remembered why Bella and I never asked to sleep in there. There were no pictures on the wall, no homey quilts on the beds. Just two double beds, made up with sheets and blankets. No dressers. No bookshelves.

Getting on my knees, I looked under the beds, hoping I might find the diaries boxed up, but no luck. Then I checked the bedrooms on the other side. Each a cozy room, ready for a family member to move into at a moment's notice. And while there were dressers and bookshelves in each room, there were no journals.

I was stunned. What had Grandma done with those books? I'd looked in every conceivable place in the entire house. There was no attic and no basement. The only other place I could think to look was the barn, and I really didn't think she would have put them there.

Maybe she'd taken them with her.

With a glance at my watch, I saw it was almost time to meet Mr. N out at the barn. Picking up my now empty cup, I went back to the kitchen and filled it again. After unplugging the pot, I left by the backdoor and walked across the lawn to the barnyard gate. After turning the small board that served as a latch, I pushed it open and walked through, closing it behind me.

I walked slowly so I wouldn't scare the chickens pecking in the grass. When I got to the barn door, I saw Mrs. N there with her husband. "Have you found a newborn interest in fishing or are you afraid I'm going to steal your husband?" I asked.

"I've always liked to fish, Miss Smarty," she answered, her voice sharp with teasing. "But I had too many chores to loaf at the pond with the rest of you lollygaggers."

"And you've decided you have time to loaf today?"

She nodded once. "Yes."

When Mrs. N had picked out her cane pole, I took one that wasn't too thick and had a large red and white float on it. Mr. N took a pole like mine, then picked up a rusted coffee can that had holes poked in the lid.

We passed through the gate that led into the pasture, then walked across the dead grass toward the best fishing hole on Grandma's farm. It took a few minutes to get there. I wondered if the Newkirks wouldn't benefit from the purchase of a golf cart or four-wheeler to use on the place.

If I were to suggest it to them, though, it would probably insult them. When we got to the water's edge, we stopped near the old willow that grew at an angle out over the pond. Mr. Newkirk sat on the trunk of the willow that was just the right height to be a bench, balanced his pole against the tree and opened the coffee can.

"Looks to me like you've opened a real can of worms," I quipped.

"Speaking of a can of worms, *why* didn't your sister come with you?" Mrs. Newkirk asked.

I smiled. "No, we aren't fighting, if that's what you're wondering. I just decided to come on the spur of the moment, and she has responsibilities at the zoo."

Mrs. Newkirk's smile brightened as if she'd been truly worried about Bella and me. "Well, I'm glad to hear that. How are your folks?"

"They're fine." If they weren't, I was sure Mom would have let us know. She was never one to keep secrets.

When Mr. Newkirk had put a worm on his hook, he pushed himself to his feet and set the can where he'd been sitting. "Gabby women. Bait your own hooks," he mumbled and wandered toward the other side of the pond.

I picked up the can and held it for Mrs. N. She grabbed a worm as if she'd done it every day of her life and baited her hook. When I had my wiggly little guy on the hook, I put the lid back on the can and tossed my hook into the water.

The float bobbed on the water for a few moments as I hiked one hip onto the bare willow tree. As I settled in to wait, I heard Mrs. N humming softly under her breath. It was such a peaceful scene with the golden shades of winter-killed grass surrounding the pond, and farther on, the russet colors of sumac bushes. Probably the same sumac bushes that first taught me about my allergy.

All so different from the mad whirl I'd left behind in Dallas.

Before long my float sank, bringing a yelp from Mrs. N, who pointed at the place where my fishing line had been yanked deep in the water.

Reverting to instructions from childhood, I jerked my line to set the hook and hauled what I assumed would by a small perch out of the water. Instead of a perch, though, I pulled out a glossy black catfish that clicked at me as soon as he broke water.

Mr. N pulled his line from the water and, carrying his pole, came around the pond to take my fish, put him on the stringer and placed him back in the water. "We can let him go later if we don't catch enough for a mess."

As soon as my catch was submerged, Mrs. N caught a large perch. We went back and forth until we had more than enough for a meal.

"I reckon that's plenty. We might as well pack up and go in for lunch," Mrs. Newkirk said, winking at me as she talked.

"Since when did 'let's go fishing' mean 'come to the pond so you can take the fish off our lines?' I didn't get to catch one because I had to help you two dag burn females," Mr. N pretended to grumble. "Jazzy, I'll carry the fish if you can get my pole as well as yours."

I nodded, happy to carry Mr. Newkirk's for him. After we got back to the barn, I helped Mrs. Newkirk put away the fishing equipment then we went into their house, washed up and prepared to fry the fish while Mr. N cleaned them. When he brought them inside, we had the breading ready, the oil hot and the potatoes oven frying.

We sat down to the freshest fish dinner I'd had since the last time I was there, and although I didn't find Grandma Maleva's journals, I didn't feel as though the trip had been a waste. Somehow, being there in Grandma's home and spending time with these two people, who she'd been so close to, gave me a feeling of renewal.

After we'd cleaned up the dishes, I told the old couple goodbye, went back to Grandma's house and packed up my car. After checking to be sure the house was locked up, I stowed my gear in the Z, got into the driver's seat and was just putting the car into reverse when I saw Mr. Newkirk coming out of his house, a large brown box in his hands. Mrs. N followed right behind.

When they saw me in my car, she started waving for all she was worth. "I have something of your grandma's and I think it's time you kept it," she called as she rushed toward me.

I killed the engine. Getting out, I went to meet them. Mrs. N took my arm and turned me, so I walked back to the car with them. "Your grandma asked me to keep these until one of you were in a position to warrant passing them on. I think you might be there now."

Mr. N held the box out to me, so I opened the lid. There inside were Grandma's journals.

"How did you know I was looking for those?" I asked, my voice cloudy with emotion.

"Just a hunch." Mrs. N pulled me with her to my car then opened the passenger door. "Put them in the seat, James. She'll want to have them close to her, I'm thinking."

"Yes, ma'am," he answered. "I aim to please."

"Oh, you." Mrs. N waited while her husband put the books inside the car then hugged him. "I'd never be able to get along without you."

"That's been my plan all along." He gave me a wink then hugged me. "Don't stay away so long next time. And tell that sister of yours to come see us and bring her beau with her."

I thought about my ultra-professional sister. "I'm afraid she'll have to come alone. She's too busy at the zoo to have a boyfriend."

"Well, she'll get over that," Mrs. Newkirk answered. "Soon as she sets eyes on the man she was meant for."

Getting back into the car, I buckled up and, with one hand resting on the journals, backed down the driveway. As I drove away from the farm, I almost wished I had a job that would make it easier for me to spend time there. But as soon as Christmas was over, I'd be heavy into cruise season. And I hadn't met a woman yet who thought she had all the clothes, or the right styles, to go on a cruise.

For some reason, the trip home is always faster for me than when I go somewhere, and this time was no exception. When I got home, I parked my car in the garage then struggled to carry my bag and the box of journals up to the apartment with me.

I got to the door and knocked, hoping Bella would let me in, but after several moments, I set the box down and flipped through my keychain for the right key. After opening the door, I put my bags inside, then picked up the box and carried it in with me.

I almost dropped it when I found Bella, sleeping on the couch in front of the TV. Setting the box on the coffee table, I gave her a shake then crashed in the chair next to her.

Finally she blinked at me then sat up, rubbing her eyes like a little girl. "Did you just get home?"

"Just this minute," I answered.

"From work?"

"How hard were you sleeping?" I asked as worry weighed in my stomach. "It's Sunday. Remember? I went to Grandma's farm for the weekend. Didn't you see my note?"

She stared at me for a moment as if she had no idea what I'd said, then glanced toward the kitchen, where I'd left the note written in chalk. "Oh. Oh, yeah. I forgot for a moment. I must have been dead for all counts. What time is it?"

"A little before six." She looked pale, which added to my worry. "Want to go out and get something to eat?"

She shook her head. "I'm really not hungry. Why don't we just warm up some chicken noodle soup tonight?"

That meal had always been reserved for only when we were ill. "Are you feeling okay?" I asked as alarm shot through me.

"I'm fine," she insisted. "Just not hungry."

Maybe if I give her time to wake up a little, she'll get hungry. Even after having that great fish dinner for lunch, I was starving. "Do we have any chicken noodle soup?"

"Yes," she answered, her tone chiding. "I keep several cans, just in case."

Deciding to humor her, I got to my feet and went to the kitchen. I opened a couple of cans, poured them in a pot and turned the flame on low under it.

"Did you get any Christmas shopping done while I was gone?" I called.

After several moments, I heard a loud yawn then Bella answered, "None. I can't begin to think what we're going to give Mom and Dad."

"Something from a store near them to make it easy for her to take back." I took crackers, bowls, soup spoons and small plates from a cupboard and set them on the table.

Bella chuckled at my joke. "She can't help it if she has discerning taste."

I snorted as I gave the soup a stir. "Her taste isn't all that discerning. She just can't stand for us to buy her something that she'd use. She wants to be the discoverer."

"Then let's give them a cruise."

I knew Bella would think of something. "Good one. But it'll have to be the best cruise around. Otherwise, she'll take it back for a different destination."

Bella giggled. "She probably will anyway."

I watched the steam rising from the pan as I tried to think of a place Mom would die to go. "We could send them on a cruise to Hawaii."

"They flew to Hawaii two years ago. Remember?" Bella wandered into the kitchen and dropped into a chair at the table. "She'd have a been-there-done-that whine if they actually took the trip."

"True." I waited a few more moments until the soup started to bubble around the edges, then ladled it into bowls and set one in front of Bella. I pulled one close to me.

Bella picked up her spoon and took a hesitant bite. Then, as if it were the best soup on the planet, she dug in.

"Taste all right?" I asked, taking a bite to see if it tasted as good as she made it look. It didn't.

"Oh, yes. It's delicious. And these crackers are wonderful. What kind are they?"

If I hadn't known Bella so well, I'd have wondered what she'd been smoking. She sounded as if she had the 420 munchies. "The same kind we always eat. Whole wheat sodas."

"Well these are great."

I took a bite of one, but it was the usual dry, crumble-into-dust cracker. She ate for several minutes, emptying her bowl, without saying a word. When she'd filled it again, I stared at her. She didn't usually eat like this.

"Didn't you eat anything at all while I was gone?" I teased her.

She looked at me as she thought, then she lowered her gaze as her cheeks turned a dull pink. "I ate while you were gone. Almost everything in the place. We'll probably have to go shopping if you're going to want anything this week."

Which pretty much explained the soup for supper. She wasn't sick. She'd just polished off the rest of the food in the place. I gave her a quick smile. "Well, a growing girl has to eat. We'll go shopping after we do the dishes."

She blinked at me as if I'd thought of something new and awe inspiring. "That's a great idea."

"And since I cooked, that means..."

"I know. I have to do the dishes." She picked up her bowl, put it to her mouth and drained it, something I hadn't seen her do since we were three. She was always so fastidious, I was shocked.

When she set it down, she glanced at my bowl to see if I had anything left.

"Sorry. I didn't save you any." I didn't try to hide the amusement in my voice.

She glared at me. I swear, if she'd been a werewolf, she'd have growled. "I'm starving to death and you think it's funny."

"No, I don't." I picked up my dirty dishes. "Tell you what. I'll help with the dishes then we can go to the store sooner."

She shook her head. "You only offered because there's not much to do."

"Right."

With a chuckle, she opened the dishwasher and started rinsing and loading while I put away the crackers, salt and pepper.

As I washed off the table and stove she finished up and went back into the living room. "I'm going to change clothes then we'll go. Okay?" I called.

"Anytime you're ready."

In my bedroom, I swiftly tossed the clothes from my bag into the hamper, put away my other things, and changed into a fresh pair of jeans and a medium weight sweater. After slipping into a leather jacket, I went back into the living room to find Bella asleep. Again.

Alarmed that she'd dropped off so quickly—I couldn't have been more than ten minutes—I got on my knees in front of her and shook her. "Bella? Are you okay?"

She jerked as if I'd startled her. "Yes. I'm fine." She tried to hide a yawn, but wasn't successful.

"Why are you sleeping so much? Didn't you get any rest at all last night?"

"Yes, I did. In fact, I didn't go anywhere. I just…slept."

That worried me. I got to my feet, then taking her hand, I pulled her up. "If this doesn't stop, we're taking you to the doctor to see what's wrong."

She sighed, but then nodded. "All right. But we'll probably find out I just need vitamins."

"Then we'll buy you vitamins."

At the store, we did a role reversal. I spent most of my time picking out healthy food and putting back the junk food Bella tossed in the cart.

Talk about an upside down world. Usually I was the one who wanted instant junk food.

When we checked out, I found that she'd been able to sneak a package of chips and a bag of candy bars into the cart. She was much better at getting the bad stuff past me than I was at getting it past her.

I should have taken notes.

On Monday I went to our storage locker and pulled out our artificial Christmas tree along with our decorations. When I got the tree set up and glowing, I yelled at Bella to come help me.

She came into the room as if her feet were made of lead. "I'm not really up for this."

"If we don't get up for it, Christmas will be over and the tree won't be put up at all." I held out her favorite ornament—an antique bulb in shades of green and gold that said, *Happy Holidays*. "I knew you'd at least want to put this one on."

Giving me a tired smile, she took the ornament and wandered to the tree.

While she did her normal "where's the absolute best possible place for this ornament" I heard my cell phone playing, *Santa Baby*.

I picked it up and glanced at the screen. Doc.

My heart danced as I flipped it open. "Hello."

"Hi." His voice warmed me all over. "Where've you been lately? I haven't heard a word from you."

"I know. I had to run out to the family farm to take care of some business." I remembered the journals for the first time since my worry about Bella had taken over my thought processes. "How are the babies?"

"The runt is doing well. I don't know what you did, but she started eating after your visit."

"I just told her the facts of life. 'You want to live, you gotta eat.'"

He chuckled low in the phone. "Well, I'm glad you spoke her language. She probably gained several ounces over the weekend."

I glanced at Bella, who finally put the ball on the tree, and wondered if she'd gained that weekend, too. The best way to gain weight was to eat a lot and get no exercise. Sleeping was the best way to get no exercise I could think of.

****

Bella curled up on the couch and stared at the Christmas tree. Why Jazzy was bothering to put it up this close to Christmas, she didn't know. She'd just have to take it down again in a week or two anyway.

Laying her head on the arm of the couch, her thoughts drifted to Spencer, which they did more and more these days. He'd told her the night they'd been together that he had to be out of town for a few days, running records at the bottom of Texas and points south. Whatever that meant.

Of course when he'd told her, he asked her if she'd like to go along.

She should have gone. At least she'd have done something besides sleep.

Like mind blowing sex. All things considered, not a bad pastime.

Heat swirling through her, she forced her attention back to the nearly nude tree in their living room. She really ought to put on a few more ornaments, just to let Jazzy know she wasn't a Scrooge this year. Or would that be Scroogetta?

As she started to get up, she realized she had to go to the bathroom. Again.

It seemed the thing she did most that weekend, after sleeping and eating, was visit the powder room.

But there was no helping it. When you've got to go, you've got to go.

When she came out, Jazzy was off the phone and back to decorating.

Bella refused to ask about Chase's brother. After all, he hadn't called even once, and she'd have sworn his mind had been blown the other night as surely as hers. "What did Chase have to say?"

Jazzy tossed her a glance and a secret smile. "He wants me to come back out and see the litter y'all are hand raising. I fed the runt the other night, and since then, she's really started eating well."

Bella nodded absently as she bit the inside of her lip, trying to think of another question to ask that didn't include Spencer. "You should come out tomorrow if you don't have appointments scheduled."

"This close to Christmas, I don't usually have many. But right after, look out!"

Spencer! Tell me what he said about Spencer. She forced herself to remain quiet while she picked up another bulb. Strolling slowly, she circled the tree, looking for its proper place.

Jazzy stepped to the far side of the tree, giving her voice a muffled sound. "He said he'd take me out there tonight, but he had to do something for Spencer."

"What?" Bella demanded almost before Jazzy stopped speaking.

"What?" Jazzy stuck her head around where she could see Bella.

"I said what did he have to do for Spencer?"

Jazzy shrugged. "I don't know. Water his plants, feed his tarantula. Something."

Bella swallowed hard. "He has a pet tarantula?"

"Just kidding. I don't remember what he said he had to do, but Spence had to go to southern Texas and Doc promised to take care of something for him." Jazzy smiled. "I think Spence told him to say hi to you."

A small shock jolted Bella's stomach then she warmed at Jazzy's words.

Idiot. You aren't in middle school anymore. Why are you acting like this? But no matter how much she chided herself, Bella couldn't help thinking about him. DGL—darn good looking—and manners, too. Who would have ever put the two together?

Suddenly, Bella was filled with energy. "Let's get finished decorating this tree."

When Jazzy looked at her as if she'd lost her mind,

she gave her a huge smile. "Come on, Jazzy. I'm starving!"

When they finished the tree, she talked Jazzy into going with her to the nearest drive-in for a burger.

As they pulled in to the old-fashioned hamburger place, Bella pushed the button to order.

"Just a Coke for me," Jazzy murmured.

"Aren't you hungry?" Bella looked over the menu as she waited for the people inside the restaurant to answer.

Jazzy shook her head. "We just ate a little over an hour ago."

Finding the double cheeseburger she craved on the menu, Bella shrugged. "But that was over an hour ago."

Jazzy shook her head, but thankfully was silent while Bella gave the girl on the intercom their order. Double cheeseburger, onion rings and two Cokes.

"Think that'll get you through the night?" Jazzy teased.

Bella gave her a sharp glance. "If you're lucky, it should."

"Maybe we should get something to keep in the fridge tonight. Then if you get attacked by the hunger monster again, you can zap it."

"Not a bad idea."

The drive-in's speaker system played Christmas music, as was every other retail establishment in Texas that time of year. And Christmas music made her think of Christmases past and the great food they always had on Christmas Eve at their parent's house.

And she got hungrier, something she often did in winter, but rarely to this degree. She could only hope what she ordered would be enough to tide her over until morning.

Finally, a girl wearing inline skates and carrying a tray with a bag of food and two drinks came out of the building, rolling to a stop at Bella's window. The girl handed Bella the food and drinks, then gave them a plastic smile. "That'll be nine fifty three."

As soon as the burger was inside the car, Bella tore it open and took a bite. Oh, that was good. As she chewed, she found her purse and shoved it into Jazzy's lap.

Rolling her eyes, Jazzy shook her head then dug for Bella's wallet. She pulled out a twenty and handed it to Bella.

Bella took the bill and shoved it into the girl's hands. "Keep the change," she mumbled around a mouthful of onion ring.

The girl grabbed the bill and skated away before Bella could reconsider.

"That was a twenty, Bella." Jazzy's eyes practically bulged.

Grabbing her Coke, Bella took a long drink. "I know."

"You just gave that girl a ten dollar tip."

Bella nodded.

"That's way too much."

Bella shrugged. "So the kid got a break tonight. And I got my food, which is delicious. Want a bite?"

"No."

"Good." Bella ate for a while before she realized Jazzy watched her intently. "What? Do you want an onion ring?"

"No." Jazzy shook her head then put her hand on Bella's shoulder. "Bella, I think you need to see a doctor."

Bella looked around the car. A double cheeseburger and a large order of onion rings as well as a large Coke. That was more than she was used to eating in an entire week, and she'd scarfed down it *after* having dinner.

Something was definitely wrong.

Chapter Twelve

Christmas Day grew near with Bella in the strangest mood I'd ever seen. I started wondering if manic depression could suddenly happen to a person, until I remembered she'd started acting this way just after she'd gone out with Spencer.

And as far as I knew, she hadn't heard from him since. There was no manic to it. It looked to me as if my sister was just depressed.

We finally got our tree decorated and our shopping finished so I was free most of the time. I'd started reading Grandma Maleva's journals from the beginning when we got a call from Mom.

"Hi, Jazzy." She always sounded so happy at Christmas; you'd think she believed in Santa. "How are my girls?"

Should I tell her about Bella? I wondered. *About the mood swings and food orgies my twin has gone through in the last several days? I don't think so.*

"We're great, and almost ready for Christmas. How about you and Dad?"

"Oh, you know your dad. As long as I do all the preparation, he loves holidays." She chuckled, warming me all over. I doubted I'd ever get too old to enjoy my mother's laughter.

"What do you want us to bring for Christmas Eve?" *How about a couple of guys we've been seeing?*

But I knew better than to ask. Unless we were married to them, making them officially part of the family, no one would be invited to our special Christmas Eve celebration.

"Nothing but yourselves." *And, of course, gifts.* She'd have a breakdown if she didn't get Christmas gifts. "Has your father made his last minute call to you for what to buy me for Christmas yet?"

"No, Mom. I haven't heard from him."

"Well, when he does, tell him I'd really like a Timarrah bag…" She went on to describe the most expensive bag in an ultra expensive line of purses, and to go with it, she wanted the matching wallet and sunglasses case. And if Bella and I hadn't found her gift yet, she'd like to have some of the company's jewelry—an overpriced gold ring with the company insignia on it—and their perfume, which to me smelled like a cat had urinated in a bottle.

"In other words, you want to be a walking billboard for them."

"No." She cut the word so short, it almost didn't get out of her mouth. "I knew I should have spoken to Bella."

I laughed softly. "Don't worry, Mom. I'll tell him."

"Without your billboard comment?"

"Yes. Without it."

"Good. We'll pick you up Christmas Eve at three." She sounded as if she were about to hang up.

"Wait, Mom!" I spoke quickly so I wouldn't have to call her back. "Pick us up?"

"I told you we were going to the farm to celebrate this year, didn't I?"

I cleared my throat to keep from barking at her.

When my mother focuses on something she wants, she can be very absent minded. "No. You didn't mention that, Mom."

"Oh. I thought I did." Her voice was almost musical. "I called the Newkirks and told them we'd be out to spend a night or two. They'll have everything ready for us."

"Mom, aren't the Newkirks are getting a little old to have to get everything ready?" I had to be careful how I worded my questions if I didn't want to start a war that would last through the holiday.

"It's not like I expect them to chop down our tree and drag it to the house for us." She laughed softly into the phone. "We'll do that ourselves. All I asked them to do was the grocery shopping. Oh, and to make sure the sheets were fresh on the beds."

I closed my eyes and thought about the old couple trudging up and down that staircase, and had to stifle the sigh that built inside me. "We could have done that."

"Why do you think they're there, dear? It's not a retirement home."

Maybe it should be. Happily, I was able to withhold my opinion. A war, especially at that time of year, wouldn't be pretty. "All right, Mom. We'll be ready at three."

"Maybe we'd better make it noon," she answered almost before the words were out of my mouth. "With the drive down, and we'll have to cut the tree then decorate it. No, let's make it ten o'clock."

If I didn't get off the phone fast, we'd have to get up at daybreak to leave. "Okay, Mom. Bella and I'll be ready." *If I can get Bella to wake up long enough to come.* I disconnected the call before I could break down and tell Mom about my worries.

It wouldn't do any good to tell her. She'd just go crazy and want to take her to Johns Hopkins or some other high dollar medical place.

I thought about calling Doc and confiding in him, but how could I tell him that his brother had broken my sister's heart? I couldn't.

I looked for Bella, but she wasn't in the room with me, so I looked around the apartment, where I found her asleep in front of the TV. "Ready to go shopping?" I asked, sitting down next to her.

She blinked awake, then yawned. "Now? Do we have to?"

"Only if we're going to get Mom what she's requesting for Christmas." I stood up, knowing Bella would follow me just to find out what Mom wanted.

"What is it this year?" She got off the couch, following me to the door. "A trip to Paris?"

"No." I laughed then shook my head. "You know Mom. Just think of the most expensive, hottest item out there."

"Not a Timarrah bag?" Bella looked horrified at the thought.

"No. Not just the bag. She wants everything they make."

Bella groaned, but having lived with our mother our entire lives, she knew it was no good arguing. If Mom wanted the entire line, she'd get it. Or we'd hear about it until the end of time. "What about the Alaska cruise tickets we bought?"

I shrugged. "I guess we'll give them to Dad."

Although several of the shops in the shopping mall

where my office is carried Timarrah bags, we decided to go to the Timarrah store itself. They'd surely have whatever was the latest.

When we got there, we looked around for a few minutes before a woman on the sales staff approached us. "May I help you?"

"Yes." I told the woman which bag we were looking for, and she led us to the display with three different sizes. Although Mom had been very specific about the bag she wanted, she hadn't told me which size. I decided it was time to call Dad.

While I was on the phone with him, Bella wandered away, looking at the jewelry, t-shirts and other items made by the company. It wasn't long before she came back and dropped into the chair beside me.

"Dad said to go ahead and get everything Mom asked for. Even though he's already bought her the necklace and earrings she wanted, he'll pay for most of this, too."

"Fine." Bella's voice was so thin, I turned to see what was wrong. The girl was so pale, the veins showed blue through her skin. In the back of my mind, I wondered how she could remain upright.

I dropped to my knees beside her. "Bella? What's wrong?"

The saleswoman sounded concerned. "Would you like something to drink? Or a plate of fruit?"

"Yes." I'd have said yes to anything just to get her to leave us alone for a few minutes.

I squeezed Bella's cold hand tighter. "What is it, Bella? Are you sick?"

"I think I'm going to be."

"Why? What's wrong?"

"Spencer just walked into the shop." She took a shaky breath and blew it out before she continued. "And he's with someone."

The woman came back with a plate of melon balls and thin slices of ham and a small cup of cola. I took them from her and pressed the cup into Bella's hands. Then I turned back to the woman. "We'll take it."

"Which?" she asked.

I pointed out the middle sized bag, the matching wallet, sunglasses case, makeup case and belt. Then I instructed her to get the ring that matched Dad's gift. No way was I buying the cat pee fragrance. She'd most likely buy it for herself the week after Christmas, but at least I wouldn't have to smell it throughout our time at the farm together.

When the saleswoman left with a wide grin on her face, no doubt thinking of her commission, Bella peeked around me to see where Spencer had gone. "I'll be in the car." Turning up her coat collar, she strode swiftly for the exit.

The clerk came back with our total, which rivaled the national debt, and I abandoned the fruit plate on a nearby shelf and fished through my wallet for a credit card. As I dug, I caught a glimpse of Spencer, leaving through the door Bella had taken.

Alarm rushing my actions, I grabbed the first card I came to and shoved it into the woman's hands. "I'll be right back."

The woman caught my wrist. "Before you leave, I need to see some identification."

Frantic to get away from her, I dug for my license. When I finally found it, I slapped it into her hand. "And I'd like everything wrapped separately."

I could tell by her near scowl that wasn't what she'd hoped to hear, but she nodded and walked away.

By the time I got to the door, Spencer walked back inside. His mouth dropped open then he focused on me with a singular intent. "I thought I saw your sister go out that door a minute ago."

"You did." Anger roiled in my stomach. I didn't bother to try to act like I was glad to see him. Why should I? This jerk had put my sister in the mood from hell for the last few weeks and made my life a misery.

"Where'd she go? I wanted to say hi."

I glanced through the plate glass at my Z, but the car was empty. She must have ducked into a nearby doorway when she saw him coming. I shrugged. "I don't know where she went."

"O-kay. Well, tell her I said—" His brows rose, puckering his forehead. "Merry Christmas. I'll call her—"

"We're going out of town." *Where she can't be reached.*

"Oh." His shoulders sagged as if he were really disappointed. As if she meant something to him. As if he cared.

Nice act. I had to bite my tongue to keep from asking him why he hadn't called her in all that time. All of Texas, as far as I knew, even the far southern parts, had telephone service. Maybe not cell phone, but some kind of phone. And postal service.

"I'll call her a few days after Christmas, then." He tried to smile, but didn't do a very good job of it. "Tell her hello for me?"

"I will." Noticing the woman he'd come in with watched us from a display of red and green bags, I tipped my head toward her. "I think your friend is waiting."

"Who, her? She's not my friend. She's…a c-cousin," he stammered.

I didn't try to hide my snort. "Right. And I'm your uncle."

I turned my back on Spencer, effectively cutting him off as the saleswoman came back with our gifts. I wasn't about to listen to his lies when I knew how badly he'd hurt my sister. Or at least I had a pretty good idea.

Signing the sales slip, I put away my card and ID, took the presents and walked toward the door.

Much to my surprise, Spencer was there to hold it for me. "Would you like some help?"

"No. Thank you." I clenched my teeth to keep from telling him what I thought. What I really wanted to do was snap his head off.

"No. You probably wouldn't. At least tell her I asked about her. Will you?"

"All right." *But I'm not going to ruin Christmas.*

****

Mom and Dad picked us up Christmas Eve morning in their SUV, so there was plenty of room for gifts. After stopping at the closest Starbucks for Cinnamon Dolce Lattes all around, we drove to the farm. When we got there, the Newkirks were waiting for us. "How do they know when we'll get here every time?" Mom murmured as Dad pulled in next to the house.

"The same way they know everything else," Dad answered her. "They just do."

Mom nodded, then with a shrug, opened her door,

got out and hugged Mrs. Newkirk.

As we unloaded our bags and presents, Mrs. Newkirk prepared a pot of coffee in Grandma's kitchen for us. Mr. Newkirk stopped Dad just as we headed inside with the last of it. "I sharpened the ax for you."

"The ax?" Apparently, Dad's mind was on that cup of coffee, not the manual labor he'd be doing in a little while.

"I thought you'd want it sharp so you could make a clean cut on the tree." Mr. Newkirk clapped him on the shoulder. "Better have your coffee and head for the tree field. We're going to get some weather this afternoon the forecasters aren't expecting."

Dad's eyebrows almost reached his hairline. "And how do you know that?"

Mr. Newkirk chuckled hoarsely as he rubbed his leathery hands together. "Feel it in my bones, boy. Always have."

After we finished our coffee, Dad, Bella and I headed for the tree field our grandfather had planted when our mother was small. It wasn't a commercial tree farm, but when we were in the mood for a fresh cut tree, we always had the freshest.

Mom stayed at the house to "get the ornaments ready," but we knew it was because she didn't want the exercise.

As we stepped out the backdoor, Dad zipped his jacket. "It's getting colder, girls. I wonder if Mr. Newkirk's bones are accurate."

"Probably," Bella murmured, not particularly thrilled to be out in the wind. "I should have stayed at the house and had a nap."

"You slept all the way here," I reminded her, then

dropped my voice so Dad wouldn't hear me. "I think you need to see a doctor."

She tripped over something in the dead grass, and when she'd righted herself, gave me a look that should have set my hair on fire. "I don't need to see a doctor. I just need to slow down a little. That's all."

I held her gaze for a moment, but she wouldn't relent.

"Come on, girls. You're lagging behind," Dad called to us.

I lengthened my step, catching him easily, but it took Bella a little while longer. Or maybe she didn't want to catch up with us.

We walked past the pond I'd fished in not too many days prior, continuing on until we came to a fence. Following the fence we found the gate, which we left open as we walked to another pasture. Finally we got to the field of pinyon and juniper trees. Mr. Newkirk had taken good care of them. They looked as if they'd been watered regularly and fertilized. We picked out a tree that would fit in the living room, where Mom had announced the tree would stand, and Dad prepared to cut it.

"Either of you girls want to take a swing at it?" he asked.

"No, thanks."

He chuckled as he pulled leather gloves from his pocket and put them on. "You used to squabble over who was going to get to take the first swing. Remember? For a while we had to have two trees so you could both have a first swing."

Bella stared at the ground in front of her as if thinking of something else. "That was a long time ago."

"Yeah. It was." He made sure we were out of his range then took the first swing. The bite of the ax sang out, bringing back memories of long ago as surely as the pinyon's fragrance filled the air.

A few blows felled the tree, and after making sure the stump he left was smooth, he handed me the ax, picked up the tree by the trunk and started toward the house. Bella followed along as if lost in a dream.

We walked along single file, no one talking until we went through the gate we'd left open. "Can you close it, Bella?" Dad asked.

"Yes." She didn't laugh or play as usual. I was getting really worried now, but Dad didn't seem to notice, and the last thing I wanted was to worry him. Because if I worried him, he'd tell Mom, and no one would get any peace until she'd found out what was on Bella's mind.

My cell phone rang, which surprised me, since I hadn't realized we could get reception there at the farm.

"Hey, Jazzy." As usual, Doc's voice made my heart go crazy. I swallowed hard, trying to keep my insides from melting like so much chocolate.

"Hi." I stopped, hoping not to lose the signal. "Getting ready for a big Christmas?"

"Yeah." Was that regret I heard in his voice? "House is full of relatives and godparents, so we're pretty much stuck for the duration. How about you?"

"We're at my grandparent's farm for a few days." I cleared my throat, trying to keep the wistfulness from it. "Guess I won't be seeing you."

"Doesn't sound like it. I just saw on TV a weather front has taken an unexpected turn toward us."

"We're going to get a lot of snow, aren't we?" I

asked.

"Did you catch the breaking news?"

"No. Mr. Newkirk, the man who takes care of the farm, told us a couple of hours ago, when we got here." I glanced over my shoulder to see how far away Bella and Dad were when the first flake twirled past me. "Said he felt it in his bones."

Doc chuckled. "Well, stay warm. I'll see you in a few days."

"All right. I'll talk to you later."

"Bye." The word was barely a whisper, but I could feel the emotion behind it across the distance. He didn't want to say goodbye. Didn't want me to be away.

I loved it.

I rushed, catching up with the others as they passed the pond. Bella had stopped to watch the calm water for a few moments. I waited for her, unwilling to leave her alone in her present mood. No matter what, I was determined to find out what was up with her *that night*.

****

Bella tugged the gate into the yard shut just as Jazzy handed Mr. Newkirk the ax. Mr. Newkirk always knew when they'd need him, but the funny thing was, she'd never paid much attention to that before. The Newkirks had always just been there, almost as if they were part of the farm.

With a shiver, Bella stuck her hands deep into her pockets. It was getting colder. Much colder. And snow had started to fall. Maybe Mr. N knew what he was talking about. He usually did.

As she watched the flakes chase one another to the ground, several piled against her boots.

"When did you get the firewood stacked on the

porch?" Jazzy asked the old man.

"I kinda figured you folks would be down for Christmas, and remembering how your mama likes a fire, I hired old Art White to deliver it," Mr. N answered.

Jazzy lifted her eyebrows and smiled softly. "Was that about the time you got that feeling in your bones about this storm?"

"Might be. Just might be. Better get inside before you catch your death." His focus narrowed to Bella. "You, too, Missy. You certainly don't want to catch a chill."

Before she could answer him, he started for the barn. The flakes grew fatter and fell even faster. "Guess we'd better get inside." Jazzy linked her arm with Bella's as they ran toward the house.

When they stepped onto the screened in back porch, Jazzy picked up several sticks of firewood. "Might as well take a load now. Otherwise, Mom'll just send us back."

Bella picked up a few pieces, stomped off the snow at the kitchen entrance and took the wood to the living room.

While Dad worked at putting the tree in the stand Mom had ready for him, Bella and Jazzy took kindling from the nearby bucket, obviously left by the Newkirks, and built the fire.

When it was burning brightly, Bella settled on the hearth, forcing herself to try and enjoy the holiday. Jazzy, never able to sit still for long, went back for more wood. After a few moments, Bella picked up a dried lavender bundle and tossed it into the flame. The small bunch burned brightly, releasing a dusty sweet fragrance into the room.

Jazzy grinned at her while she stacked the firewood. "I love that aroma, especially mixed with the fresh pinyon. Let's take some home with us to use there."

Bella couldn't help but smile as the memory of their childhood flooded back. When they'd been small, Grandma had grown lavender, mainly as a ready source of food for her honey bees.

Rather than let all the blooms dry up and fall to the ground, Bella had gathered part of them and hung them to dry from the ceiling joists of the back porch.

"Why are you doing that?" Grandma had asked, an odd light in her eyes.

"So this winter when you build a fire, you can throw them in and make your house smell good."

After that, Grandma and Bella had collected the purple blossoms together and dried them on her back porch. It had been their special project. Must be Mrs. Newkirk who tended the good smelling herb these days, and left them bundled in the basket.

Dad finally had the tree upright in the corner Mom had chosen. "All right, Bella. Get some water for this fella. He's got to be thirsty."

Shoving to her feet, Bella went to the kitchen, found the spouted can under the sink, and filled it with tepid water. Taking it back to the living room, she poured it in the reservoir then took the can back, where Mom started the Christmas Eve meal.

Passing the kitchen window, all Bella could see was snow. The world outside was a white blur with nothing distinguishable. The sky was white, the ground, the trees. Everything, even the wind, was the same heavy white.

Thankful she wasn't out in it, she went back to the front room, which was considerably warmer than the other parts of the house, and helped decorate the tree. When they finally had the garland on and Mom pronounced it "perfect," they put one of Grandma's handmade quilts under it, then piled on the presents.

With the room lights off so they could appreciate the old-fashioned ones on the tree, the glow of the firelight drew her attention. "Uh-oh. Looks like we need to bring in more wood."

Mom rubbed her arms as she moved closer. "I hadn't realized how cold it was getting." She went to the door and looked out the front. "It's really coming down out there."

Bella went to stand beside her. Even looking across the screened in porch, she could see the whiteout conditions hadn't changed. They'd been hit by a blizzard, and anyone caught out in it would be in real trouble.

"Well, come on Bella baby, peel potatoes for me."

Exhaustion making her bones ache, she wished she could whine and say, "Make Jazzy do it." But knowing what Jazzy's answer would be, Bella nodded and followed her mother into the kitchen.

When almost all the potatoes were peeled, something banged several times against the backdoor. Bella startled, dropping her potato and the peeler in the sink. Eyes wide, Mom looked at her in surprise then they both rushed out to see what it was.

There, covered with so much snow he was almost indistinguishable from the storm, was Mr. Newkirk. As he shuffled onto the back porch, a snow mound behind him that Bella hadn't noticed moved.

Mr. N stomped the snow off his feet. "I found this fella coming up your driveway."

Bella stared for a moment at the man brushing off layers of snow from his arms and legs.

Spencer.

Her heart stopped. Was he there or had she conjured him?

Mind reeling, she turned and shoved her way back into the house. The warmth of the kitchen after the frigid temperature on the porch made her fingers tingle. If hers hurt from that short time on the porch, how must his feel?

Could it really be Spencer? Was this a cosmic coincidence or had he actually followed her all the way there?

Hoping not to look like a spoiled kid who'd run away and hidden, she hurried to the bathroom for a stack of bath towels and rushed back to the porch.

"Oh, good. Here she is now," Mom said standing well away from him as if she were afraid he might get her wet.

Dropping the stack of towels on a chair just inside the kitchen door, she unfolded one and handed it to him. He held it to his face for a moment, as if to thaw, as well as dry it.

With a glance at Mr. N, she picked up a towel and held it out for him, but he shook his head. "I'd best be heading to the house. The missus will be missing me if I don't get back. G'night."

"Be careful going home. And stay out of the storm!" Mom called after him, then turned to Bella. "I'm going to finish those potatoes and get them on the stove."

Spencer pushed the towel up to his hair, dragging off the snow laden knit cap on his head with a regretful smile. "Guess this wasn't the best idea I've ever had." When he spoke, his words were tight, as if his jaw had frozen. Or maybe he was working hard to keep his voice from trembling with the cold.

"What idea is that?" Fighting hard not to read too much into his presence, she reached for another towel.

He waited until she faced him again before he spoke, then, eyes doubtful, he rasped, "The idea that I had to be with you tonight. That no matter what, I couldn't live through Christmas Eve without you by my side."

Stunned by his words, she stared at him for a full minute before folding the towel lengthwise. His gaze kindled. As she stood on tiptoe to fit the towel around his neck, he slid his arms around her and, ignoring his frozen, wet clothes, he pulled her to him.

Something inside her eased as his mouth closed over hers.

"How are things—" Her mother caught her breath in surprise.

Not the least embarrassed, Bella slipped from his arms and turned to face Mom. Water dripped from her chin, but rather than wipe it off, she caught his hand. "Mom? This is Spencer."

"I guess you know him then." Mom's voice was dry, filled with humor.

"Yeah. I've met him before." Bella didn't try to hide the grin pulling at her lips. Why bother? Mom would figure it out soon if she hadn't already.

"Well, let's get him inside before he refreezes."

Bella tugged him in the door, but he resisted long enough to pull off his boots. In the kitchen she helped him remove his outer layer of clothing—coat, mittens and insulated coveralls—before she took him into the living room to let him warm by the fire.

Surprise filled Jazzy's face. "Spence. Where did you come from?" Her gaze flew to the empty doorway behind them.

"I decided to drop in on a whim." His brow puckered in a frown. "Sorry. I'm alone."

He removed another two or three layers until he stood near the fire in a snuggly pair of long underwear.

Bella picked up one pair of jeans to spread them by the fire. "You look as if you were prepared for the Iditarod."

Spencer snorted then nodded. "I wasn't sure how close I could get before I'd have to walk. Had to be prepared."

"I believe you." Feeling something in the pocket, she pulled a small, gift wrapped box out of the pocket and handed it to him.

Giving her a half smile, he laid it on the mantel. "To be truthful, nothing could have prepared me for this."

Bella had the feeling he wasn't talking about the weather.

"Doesn't surprise me." Jazzy picked up a piece of firewood, but Spencer took it from her and tossed it on the fire. "Few people are."

Mom and Dad came into the living room from the kitchen. Mom introduced Spencer to Dad then said, "I have an idea. Let's move the dining room table in here, in front of the fire, so we can stay warm while we eat."

"Okay, darlin'." Dad glanced their way. "If you girls can get the chairs Spencer and I will get the table."

Jazzy nodded and went to work, but Spencer caught Bella's hand before she moved away. It was just a touch, a stroke of his palm against hers, but it warmed her entire body.

Hating to move away from him, she went in to help with the heavy chairs. When they'd put them in the living room, Dad and Spencer hefted the table and walked with half steps as they carried its enormous weight to the area in front of the fire.

"There!" Dad expelled the word on his pent up breath. "Now, Jazzy, why don't you come with me and we'll find out what your mom wants us to use to set this table?"

Bella turned to Spencer, but instead of focusing on her, he reached for the tiny box he'd set on the mantel.

Chapter Thirteen

She forced her hunger for him aside. "What's that?"

"Gift." His sexy half smile sent her brain spiraling until she had to concentrate to remember what she'd asked.

"Oh." Lame answer. *Is it for me?* she wanted to ask, but her tongue would only form the words *hold me*, and no way she would beg for that.

He walked around the table to place the gift in the higher branches of the tree as if it were an ornament. When he was sure it wasn't going to fall, he moved back to her side and took her in his arms. Finally. She snuggled against him, the perfect fit—as if he'd been created with her in mind.

As naturally as a flower turns toward the sun, he covered her mouth with his. He stroked her tongue, taking the kiss deeper until her knees lost their strength, and if her parents hadn't been in the next room, preparing to come in at any minute, she'd have pulled him to the floor.

Just as they'd done in his house the last time they were together.

She thought longingly of the bedrooms upstairs. Unhappily, there were no fireplaces in those bedrooms. In fact, there was no heat up there at all, which meant they had to sleep under several layers of quilts anytime they were there during the winter. Not exactly conducive to wild lovemaking, but it wasn't impossible either.

Much too soon, Dad and Jazzy came back into the room. Feeling as if she were losing a vital part of herself when Spencer broke their kiss, Bella stepped away from him. But she couldn't go far.

Jazzy spread out the tablecloth she carried, then demanded Bella help her straighten it. While Dad set down the family heirloom china, Jazzy went back for the good silverware.

Bella gritted her teeth as she watched her twin move around the table, to the kitchen and back, in an unusual show of home keeping. She was practically bustling.

When she'd done everything she could to look like Martha Stewart, even carry in the side dishes and light white tapers she'd placed in pewter candlesticks with a long match, Jazzy dazzled them with a smile. "Looks like we're ready."

"Great." Dad reached for the light switch and turned them off. "All right, honey. Bring it in."

Apparently, Mom had accepted the fact that they had no choice about a visitor for Christmas, and made her annual dramatic entrance, carrying a crown roast filled with stuffing on a huge silver platter. After pausing in the doorway, she swept to the table and set it in the center between softly glowing candles.

Dad opened a bottle of wine and poured a glass for each of them, and with a glance out the window said, "None of you were planning to drive later. Right?"

Spencer gave a bark of laughter, but Jazzy and Mom just chuckled softly at Dad's annual joke.

As everyone started eating, Jazzy glanced across the table at Spencer. "So...why are you here?"

Unable to believe her sister would ask such a rude question, Bella couldn't find the words to admonish her. Heads together, Mom and Dad talked softly, missing Jazzy's missile.

Spencer set his glass down and gave Jazzy an easy smile. "I couldn't get through Christmas without being with Bella."

"You sure made it through the last—how long?—without seeing her." Jazzy took a long drink of her wine. "And you didn't seem to be suffering much when I saw you yesterday."

He blew out a soft sigh. "I was with Karla, my godparents' daughter. She was helping me with...a Christmas gift."

Surprise flashed in Jazzy's eyes. She lifted one eyebrow then glanced at Bella before stabbing him with her gaze again. "Really?"

"Really." He tipped his head toward the tree. "It's in the upper branches."

Finally one corner of Jazzy's mouth tipped up. "Score." Then she leaned back in her chair, a full smile spreading across her face. *Can you believe this guy?* she whispered to Bella in her mind. *According to Doc, he spent all of last week and part of the one before working to secure new leases for their oil company. Missed several holiday parties, too. And now he's driven all this way to be with you.*

If he'd waited only a couple of days, you'd have been back in Dallas. Easy access. Putting her fingers on her temples, she massaged the ache their twin speak caused.

Maybe he didn't want to wait.

A smug look curved Jazzy's lips and brightened her eyes. *Any idea why?*

No. But I'm glad he's here, Bella answered.

What about that woman he was with? His cousin?

His godparent's daughter. Bella lifted her shoulders in a slight shrug. *Who cares who he was with? He's with me now.*

Being with her had to be important to him, didn't it? The long drive, after the trip he'd just returned from, and impending weather would have been enough to stop most men. But even with his close knit family, Spencer was here with her. The thought thrilled her, sending a buzz jangling along her nerves.

Mom glanced down the table. "Did you park out back, Spencer?"

He shook his head. "No. My car's out on the county road, somewhere between here and town."

A frown of concern puckered Mom's brow. "You *walked* in this weather? Why, that's dangerous. People freeze to death in temperatures this low. How far did you walk?"

Spencer chuckled. "Far enough to give a snowman frost bite. Luckily I was prepared."

"You knew you'd be running into weather this bad, and you came anyway?" Shock sharpened Mom's voice.

Spencer refocused his gaze, settling it on Bella. Summer heat slid down her spine. "I couldn't make myself stay away."

****

We were almost finished eating when we lost power. Not that it's unusual for the electricity to go out at the farm. Any kind of inclement weather can send darkness crashing in on us. That's why we kept several hurricane lamps and a supply of lamp oil handy.

Luckily, I'd thought to add candles to our holiday table, so we weren't flailing in the darkness when it happened. Once we were over the initial surprise, we finished eating and started cleaning up—not an easy task without light.

After helping carry in dirty dishes, I started washing with water from the huge kettle Mom kept heating on the stove while Bella and Spencer dried. Mom and Dad put away leftovers and straightened up the living room.

I hated being the only one alone on a holiday like this. I'd never felt so desolate in my life. And watching Bella and Spencer only made it worse. The more I tried not to, the more I missed Doc.

A rogue thought attacked me. If Spencer had come, why hadn't Doc come with him?

Anger sizzled along my nape while my crippled ego curled in my belly, firing me with energy so I practically scrubbed the pattern off the china. My assigned chore was completed in record time.

While Bella and Spencer messed around, spending more time touching one another when they thought I wasn't looking than drying dishes, I moved through the kitchen, putting away condiments and candle sticks. Then I stormed to the living room to carry the chairs back where they belonged, and I would have moved the table back, but Dad stopped me. "That's too heavy for you to lift. Let Spencer and me do it."

I started to argue. "It's not too heav—"

"Yes, it is." Dad's voice was sharp. A tone I hadn't

heard from him since high school. "Lifting things that are too heavy might keep you from having babies—"

"Mark!" Mom's shocked yelp stopped his tirade.

Dad stopped practically mid-word, and I was glad he had. No way I wanted to discuss reproduction and whether lifting heavy weights could make a woman sterile—which I firmly doubted, but Dad, undoubtedly believed.

Thankfully, Mom was there to change the subject. "Remember the year we came down for Christmas, and were snowed in for days?"

"Yeah," Dad answered, a half smile creasing his face. "The girls were just little, and both of your parents were still with us."

"That was…quite a Christmas." Mom glanced at me, then at the floor as if by looking at me, she might let the dark family secret escape.

I remembered that Christmas very clearly. Bella and I were nearly three, and the full moon was almost upon us. That was when Grandma Maleva took me aside and taught me about my heritage.

I learned how to control my gift rather than letting it control me. And I'd learned that year just how wonderful being a werewolf could be.

Grandma Maleva and I'd grown closer than any grandmother/granddaughter pair I've ever known.

I only wished she were there with us that night. Maybe she could have told me how to expend some of the energy building along my muscles. What I really needed was to go out for a run. But with the snow coming down like it was, Mom would never let me out the door. And if I could get past her, Dad and Bella would be there to block me.

As if I could get into trouble. Who'd ever heard of a wolf freezing to death? Or getting lost in the snow? But trying to convince my family of that was a practice in futility.

I didn't bother to try.

Still hoping to work off the blistering energy, I carried in several armloads of wood, used some of it to pile the fire high, swept up the wood dust and tossed it in. I went through the French doors, kept closed to encapsulate the living room heat, and up the stairs to my bedroom, built alongside the chimney for a modicum of heat. I quickly found I couldn't stand being caged there, and jogged back down.

Finally I grabbed my jacket, went onto the screened front porch—the width of the house—and prowled. I walked the length of the enclosure again, and the entire time, I thought of Doc. I could envision his eyes as easily as I could blink. The memory of our night in his bed was as alive within me. To conjure his scent, I only had to take a deep breath. Now if I could only make him appear, too, life would be perfect.

But there are some things even a werewolf can't do.

The front door squealed in protest as it opened. Spencer stepped out on the porch, tucked his hands in his pockets and moved close enough to me he wouldn't have to yell over the blizzard. "Want me to tell you why he's not here?"

I wanted to act as if I wasn't sure who he was talking about, but I've never been able to pretend to have a feather brain. I stopped pacing and stared out at the storm. "I guess." My voice was so husky, I wasn't sure he'd heard me over the wind.

Leaning his shoulder against the door frame, he watched me. "He was on duty at the zoo. And even then he might have come, but there were several emergencies. Then the wolf cub you got to start eating suddenly took a turn for the worst. He didn't feel he could leave her."

My heart thumped with pain as I thought of the small animal. "Poor baby. Is she going to be okay?"

Spencer shrugged, a look of sympathy on his face. "I don't know. He promised to call when he knew something, one way or another."

"If he can get through. We usually lose phone service not long after we lose our power."

"He can always call on the cell."

"Hopefully." I forced myself to smile. "Reception isn't always the best here."

"Kind of like where I've been for the past few days." He matched my smile then touched my arm. "Aren't you freezing? What you're wearing isn't heavy enough for this weather."

Although the gift is mine, its secret was Bella's to share with Spencer, or not. I couldn't tell him that frigid weather was the least of a werewolf's worries. "Now that you mention it, it is a bit nippy."

He chuckled at my lame joke then turned with me toward the door. When we went inside, Bella sat on the hearth, watching the door. "Are you okay?"

I glanced at Spencer, wondering if there was something he hadn't told me. "I think so. Why? What's going on?"

"He told me about the wolf pup."

I sat by her on the hearth. "I'm fine. I just hope Doc doesn't have to miss Christmas."

"Are you kidding?" Spencer rested his hand on Bella's shoulder as casually as if she were an extension of his body. A part of him. "He never misses anything. If he has to work on a special occasion, Mom makes sure somebody takes him dinner and keeps him company."

I could only hope it wouldn't be Spencer's godparent's daughter.

Glancing around the room, I realized Mom and Dad weren't there. "The 'Rents head for bed?" I asked, using the shorthand name we'd teased them with when we were kids.

"Yeah. I think all the firelight and candlesticks got to them. They snuggled on the couch for a few minutes while you two braved the elements then decided to go to bed." A naughty grin curled Bella's lips. "Told us we should make pallets here in the living room, since upstairs we'd probably freeze to death. Then they shut the door."

"Sounds like a Santa thing to me," I said, referring to Dad's old excuse for putting us to bed early—so he and Mom could head for theirs on Christmas Eve. I always blamed Christmas lights for stirring up Dad's libido.

Bella and Spencer chuckled then glanced at one another. I could almost hear their thoughts. *What excuse can we use to sneak away?*

I didn't have a wrapped present to give Spencer the next morning, but I had an idea for a gift he'd like better, and that would mean more to him than a new tie or belt—time alone together with Bella.

I feigned a yawn, then leaning close to the firelight, glanced at my watch. "Wow. I can't believe how tired all that cold air made me. I think I'll head for bed."

My words took a moment to register with Bella. Clearly her mind was someplace else. Finally she asked, "What?"

Spencer gazed at me for a moment, gratefulness in his eyes. "Please don't feel—"

I did my best to look coy, but brazen is more my thing, so I winked at him. "Thought I might try to give Doc a call."

He tossed my wink back at me, put his arm around Bella and pulled her against him. "That's a great idea."

I lit another lamp and said goodnight. After going through the French doors into the frigid air that filled all but the heart of the house, I made my way up the dark stairs. I checked the house phone that sat in its niche in the upstairs hall, but as I'd expected, found it dead. I pulled out my cell, but there was no reception. I walked the length of the corridor, frustration filling me. Still none. I went into my room and Bella's. Nada.

Finally, in the large, extremely cold room across the hall from mine, I got a tiny bit of signal. Setting down the lamp, I quickly called Doc.

"Hello?"

The static was so bad, I could barely hear him. "Doc?"

"Jazzy?" The noise grew worse, but his voice was like a damper to my exasperation. "—can hear me…a mer—"

I'd lost him.

The quelling of my fiery energy left me almost languid. I picked up the lamp and went to my room where I put on a pair of sweats, unfolded an extra quilt and crawled into bed.

The next morning, the worst of the storm had past. Flakes the size of quarters still fell, but without the ferocity of the night before. I quickly dressed and went downstairs, where I found myself all alone.

In the kitchen I flicked on a light switch but found the power still off, so I got out Grandma's old enamelware coffee pot, filled it and set it on the stove. Thankfully, Grandma always cooked with gas, but if she hadn't, I'd have made my brew in the fireplace. Coffee is a necessity of life.

While I waited, I carried wood to the living room and built up the fire. Maybe I could have the room comfortable, and the icicles melted from the tree, by the time the rest of the family got up.

There wasn't much to do once I had the fire going strong, so I ran back upstairs for Grandma's journal. I lit my lamp and set it on the dining room table. After pouring a cup of coffee, I read until Mom and Dad got up.

When I heard them stirring, I hurried to my room and packed away the diary. On my way back down, I tapped on Bella's door. "Merry Christmas." Then I scooted back to the living room. Whether or not she was alone was TMI—too much information—and none of it mine.

By the time I got back to the living room, Mom and Dad both had mugs of coffee and were all but mainlining it.

"Morning," Mom murmured, cup at her lips.

"Good morning." I glanced at Dad. "Do you feel okay this morning? You look like a house fell on you."

Dad gave Mom a startled glance then shrugged. "I'm fine. Or I will be when I have one of those rolls

Mrs. Newkirk baked for our breakfast. But no. Your mother—"

Mom made a face. "Oh, for heaven's sake, Mark. Go ahead. *Eat* Christmas breakfast before everyone is down."

"Everyone should be down by now," Dad grouched, then glanced at the stairs. "Think I ought to go wake that…"

"I'm sure he'll be down soon." No matter what Dad said at this point, Mom would take the opposite side. Good thing he'd had his Christmas Eve last night.

"Good morning." Bella came into the room, and in a few moments, Spencer followed her.

"Finally." Dad's whisper was loud enough for the Newkirks to hear next door.

Mom rolled her eyes. "Come on, guys. There are hot sweet rolls in the warming oven. We'd better eat them before they dry out."

"How in the world did one of the Newkirks get over here in this snow with hot rolls?"

Mom shrugged. "I don't question their generosity. I just appreciate it."

We each took a roll then went back to the dining room table. The spicy sweetness of the rolls struck us dumb, so we ate in silence. I forced myself to quit after the third roll, as did Mom, but Dad, Spencer and Bella had no such compunction. Dad fell out after the next round, and Spencer after the next, but Bella lasted through six.

We all watched in amazement as she all but licked her plate. And when she finally finished, she had syrupy cinnamon on her nose and chin. She glanced at her audience with a shy smile. "Well, that was good."

I laughed at her. "You're going to have to wash off a few layers of sugar before we can open presents."

She flashed me a smirk then with the dignity of a queen, left the room. The rest of us moved into the living room. Dad threw some wood on the fire while we settled in.

We took turns with our presents because Mom believed that the gifter enjoys seeing them opened as much as the giftee enjoys unwrapping them. To put it mildly, our Christmas mornings are known to be drawn out celebrations. That Christmas was no exception.

Mom gave Bella and me the exact purse that she'd demanded Dad give her—as well as the same jewelry and the cat pee perfume that I wouldn't buy. When she realized she hadn't received the fragrance, she pouted just a little until we gave her the cruise tickets and Dad promised to go.

Mom and Dad gave Spencer a set of pajamas that I was certain had been purchased with Dad in mind. And Bella gave him a beautiful antique pocket watch.

And finally, after every other present had been opened, Spencer took the small box from the high boughs of the tree. Holding it in both hands, he held it out to Bella.

Bella stared at the present without touching it. Without her telling me, I knew what she thought. The box was the right size and shape to be an engagement ring, and that in itself was a scary thought. They hadn't known one another long enough—at least on a friendly basis—for him to ask her to marry him.

Had they?

He had to practically force the gift into her hand. "This is very dear to all the Hollidays."

As she took it, her thoughts reached me. *What if it's a ring? A family heirloom?*

Look at him, sis. He's not stupid.

She glanced up at him. *You're right; he's not.*

I lost her thoughts then. Well, I really didn't lose them. They flowed away from me as her fascination with him took over. Very slowly she tore the paper from the box then pulled off the top. Inside was another box made of leather. Pulling it out, she opened the hinged lid and looked inside.

"It came through my mother's family. It's a piece of some sort of reward from a great-great somebody. I don't remember the whole story, but it's a good thing." He sounded almost like a little boy, hoping his gift would be the most highly regarded.

Bella blinked hard as she gazed into the box. Wishing I could snatch it away from her and have a look for myself, I peeked over her shoulder.

There on a chain was a golden coin that looked as old as Christmas. "Wow. Looks like someone found the end of the rainbow."

Spencer chuckled, then took the box and pulled out the necklace. Stepping behind Bella, he put it around her neck and fastened it. "I...hope you like it."

Bella put both hands on the necklace then turned to him. Tears filled her eyes, making them luminous as she smiled. "I love it."

****

Christmas morning, Chase paced the wagon wheel. First his home, then the garden. It had been too long since he'd seen Jazzy. And way too long since he'd held her.

With the blizzard blowing in the panhandle, it was

likely to be a while before he saw her again. Damn phone service was out. Damn cells had no reception.

Damn. Damn. Damn!

He grabbed the phone as it rang. Jazzy's smile played with his libido as he put the receiver to his head. "Hello?" *Please be Jazzy.*

But he was disappointed. "Chase, darlin'?" Disappointment leached his excitement as his mother's voice reached his ears.

He couldn't quite stifle the sigh that built within him. "Yeah?"

Her light chuckle told him she understood way more than he hoped. "Come eat breakfast. And if you have gifts for anyone, bring them now so you won't have to go back later."

If he had gifts for anyone? *If?* As if he'd forgotten to buy gifts more than once in the last few years?

With a snort, he hung up the phone, grabbed the pile of gift bags he'd left on his kitchen counter and stalked out the back door. A brisk walk through the center garden didn't help his mood much, but the heady fragrance of breakfast made a real difference. Especially the coffee. He walked straight to his mother and took the steaming mug she held out for him before depositing his presents under the tree.

Putting the cup to his lips, he savored a careful drink. How did people live without coffee?

"Breakfast is ready," Mom announced to the room. "Since we're all here, why don't y'all go to the table while I bring it out?"

Mack and Drew argued good-naturedly while everyone took their places.

Mom brought a huge fruit laden pizza to the table.

"There's another one just like this in the kitchen, so don't hold back." She sat opposite Dad.

Chase snagged a couple of pieces then passed the platter to Dad before Mack and Drew could take most of the pie for themselves. After waiting for everyone to serve themselves, he took a bite then closed his eyes to enjoy it while he chewed. The slightly tart fruit on the sugar cookie crust was delicious, but it was the sauce, some kind of super sweet white stuff, that made it spectacular.

Before he knew it, Mom brought in the second pizza and he and his Dad and brothers finished it off, too.

When the last piece disappeared, Mom quickly stacked the plates. "Mack and Drew, since you ate the lion's share, you get to do the dishes."

When the pair started to groan, she held up one hand. "After we open presents, that is."

The boys grinned like a pair of death row inmates who'd been handed a reprieve then they jumped from their chairs. "Last one to the tree has to be Santa," Mack yelled as they sprinted for the living room.

Dad shook his head as he stood. "I don't know that those two will ever grow up," he said to no one in particular.

Mom slid her arm through his. "They will someday, Sam. I promise."

Dad walked her to the most comfortable chair in the room, which Mack was in, and they stood next to it until Mack looked up. "Your mother would like to sit down."

Mack shot them a sharp smile then glanced around the room at the furniture. "Well, she can si—"

At Dad's sharp intake of breath, Mack stopped speaking as he shot out of the chair. "Yes, sir. Just kidding."

Dad closed one eye in a slow wink. "I thought you were. You had to be. No son of mine would be disrespectful t—"

"No, sir. I wouldn't be disrespectful to Mom anytime. Ever."

"Good."

Once they were all gathered around the tree, Mack was appointed to hand out gifts. Chase joined the chaos half-heartedly as everyone tore through wrapping, opened boxes and bags. As he opened the usual belts, boots and Stetsons, he couldn't keep his mind off Jazzy.

When Spence had told him he was going to the panhandle for Christmas, he'd been only too glad to have a reason not to go with him. Not that the idea of being snowed in with Jazzy for a week or two wasn't appealing. It was. But if he spent that kind of time with her, he'd be tempted to make a commitment—maybe do something permanent—and they weren't ready for that.

Make that, *he* wasn't ready. Until he could bare his soul to her, he wouldn't allow himself to go there. And he was pretty sure his soul was unbearable.

But going over it again and again in his mind didn't make not seeing her any easier. When the boys went to wash the dishes and Dad followed them in search of more coffee, Chase cleared his throat. "Uh, Mom?

Beatrice looked up from the book she'd received from Mack. After a searching look, during which he hoped she couldn't see too much, she smiled. "What is it, Chase?"

"I've got to run out to the clinic." He cleared his throat, hoping to keep from blurting all his reasons for going. She didn't need to know he couldn't sit still because he missed Jazzy so much it was like a pain in his gut. And she couldn't know that every time he visualized Jazzy's face, he grew hard with wanting her. "I'm running a research test that I need to check on."

Her brow furrowed slightly as concern stole the smile from her mouth. "Is it that critical?"

Only if he was going to stop a whole new crop of neophytes from being loosed on the citizens of Texas. "Yeah. I think it is."

"Then definitely. Go." She closed the book and laid it aside. "If we can do anything, call. You know we're here for you."

****

Pulling into the zoo, Chase stopped to check in with the security guard then drove to the clinic. Being a holiday, only the lightest of skeleton crews would be there, so he shouldn't be interrupted.

Not wasting any time, he went to the lab where he took out the specimen he'd grown from a small sample of Tony's blood then injected the antigen. If all had gone well, the healthy growth that had been there yesterday should have stopped growing completely.

He removed the lid from the Petri dish. The clock slowed as he prepared a sample and slid it under the microscope. Then time stopped completely.

The antigen not only hadn't stopped the infection. It appeared to have fed it. The werewolf infection must have developed a sub-strain that wasn't just resistant to the antigen, it thrived on it.

He glanced at the calendar. Not quite two weeks before the next full moon. Not much time for what had to be done, but was it enough? If he could find what he needed, he'd have to get with it to make the new antigen.

And the first thing he'd need was Jazzy.

Chapter Fourteen

Christmas afternoon as I watched Bella and Spencer watch each other, touch each other when they thought no one would see, I thought I'd go crazy. Were they so stupid they couldn't tell I was about ready to bite a hole in both of them? Or didn't they care?

Finally I couldn't sit still any longer. I lunged from my chair and headed for my room. "I'm going to put on a few layers and go out."

"It's cold out there," Dad called through the open door of the bedroom where he'd gone to take his annual after-the-festivities nap. "It might be Texas, but the temperature is still low enough to freeze your nose off."

I tried to hide my scowl, but I heard Spencer chuckle softly as I went through the door into the stairway.

I took the stairs two at a time, hoping to dress and get outside before I exploded. I slammed into my room, threw on the clothes and my boots and was just heading out when my text message signal beeped. I opened my phone and focused on the message as I jogged back down the stairs.

It was from Doc. *In desperate need of your help, Jazzy. I'm coming to get you. Be ready to leave by three.*

Coming to get me? Without telling me why he needed my help, he expected me to leave my family at

Christmas and run off with him? My explosion was going to happen at any moment. I stormed through the living room, out the front door and across the yard.

It was almost two o'clock now. He'd be here in an hour, and he was just now letting me know about it? As if he knew for certain that I'd go?

Ha!

I turned and started for the pond, digging in my heels as I walked to keep from sliding. The snow had all but stopped falling with just a few flakes coming down from time to time.

I blew past the barn and was almost to the pond before I realized how much had disappeared beneath the white blanket. Small depressions, rocks, grasses—anything less than eighteen inches high was lost in the blue-white world.

Would I be able to tell where the edge of the pond started or would I walk out on the ice where I could very easily fall through? Taking a wide track, I circled the pond, hiking all the way around before climbing the rise on the far side. After gazing down at the small creek, which was now mostly obscured by the snow, I turned back.

I stopped at an outcropping of rock above the pond and, clearing a small area, sat down.

The sun peeked out for a moment, casting a whole pot of glittering gold coins across the landscape. The beauty of it stole my breath away. But as I admired the scenery, my thoughts circled like so many vultures. The kernel of envy that had lodged high in my chest when Bella opened her necklace began to burn with life.

Surprise straightened my spine as I sat there. I'd never in my life been jealous of Bella. Usually I carried a little sympathy for her because she'd missed out on the Lycan in her life. How could I be jealous now, just because she'd received a coin necklace?

But it wasn't the necklace. It was the feeling behind it. The love I could see in Spencer's face each time he gazed at her. The emotion that colored hers when he was near.

Okay, maybe I was jealous, but I could get past it. After all, I'd have to live with it someday. She'd marry and go on to have a "normal" life. But unless I found an open-minded man who loved me—every facet of me—which would have to include a love of animals and sudden volatile changes, I'd be forever alone.

That necessitated putting Doc from my mind when it came to my future. He'd never be able to love all my components. A man who'd made it his life's mission to put an end to Lycans couldn't love one, could he? Not the kind of love I needed. I had to have someone who would support me, even if he didn't understand me. Who would evolve with me as I grew.

No. Doc was the kind of man who set himself a future, and then charged toward it at full speed. Never changing. Never adjusting.

A sigh filled me until I ached with it. I'd have to get over this before I went back to the house to meet him. After he told me why he needed me so badly, I'd decide whether or not I'd go.

I returned my thoughts to the coin in Bella's necklace. Where had it come from? Why had the family been gifted with them, and more interestingly, why didn't Spencer know more about it? Or did he know and just not want to talk about it?

At least now I understood where their family

money had started.

Getting up, I dusted my behind. I had to go back and pack my things in case I decided to leave with Doc. And I couldn't forget to take Grandma's journals, which I'd had only a little time to read since we'd left Dallas.

As I walked, the sun disappeared again, replaced by bulging clouds, hanging low overhead again. I glanced at my watch and saw it getting dangerously close to three. If Doc hadn't run into the same kind of trouble that had put Spencer's car out of commission, and he'd calculated correctly, he should be at the house soon.

As I turned back, a tingle of excitement sizzled through me. If I looked into the face of that exhilaration, I realized it was my feelings for Doc that caused it.

I tried to tell myself it was a physical thing. That we were simpatico physically, so naturally I'd look forward to being with him again.

Deep down, I knew better.

Snow started falling again. This time the flakes were smaller, but there were more of them and they were coming down faster. For a moment the entire world became a white blur, startling me into pausing. What if I got off course and missed the house? People got lost in snowstorms, didn't they? And sometimes they froze to death. Then self-awareness spurred me toward home.

As I passed the barn, which I could barely make out, a ghost materialized in the storm. When the apparition hovered closer, I realized it was Doc.

He caught me to him, practically knocking the

breath out of me as he took me in his arms. His kiss seared the chill right out of me.

I wanted him. Couldn't wait to be alone with him. I knew I'd never be able to ride in the car with him all the way back to Dallas. We wouldn't get far before we'd have to pull over and make love.

The barn was close, and the loft more private, at least for the moment. Taking his gloved hand in my mittened one, I dragged him with me.

Shoving the door open in all that snow proved harder than I expected, but somehow Doc got it done. We stumbled into the dim, dusty atmosphere, past the stored garden equipment and climbed the ladder.

Mr. Newkirk always bought straw in the fall to use in the hen house and to mulch the garden, so I knew we'd have a sweet smelling bed if not a particularly comfortable one.

Without a word, I rushed to pull a bale apart. The storm blowing outside would cause everyone in the house to worry and come looking for us. I didn't want to waste a nanosecond of our time, and the last thing I wanted was to get caught.

The threat of being found naked with my lover put an edge to our lovemaking. He took my face between his hands and kissed me until I was nearly senseless. "I've missed you."

I tried to catch my breath so I wouldn't sound like a bad Marilyn Monroe imitation, but with my heart pounding a million times a minute, it was impossible. "I missed you, too," I gasped.

He didn't say anything else because he kissed me.

My joints turned to warm butter, my muscles mush. I sank to the straw and pulled him on top of me, relishing the weight of his body against mine.

Taking off his gloves, he reached under my jacket where he found the layers of sweaters and shirts. Burying his face in my shoulder, he started to laugh. Each chuckle sent spirals of desire through me.

I shoved him to his back, and straddling him, I rocked against him. His laughter morphed to moaning as I rotated my hips. He reached for me, but I pushed his hands away. Two could play that hand of poker. He was going to be as needy as me before I relented.

But rocking my hips to entice him made me want him so badly, I couldn't stand it. No, I *wouldn't* stand it.

I sucked a long breath. "Doc."

Scrambling off, I rushed to loosen just enough clothing to give him access to my body while he hurried to do the same.

Then, finally, we were one. I couldn't help but think for a brief moment that at last, I was complete, and he'd made me that way.

It wasn't only the physical part. Something in him made me better than I was alone. It was as if he made me whole. And I him. When we weren't together, we were only a portion of what we were meant to be.

And the sex wasn't bad.

Even with straw creeping into places it was never supposed to go, frigid air biting tender body parts and the barn cat nosing around, it was spectacular.

As we moved together, making love as though we'd been at it for years, he fulfilled my secret yearnings and I stroked places that made him shiver all over.

He rolled me beneath him, moving as if his life

depended on it. The end spiraled dangerously close, my love arcing as I neared the end. I barely controlled the bristles charging my skin as a howl lodged in my throat.

Would I be able to do it? Would I be able to finish this perfect love making, handle the explosion of my climax along with my love for him without morphing into my animal state? Did I really want to?

But as the howl crept up my throat, he arched over me. Then something happened. Just when I thought he was going to explode with passion and take me with him, he died. It was as if we'd just worked to build a beautiful, raging wild fire, then at the last moment he'd turned and dropped a wet blanket on it.

He finished without so much as a whisper and my howl of joy wilted to a groan of disappointment.

What happened? Was it something about me that gave him such an inadequate climax? Could I live with that kind of finish again?

He rolled away from me and stared at the barn roof for a long moment. "Guess we'd better get a move on before your folks get worried."

They couldn't worry half as much as me. My heart in turmoil, I forced a smile, rearranged my clothes and headed for the stairs without so much as a kiss. And I'm afraid he was as disenchanted as me.

Maybe we weren't truly right together. I could have been wrong when I thought nature had picked him as my mate, couldn't I? Would I be cursed for life with a mate who was perfect in every other area but who lost it in what I thought of as the most crucial area?

We walked back through the waning snowstorm to the house. Spencer met us at the back door. "Got caught in that squall, didn't you?"

Doc smiled, but I could still see the sadness in his gaze. "Yeah. We stopped at the barn until it slowed."

I have to give Spencer credit, he didn't even grin at Doc's words as most men would. Didn't poke him with an elbow or make a smart remark. In fact, he seemed almost sympathetic, which made absolutely no sense. "Well, according to the weather map, we're going to have a respite. Another front is coming through in a few hours."

That's when I noticed the lights were back on.

"We'd better hit the road then." Doc turned to me. "I told your parents when I met them earlier that we'd be leaving as soon as possible. They must be used to your surprises, because they were okay with it. Want me to get your suitcase for you?"

No way I wanted him in my bedroom again. Not until I could figure a way to snatch that smothering blanket away from him. "No, thanks. I can manage."

I rushed through the house and up the stairs. While I checked to be sure I had everything, a tap sounded on the door. Bella pushed it open and peeked inside, her hands full. "You wanted to take some of the lavender home. Remember?"

Trust Bella to remember, even with everything else going on. I gave her a quick hug. "I'd forgotten. Put it in my bag, would you?"

"No." She was aghast at my idea. "It'd be dust by the time you got it unpacked. I'll find a box for it."

When she'd found the box then tucked used Christmas tissue over the herb, she closed it securely.

I double checked I had everything, especially Granny's journals and closed my bag. Together we went down, me carrying my bags, Bella the box.

Apparently, Doc had explained things to my parents, because Mom, Dad, Bella and Spencer waved happily to us from the front porch as we got in the giant black Hummer and started up the road. "No wonder you didn't have problems getting here. Doesn't the army use these for fighting wars in Antarctica?"

He pulled his gaze from the road just long enough to glance at me. "I think so. Wasn't that last fight called The Battle of the Ice Chip?"

If I hadn't been so upset, I'd have made a joke about the ice maiden that started it all, but I wasn't happy enough to do that. In fact, I felt mourning coming on. "I guess you'd better tell me what this is all about."

"It's Tony." He hesitated as if trying to figure how to tell me. "I grew a culture of his blood, and when I used the normal antigen to cure it, the culture didn't die. It thrived."

I hadn't expected the anger that took root within me. "So since your antigen won't kill the infection, you want me to help you kill Tony?"

"No!" Shocked, he drew his eyebrows together. There was something he wasn't telling me. I could see it in his face. "I need you to help me take another sample of his blood."

"You came all the way to Winnie Rose to get me to help you draw his blood when you did it by yourself the last time?" Disgusted, I shook my head. "I don't believe it."

"The blood I used to make the antigen the last time was apparently from the wrong line. It could have been *too* rare. And I want to use yours to make a new one."

"Mine?" I all but shrieked. "You want to use my

blood to stop a werewolf. What's next? Do you want to use it to wipe out the gene, too?"

He shrugged, apparently unaware of the fury he'd sparked in me.

I tried to mute my anger. "Tell me something."

He nodded as casually as if a werewolf capable of tearing him to bits weren't riding by his side.

I lowered my voice so he had to strain to hear me. "Why do you hate werewolves so?"

"I *don't* hate werewolv—"

"Don't hate them? Then why do you want to eradicate them from the face of the earth?"

"I don't want to eradicate the *people* from the face of the earth. Just the infection that causes them to be werewolves."

"But I don't have an infection." I turned completely toward him. The desire to make him understand ached deep within me. "I was born with the gene. Being a werewolf isn't just something that happened to me. Doc, it's *who* I am.

"I *love* being a werewolf. Love having the strength at my fingertips to do anything I need to. Love being able to evolve and then change back. The freedom. The clarity. The pure joy. Why do you want to get rid of that?"

"You like being a werewolf?" If he'd changed "werewolf" to "scum of the earth," his tone and expression would have remained the same.

"Yes!" I put all my deeply held feelings into that word then dropped my voice to a rough whisper. "I love it!"

"You love losing control? Not remembering where and who you are while you're gone?" His tone grew terse as he spoke. "And the new werewolves..."

"Neophytes," I supplied the word for him.

"Yes, neophytes. They come from somewhere. It has to be a Syzygian werewolf that starts that little problem."

"But very few Syzygian werewolves do that kind of thing. Why punish all of us?"

"If we cure all werewolves, we'll be sure we get the bad ones."

I tried not to think of persecuted peoples through the centuries, but the more I tried, the more the horrors of genocide came to mind. Auschwitz. Dachau. American Indians being given smallpox tainted blankets. Having their food supply systematically eliminated. Sand Creek and Wounded Knee, where innocent men, women and children were murdered.

While he wasn't going to commit murder, he wanted to wipe out the future of my species. Could I stand by and be a party to it?

I tried to force my mind from the turmoil. "How is Tony physically?"

"He's pretty much out of it with all the meds they're giving him." The car started to slide as Doc took a curve too quickly, but he almost immediately controlled it. "Which is good, since he'd be worried sick about his son otherwise."

"Why?" I knew he hadn't been home since the attack, and I doubted the hospital would let a small child in to see him, so the kid couldn't have been bitten.

"Because Tony's a single father. His ex-wife is on her way from New Zealand to get the boy."

"Tony had custody?" I stared at him, having trouble believing what I heard. "How'd he do that?"

"Lucked onto a judge who didn't want American kids raised outside the country." Doc slowed as he met a car taking his half out of the middle of the snow packed roads.

My heart sank a little deeper as I turned back to face the gray world. "Not much is fair in life. Is it?"

For a very long moment, I thought he wasn't going to answer. Finally, in a voice I could barely hear, he said, "No."

When at long last we drove out of the storm, we made great time back to Dallas. We drove straight to the hospital. As promised, I went with him to Tony's room to serve as a lookout as he drew blood.

It was obvious the full moon was getting close by Tony's restlessness. Even in his "coma," he'd been restrained by the staff so he wouldn't hurt himself thrashing. But that didn't stop him from murmuring and tugging against the ties every few moments.

There were a couple of machines in the room. One that bleeped out his heartbeat, and one dripping something into his veins.

After watching a while, we saw Tony was still for a few minutes between his spurts of activity. So the next time he lunged against his restraints, Doc was ready. I stepped to the door and leaned against it, as if I were giving the pair space. In reality, I was there so I'd feel the first movement if someone tried to come in. And I would stop them.

As I watched, Doc inserted the needle. The machine marking his heart rate bleeped a little faster, but otherwise nothing changed. Doc filled a large vial with blood. As he removed the needle, Tony opened his eyes, turned his head and looked directly at me. As our gazes met, my stomach bottomed out.

In his face was the question, *How could you betray me?*

Talk about feeling like a rat. How could I have betrayed him? But if I'd left him to attack the innocents of Texas, wouldn't I be worse? He was a phyter. Without years of training, he'd never have the self-control to contain himself.

He'd be killed like a rabid dog in the streets.

It was damned if you do, and a sharp smack if you don't.

Doc held something over the tiny wound he'd made to stop the bleeding. One good thing about being a werewolf, even a neophyte. We heal quickly.

The door bumped my back as someone tried to open it. I thumped around as if I were trying to get out of the way, while Doc quickly put away his supplies. When I heard his, "Yeah," I let her in.

"Sorry. I didn't realize I'd leaned against the door," I lied.

The woman was young and well dressed, her shoulder-length hair pulled back in a low ponytail. "Hey, I understand completely. I'm Catherine. Tony's ex-wife." She held out her hand to shake mine.

"I'm Jazzy. I'm with, uh, Chase Holliday." I tipped my head toward Doc by way of introduction. "One of your husband's coworkers."

"*Ex*-husband," she clarified, then caught her breath as she turned toward the bed, her brows drawn together, her gaze clouded. Very slowly she moved across the room to stand near Doc.

"I'm Chase." Doc kept his voice low as he held out his hand to the woman.

"Catherine Baldred," she answered as she kept her gaze on Tony.

"It's nice to meet you."

"How is he?" Catherine asked. "Have you talked to the doctors?"

"It's been kind of touch and go." Doc glanced my way for a mere moment. "I think he's going to be okay now, though."

"I hope so." She tilted her head to one side, and while I couldn't see her face, I could imagine the emotions registering there. If Tony was okay, she'd have to leave her son and go back to her current husband, halfway around the world. But if Tony died, while her son would be with her all the time, the boy would be fatherless.

She took one of Tony's tethered hands in both of hers.

"We'll leave you alone with him," Doc said as he backed toward the door.

Catherine turned toward us, her face tear stained. "You don't have to go on my account."

I shook my head as I opened the door. "We've been here too long already. See you later."

She'd turned back to Tony before I'd finished talking, and I really wasn't sure she heard what I said.

I went with Doc to the zoo clinic. While he went into the lab to do something with the blood he'd taken from Tony, I went out to check on the wolf pups. I picked up the little female I'd fed and snuggled her close. She was growing so rapidly, you could barely tell she'd been a slow starter.

Doc came out and I put the pup back. "Ready for me to take some of your blood?"

I shrugged and followed him back to the lab, where I climbed onto one of his uncomfortable stools. He did a little rummaging then turned toward me with a huge needle in one hand and an alcohol swab in the other.

"Nice needle." I stared at it before extending my arm. "Couldn't you find one the size of a soda straw?"

He chuckled as he took my wrist with one hand and cleaned the site where he planned to stick me with the other. "Quick your snarking. It'll be over in a minute."

I bit down on the inside of my cheek to keep from growling for real as he stuck the needle into my vein. To be honest, once that initial pain passed it was fascinating to watch my blood fill the vial.

Dark, rich and red, it looked just like Tony's had. And, I knew for a fact, the same as Bella's and every other human's in the world. Lycan or not, black or white, Jew or Indian, you couldn't tell whose it was by looking at the blood.

Mine just carried a gene that most didn't.

He took the needle out and held sterile cotton over the site a moment. The hole had already started healing. By the time we were ready to leave the clinic, I knew it would be completely gone. Not even a tiny scab to show for it.

Apparently Doc didn't notice, because he didn't seem surprised. Or maybe he knew more about werewolves than I realized.

"Do you mind going by my house before I take you home?" he asked.

"Not at all." I couldn't figure why he'd want to go to his house, but I didn't mind. We drove most of the way in silence.

When we finally got there, he pulled into his driveway but not the garage. This time, we went in the front door. The house wasn't decorated for Christmas, which didn't surprise me, but there was a gift with a huge red bow lying on his pool table. I followed him to the table. His gaze held mine as he handed it to me. "Merry Christmas."

My heart lost some of its buoyancy. The box was long and flat—definitely not a coin necklace, but I forced myself to smile anyway. Carrying the box with me, I walked over and sat on one of his recliners.

Doc knelt beside the chair—I guess so he could see the look on my face as I opened it.

Very slowly I slid the ribbon off the package at one end then pulled the tape loose. Turning the box, I released the tape on the other end, then on the back.

"I didn't know anyone could take so long opening a present. Especially at Christmas."

"It's always been a contest between Bella and me. Who could go the slowest? Bella usually wins."

"Doesn't surprise me." He shook his head as he gave me a sexy half smile. "But it does surprise me that you don't just blow that contest off and tear through it."

"Oh, I can do that, too."

I ripped the lid off the box and tore out the tissue paper. There inside, in a very expensive frame, was an antique poster from the 1935 version of the movie, *Call of the Wild.* And it had been autographed by both Clark Gable and Loretta Young.

Then it hit me. *Call of the Wild.* I started laughing, delighted that he'd found such a gift for me. "Where in the world did you find this?"

"Family heirloom." He got off his knees and sat in

the adjacent recliner. "My granddad was the veterinarian on that movie. He made sure that there were 'no animals harmed in the making of this film.'"

"Don't you think you should keep it in the family?" I asked, shocked that he would give away such a treasure.

His smile grew slowly, his gaze kindling. "We have other heirlooms from his stint in with Hollywood. I just thought you'd enjoy that one."

I leaned the poster against the chair, careful to keep it from falling. "It's me, all right."

With a move I didn't see coming, he reached out, grabbed my hand and yanked me into his lap. His kiss made my head reel as I settled my body against his. I could have spent years getting used to that seat, and loved every minute of it.

He ended the kiss—I could have kept it going all night—and whispered in my ear, "You know, tomorrow night is the waxing moon."

Talk about a crash to reality. I hid my face in his shoulder for a moment, wishing I could hide as easily from what I would face the next night.

I would have to find the neophyte or let him find me. And I would have to stop him. I only hoped I was up to the task.

Doc went on. "We'll have to post patrols to lookout for this guy, whoever he is."

I straightened, slid off his lap and moved to the other chair. "No."

He looked startled, but I'm not sure if that was from my answer or me leaving his lap. "What do you mean? He's dangerous, and he has to be stopped."

"I know he's dangerous, but I'm the one who's

going to stop him. With patrols, you'd just have more people getting hurt. And possibly infected."

His face hardened. "You think you can—"

"I *know* I can." Not that I did, really, but he couldn't know that. And he couldn't know that I'd tried to stop this phyter before and failed. I had to make him believe I could take care of it.

"All right." He got out of his chair and walked to the door, where he waited while I grabbed my poster and followed.

All the way back to my apartment, he didn't say a word. After trying to start a conversation a few times, I gave up, too.

The drive took longer than normal, or at least it seemed so to me. When we got there, he carried my bags to my door, but refused my invitation to come inside.

When he left, and I was alone, and filled with a sense of loss greater than I'd ever experienced in my life.

I locked the door and went to the bathroom for a long, hot soak. When I finished, I wrapped up in my oldest, most comfortable robe and crashed on the couch, my heart in too much chaos to sleep.

I pulled out Grandma's journal, and read until my eyes were grainy. Just as I was ready to put it away and get some sleep, I read about a love Grandma had before Grandpa. A love with another werewolf. The innerconnection she wrote about had been so deep, so pure it was painful to read even after so many years. For several weeks, the young woman, Grandma, had spilled her love for Charlton onto the page. Her absolute surety that he was her life mate was there in the faded ink.

But something happened. Grandma hadn't spelled it out in the diary, but there was a gap of several days, then, *June 3rd—Charlton has been called away. An emergency, he says. But I'm not sure. I know there's no emergency that could force me away from him.*

Several more days had been skipped. *June 8th—I haven't heard from Charlton except for one letter telling me he'd reached his destination. It's been two weeks. I'm sure his family would let me know if he was ill or hurt. Am I so easily displaced from his mind? His heart?*

June 15th—I got a letter today from Charlton. It's cold, so impersonal. I know he's busy, but...

There were a few entries about normal day to day life. *June 27th—A letter from Charlton. He'll be gone for at least six more months. Six! And he hasn't mentioned a word about me coming to be with him even once. The rest of his life means more to him than I do. Even more than our love, which he hasn't mentioned once in any letter he's sent me.*

I can't go on this way

July 3rd—I've decided I'm going to write to him. Tell him exactly how I feel. Even the humiliation I'd experience if he told me he was mistaken, that he didn't love me at all, would be better that the hell I'm living in now.

With the letter I'm sending him the gold coin he had set in a necklace for me. Surely when he sees it he'll realize how upset I am. I'm lost. Frightened.

And finally, *July 24th—He doesn't love me. He doesn't say it in the letter exactly, but it's there, between the lines. "Your love, so much deeper. Could mine ever match it? I don't..." But I won't burden him* *with mine any longer.*

I'll end it now with the Tumuld Argamelino.

So she'd constructed a hedge to protect her heart, and described it in detail. She'd built a small fire during the dark of the moon. Sitting before it, she'd placed on it small bundles of lavender. With each addition, she'd named an attribute that had made her love him. At the end, she'd added the most precious thing he'd given her. A locket with his picture in it—his gift of the heart.

Could I live my life, loving a man who disapproved of not only who but what I was? A man whose entire goal for his life was to wipe out what I loved most about mine? No. And I *wouldn't* spend it making love with someone who was so controlled he was a silent, uninvolved lover.

I knew what I had to do. But where would I get dried lavender?

Then I remembered Bella had packed a box of it for me. Was that the reason Grandma had grown the plant all those years? As a remembrance of the protection she'd built to block her love? Or the man who'd caused her to do it?

I found the box where Doc had left it when he brought me home, just inside the door, and carried it back to the fireplace.

Sitting cross-legged, I built a small fire then turned off the gas jets. The flames were clear and bright. Almost hypnotic.

I pulled off strips of tape and opened the box. After tossing the tissue aside, I took out the first bundle and gazed at it. The stems were brittle, the green had changed to gray, and I knew if I shook it very hard, the heads would scatter.

Did I want to do this? According to Grandma, a hedge once built couldn't be torn down. My love would be obliterated. Forever.

I drew a breath, shaky and thick with tears. "I love Doc for his humor." Steeling myself, I threw the plant into the fire where it burned brightly for a moment, the dusty fragrance filling the room. Would I ever smell that scent again without my heart aching, even a little?

"His compassion for animals as well as humans." Another sweet-smelling packet went in.

"His smile and the light that sparkles in his eyes."

I continued, naming everything I loved about Doc. Everything that made me hot for him. Everything about him that made me smile.

When I'd finished, all the lavender was gone. I picked up the discarded tissue and threw it in. Then took the poster from the frame, rolled it into a long tube and laid it on the fire. Tears burned my eyes and nose. My throat thickened until I could barely draw a breath, but I had to finish. "I destroy my heart. I burn my tender emotions. I incinerate all the love, the joy, the wonder, even though it reduces to ashes the heart in me. Kapoia bavatoo. Kapoia bavatoo. Kapoia bavatoo." By the last words, I could barely whisper, but by then I couldn't cry. All I could do was stare at the flames.

It took a moment for the poster's old paper to catch. It smoked heavily, charred and caught fire with a *whoof*! I stared until the beautiful old poster was burned up. And I stayed there, watching until the entire fire died down and was nothing but a pile of cold ashes. With my heart now dead, I didn't feel like getting up and doing anything. I didn't care to unpack, put away Christmas gifts or even make a cup of tea.

For some reason, the construction of the wall around my heart made what I had facing me the next night just a bit easier. I now knew one thing—as of that night, there would be one less werewolf in the world.

But whether it would be a neophyte or Syzygian, I couldn't be sure.

Chapter Fifteen

The next morning dawned clear. I still lay on the couch, still wide awake. Finally I turned on the TV. The weatherman sounded as if the storm out west would soon be clearing. That meant the roads would be passable before too long.

I just hoped that didn't mean Bella would be home before moonrise. I didn't want her to worry about me when I went out that night. And I didn't want her here if anything happened.

She couldn't help, and she'd only blame herself. I could almost hear her—*If I hadn't taken that job, she wouldn't have been around when the phyter started his rampage. It's all my fault.*

Just imagining her whine made me want to smash something of hers. To be honest, I'd rather be dead than listen to her wailing about it.

My bizarre thought pattern was so strange I couldn't help but laugh, which lightened my inner turmoil enough to snuggle down for a quick nap.

I slept away the entire morning, then got up and dressed in black sweats for the night. Just as I was about to leave to get something for a late lunch, there was a knock on my door. Slowly I opened it and gazed at the man standing there.

Doc.

Just to be sure my ritual had worked, I tested my

heart as he stepped close for a quick hug.

Nothing.

Inside me was as cold and dead as the remains of last night's fire—with the same potential for resurrection.

Doc had a look of permanent worry clouding his face. "Have you eaten?"

"No. And I could eat a horse." I kept the tone in my voice light.

He lost the worried look and smiled. "Not at my zoo, you don't. But I'll see if I can find something for you on the way."

"Steak will do." We went back to Pete's and I ate the best steak of my life, which I realized was possibly my last meal. It was so rare the juices ran red, clear and delicious.

"Have you heard from your folks?" Doc asked as we waited for the check.

"No. But the phone service is usually slower coming back than electricity out there."

He looked as if he'd expected as much. "Bad cell service?"

"I guess people out there don't use cell phones. Or else they use a different company than we do." I was quiet as the waitress brought the check and Doc tossed down his credit card. "But I saw on TV that the weather should clear up out there in a day or two."

"Then they should be home in three."

If we were lucky, that would be after the waning moon. "Did you check on Tony today?"

He nodded, a smile easing some of the worry lines. "Yeah. With your blood, I was able to make a serum that worked. I injected him before I came to get you. I think he'll be okay."

Relief spread through me, giving me a small measure of success. At least in my life, I'd been of some help.

As we left the restaurant, the sun hung low in the sky, the colors around us changing to pastel. My heart thumped as I realized how late it was. "We've got to hurry. The moon will rise soon."

The worry creasing his face hardened until he looked grim. I was just glad he wasn't psychic and seeing something in my future that he didn't want to tell me about.

Tension grew inside me as the sun sank lower in the sky. My spine became a steel rod, keeping me from relaxing as we drove.

This was it—my night of reckoning. Would I be strong enough to stop this neophyte?

No.

I knew from the last time he was stronger than me. He could outrun me, too, so my only hope was to outsmart him.

And if worse came to worst, I'd have to make sure he died, too.

Too bad Bella didn't have the Syzygia Gene. Together we could have confused the heck out of him with our twin speak telepathy. I wanted to smile, share my thoughts with Doc, but my mouth refused to curve. My voice wouldn't rise in my throat.

I was scared to death, but I couldn't let him know. If he realized how much I knew I couldn't do, he'd never let me go.

So we didn't talk all the way to the zoo. From the parking lot to the clinic, into the sanctuary of his laboratory, we didn't say a word.

Rather than go alone into the night, I took off my clothes and, with Doc looking on, I sat down on my heels and gathered all the anger roiling through me in my chest.

If it weren't for this neophyte, I wouldn't be putting my life on the line. I'd be going about my life as normally as possible for a werewolf.

I thought about the future I most likely wouldn't live to enjoy. How Bella would have to go on without me.

I thought of the kind of woman Doc would find. Of building the barrier around my heart—never again experiencing love—and anger exploded.

I morphed in record time. My bones elongated and reconfigured so quickly, I ached with the change. The bristles bursting through my skin were like a fire, spontaneously combusting all over me.

The surprise on Doc's face was almost worth the pain I experienced that evening.

Turning out the lights, he opened a door off the back of the clinic and I padded into the night.

On silent feet, I rushed away from the compound and found a place in the brush where I could hide. As soon as I was secure, I sniffed the air.

I could smell the neophyte, his ire, even at this distance. His anger was greater than mine, greater than even the explosion of fury I'd experienced when I thought of Doc and my now stone heart.

What was wrong with the phyter? I'd never known an animal—especially a werewolf—to carry that kind of anger. By the time a full moon has risen and a new werewolf has gone through morphing into the wild life, most carry little residual wrath or memory of what was before. The experience taking them outside their bodies and usually, minds, so confuses them they can't remember to be angry.

The rage in this one had to have started within the man. I couldn't begin to fathom what might have happened to make him that way.

And it didn't matter, really. I couldn't resolve his rage. Nobody could realign someone else's passion. All I could do was stop him, and that would be next to impossible. As with all new werewolves, he grew stronger with each full moon he experienced.

If I failed tonight, he'd be stronger tomorrow night. Even if he got me, I had to find a way to take him out, too.

Otherwise, there was no telling the number of lives he'd destroy.

I stayed low, skirting the brush as I followed his scent. We moved away from the compound. Away from human contact. As I trailed him, we left the zoo property altogether. I followed him to Lost Canyon, where Doc and Bella had taken me in the tiger striped truck all those months ago.

It was some of the roughest country in the area, silvered by the light of the full moon.

I stopped near the edge of a bush at the top of a small rise. After sitting on my haunches, I scrutinized the area with my eyes as well as my nose.

I turned my head. There! His scent was strongest to my right. But even as I rose to all fours, his odor came to me more heavily from behind.

Was the wind changing or he was he circling? Stalking. Getting ready for the attack.

Unsure, I looked for a secure area. Someplace where I could put my back to something solid so he could just come at me from one side. But even as I considered a boulder that was not far off, I realized what a foolish idea it was. The last thing I wanted was to be trapped against a solid wall with him tearing out my throat. I'd have no place to escape.

Escape. That's what I needed. A small space—a recess—where I could escape and he couldn't follow. Then maybe I could get a lucky bite in and get away, before...

If I could only find that jumble of rocks.

But I had to take him with me. Lifting my face to the moon, I howled at the top of my lungs. *Come and get me. Come and get me.*

I trotted to the bottom of the rise. Now I *had* to find that rock. I flashed my tail as if I owned that section of the woods then, hearing a not too distant snarl, had to fight to keep from tucking it as I scampered around a tree.

I ran as hard as I could, looking for the boulders. They had to be here, somewhere. But as good as my wolf-sight is by the light of the full moon, it wasn't good enough to find what I sought.

He gained. I could tell by his fetid stench, which grew stronger by the minute.

Just as my tongue was ready to hang out of my mouth in exhaustion, I found the road. It couldn't be far.

Desperate, I dashed around a rock the size of a small army tank, and there it was. The pile of building block boulders I'd used to sooth my headache the day after the Halloween party. I almost panicked when I didn't immediately spot my crevice, but on a second look, I found it.

Running full out, I slid to a stop next to it.

Either because I'd run so hard and so far or because I was scared out of my mind, my heart wouldn't slow enough for me to catch my breath. I couldn't let him see my exhaustion though. Or fear.

Curling my lip, I raised the hair on my scruff and growled as I waited for him. Tonight was the night, I thought as I embraced every bit of anger within me. *I will stop him, one way or another. I can't let him escape.*

Then he was there. Not in front of me, as I expected, but to the side—standing on one of the boulders, ready to attack me from above.

Before I could whirl to face him, he leaped and, hitting my shoulder, knocked me rolling. I scrambled to get back on my feet, but he was on me. Like a natural born killer, he went for my throat.

I fought for my life.

Using everything I had, I struggled to get out from beneath him. But his weight was too great. Almost immediately, his fangs were on my throat.

No! I couldn't lose already.

I snarled, loud and threatening, hoping my confidence would surprise him enough I could break his hold. Kicking both my hind feet, I caught him in a part of his underside that was particularly vulnerable.

His yelp almost made me laugh, but there wasn't time. I rolled to regain my footing.

I hurt everywhere, and was bleeding from several places. I could feel the warm rivulets streaming through my fur, but I couldn't stop. As soon as I was up, I went after him. He met me and we went at it like that old movie with the yellow dog and the mad wolf, except this time there were two wolves. And we were both mad.

Using all my skill, I got the upper hand for just a moment. But his weight and muscle were too much. Unless I could get a lucky bite in, I was toast.

He pressed me against the boulders, holding me there as he attacked so I couldn't maneuver away from him. Couldn't escape.

He wanted me dead.

Which was only fair, because that's what I wanted for him. Now the rock was his ally, stopping me when I tried to turn, a weapon to knock me into unconsciousness if I pulled back too hard. I was trapped.

I couldn't even turn my head to find my hole so I could make a dash for it—if I had the chance.

My strength ebbed, flowing from me along with the blood, streaming from one of a myriad of cuts. I ached all over while my muscles stiffened and slowed with exhaustion.

My entire body failing, I was ready to end it.

I wished I'd seen my family one more time.

Then, just as I was trapped, vulnerable, on my back, just as he fitted his fangs to my throat for what I knew was the last time, a flash of white.

Something hit him from the side, sent him rolling with a painful yelp.

The wolf from my vision in Colorado was there, protecting me. In my wounded state, I wondered if he were my guardian angel—er, wolf.

With an effort I struggled to my feet, then stumbled

to put my shoulder next to his as together we faced the neophyte.

Get in that hole.

Sudden confusion made me dizzy. I stopped. Shook my head. My guardian wolf had a terribly familiar voice. *Doc?*

I couldn't get my mind around it. Was this werewolf Doc? The man who hated werewolves so much, he wanted to wipe their very gene off the face of the earth?

I gaped at him, fury overwhelming me. I'd murdered my own heart to find out just hours later that he was actually a werewolf?

I wanted to go for *his* throat.

But I wisely decided to wait until later to do it.

Go! he shouted. *Now!*

The phyter sprang, fresh as if he hadn't fought with me at all. Doc managed to shove me with his shoulder even as he rose on his hind legs to meet him.

I scampered to the crevice, which I was surprised to find was right behind me.

The fight was almost too horrible to watch, but I couldn't tear my gaze away. Although the wolves were about the same size and weight, the phyter had the advantage of his rage. Again and again the neophyte attacked, twisting, turning, biting, tearing.

Again and again, Doc fought him back. They battled in front of me, their mouths wide, each trying to get a hold on the other's throat.

Blood scent filled the air.

Doc glanced my way, making sure I was safe in my hole. But that was all the opening the neophyte needed. He slammed into Doc, biting hard as he tried to maneuver him onto his back.

Doc wrenched away, but he now had a limp, and his right front paw bled heavily.

Maddening at the sight, the neophyte went in for the kill. Dipping low, he knocked Doc's head up, throwing his weight onto his bad leg, which gave way immediately. He fell onto his side.

As if in slow motion, I saw the angry werewolf flip him to his back.

This was it. In the next instant, he would tear Doc's throat from his body. I couldn't let him. I *wouldn't* let Doc be killed.

"No!" I roared as I flew from my hole.

I hit the phyter with everything I had. In my fury, my blow sent the wolf sprawling, which gave Doc enough time to get to his feet. *What are you doing? I told you to stay in that cave.*

I don't give a damn what you told me. I snarled at him, unleashing my fury with my mind. *If we're going to stop him, we've got to do this together.*

He winced as he put his injured paw down to brace for the next attack. Then he nodded.

Don't tell me to tuck my tail if things start going bad. We're going to finish this. I would have shouted the last words if I could have spoken. I whirled as I realized the other werewolf had eased through the rocks around us to get the high ground. He planned to come at us from the boulders above.

But from which side?

Doc turned to face the other way. We were tail to shoulder, watching each other's backs. As the seconds ticked by, I heard Doc's blood dripping from his paw to the ground. How long before he was too weak to fight?

To stand?

Was that why the other werewolf was taking his time? Anxiety filled me like a balloon too full of air. I was ready to burst at any moment.

Then he came at us again. But rather than pouncing from a boulder behind us, he leapt from the army tank rock.

His jump was aimed perfectly to catch us both in the middle of our backs, possibly breaking one or both of our spines. But I heard a stone skitter on the boulder as he pushed off. Doc and I whirled just in time to catch the neophyte in midair.

We slammed him to the ground where he hit his head, leaving him unconscious.

Almost immediately, he changed back to a human. A very large, very naked human.

Moving closer, I sniffed the strange man's chest. *Do you know him?*

Doc sat on his haunches, studying him. *Barely. His name is Garcia, and he's a canine specialist. He's not been here long. Moved up from Mexico to work with us several weeks ago.*

About the time the outbreak started.

Doc nodded. *Right. Probably brought the virus from Mexico with him.*

Leaving the man—what else could we do?—we limped back to the compound where we slipped into the clinic, became wholly human again and got dressed.

Doc looked as if he'd been in a fight with a chain saw, and I was dirty, aching and bleeding in several places. He called 9-1-1 and reported seeing an unconscious man in Lost Canyon when riding his dirt bike. Then he cleaned and bandaged his hand with a little help from me.

"Should we should stop at the ER and let a doctor look at this?"

He cocked a smile at me. "It'll be fine. I do know a little about doctoring, you know."

I nodded once, turned on my heel and walked out the door.

I was so angry with the man, I shook all over. How dare he lie to me about who he was for so long? I'd been so worried about fitting into his life—him learning to cope with mine—and all the time, he'd been a werewolf. But it was too late for me.

My heart was dead.

Damn him.

I shot him a glance, hoping to see his hair catch fire from the angered thoughts I'd tossed his way. No such luck.

When we reached my apartment, I unlocked the door, stalked to the bathroom and quickly locked the door. I didn't want him joining me in the shower.

Rather than dimming, my anger flashed as I mulled over the night. Why hadn't he told me he was a werewolf a long time ago? He'd used me. *Lied to me.*

What kind of relationship was based on a lie—at least one that wasn't absolutely necessary.

Grabbing the soap and my scrubby, I tackled the dirt on my legs, yelping the first time I hit one of the cuts.

"You okay in there?" Doc called through the door.

"What're you doing?" I shouted back. "Listening at the door?"

A bark of laughter was his only answer.

I clamped my jaws shut. If the soap had been a

blazing coal, I wouldn't have made a sound. When I'd finished, I wrapped a towel around my hair, then wrapped a huge bath sheet around my body. I wasn't going to give the guy any glimpses.

I pulled out a clean towel, which I left on the rack for him.

Anger made me stiff, so I stalked out the door, and without looking around, went to my bedroom. As I dressed, I listened for the shower to come on. It still hadn't started when I had my hair combed through.

A niggle of worry sidled into my gut. Was he hurt worse than I thought? What if he'd lost too much blood and was too weak to call out for help?

Unable to stand it any longer, I threw open my door and flew through it to the living room, where I found him snoring on the couch.

Damned man! How could he sleep at a time like this?

I glanced at his hand, but it was still bandaged, the wrappings clean. Frustration piling on top of my anger, I stormed to the kitchen and started a pot of coffee, then looked for something to work out my emotions since Doc was obviously going to be out of it for a while.

Restlessly my mind ricocheted from one thought, bouncing to another. Then another. I could go for a run, but my leg muscles just weren't up to it. I could go to the computer and work on a new wardrobe for Mrs. Whitten, which I was contracted to do twice a year, but my heart wasn't in it.

Finally I remembered my spinning wheel. I'd ordered it online just after our trip to Colorado, but hadn't had time to try it.

I went to my room and took it from the bay

window where I'd left it. Removing the wool I'd ordered at the same time from my drawer, I carried them both to the living room. I flipped on the TV, found an old B & W that Bella would have loved and started spinning.

As I stranded the wool, euphoria stole over me. My blood pressure dropped by at least twenty points. The steel rod that had lodged in my spine gave way. My arm muscles changed from concrete back to human fiber again.

After watching the entire old movie on our big screen, I had a good beginning on a ball of yarn and was ready to join Doc in his nap.

But just as I put the spinning wheel away, I heard a key in the front door. *Bella's home!* Rushing back to the living room, I got there just in time to see Bella walk in. With a squeal, I threw myself at her.

I took a breath, ready to launch into all the million things I had to tell her. She didn't know anything about us finding and subduing the phyter. But before I could begin, Spencer came in the door behind her.

With a sigh, Doc woke up. "Well, Spence. We were beginning to wonder if you'd ever come back home."

Spence laughed at what must have been a family joke—after all, they'd been gone less than a week—then he sobered. "I'm back. But it's not by choice."

Doc frowned, lifting an eyebrow. "What are you talking about?"

"I mean I'd rather be off somewhere with Bella." He turned, faced Bella squarely as if by doing so he could erase everyone else in the room. "Like on a hot and sandy beach, celebrating our marriage."

Shock flashed across Bella's face and was quickly replaced by joy. But before she could answer, Spencer continued, "Bella, I know you love me. That's why you've been so exhausted and sleeping so much. Why your emotions have been so out of control. Falling in love with a werewolf isn't like falling in love with a human. Until you're used to it, you feel the affect all over. But I can't ask you to marry me—"

"What?" Bella squeaked as tears flooded her eyes.

"—until I tell you something." As if he were unable to stand being so far from her—all of twelve inches—Spencer took her in his arms. He dragged in a breath. "Bella, I'm a werewolf. That's how I made it through the blizzard to the farm."

My heart stopped while my mind froze. Spencer, a werewolf? Both he and Doc had received the Syzygia gene? My heart slowly resumed beating as I tried to reason my way through the new development.

Bella swallowed then gave him a tremulous smile. Obviously she'd accepted the fact without too much trouble.

He tossed a glance my way. "Doc's a werewolf, too."

Bella just glanced at me long enough to grin, then gave all her attention to Spencer as he continued. "Not only Doc, but my whole family. We're all werewolves—of the Dux Ducis line. It doesn't mean much unless you understand the werewolf world. But I'll warn you now, all our children are born werewolves."

Struggling to make sense of Spencer's words, I turned to Doc. "*Everyone* in your family is a werewolf?"

Slowly he nodded. I couldn't bear discussing this in front of his brother and my sister. I fled to my room.

He followed me so I asked, "You've been searching for a way to wipe out werewolves while everyone you're kin to—"

"Not werewolves," he tried to correct me for the millionth time. "Syzygia. The gene that causes Lycanthropy. Because of it, I've never allowed myself to experience an honest emotion. I was taught from the cradle to hold back. Always.

"I was never able to lose my temper and have a normal fight as a kid for fear I'd morph. I couldn't put my heart into a race; I couldn't even lose myself making love because I might transform right there."

"I want future generations of my family to embrace what they feel without worrying they'll turn into a monster in plain view of the public."

"It doesn't matter." I dragged air into my aching lungs. "Since the night of the dedication, I've known there was something special between us. Something that could have lasted a lifetime." Thinking of what I'd done, I folded my arms and held on tight.

He laid his hand on my forearm, but wisely removed it before I did it for him.

I drew a ragged breath. "But because you'd dedicated your entire life to wiping out werewolves, I knew there could never be a way. *You could never be my mate.* I've suffered each time we were together. So I performed the ritual to build the impenetrable wall around my heart—my every emotion—because I knew I could never fall in love with you."

I couldn't stop the tears that blurred my vision. "I read it in my grandma's journals. Once a werewolf constructs that wall, it can never be destroyed. It's over. Forever."

He drew his eyebrows together, his faced creasing as if he were about to cry. He opened his mouth, but nothing came out. Nothing.

He looked as if I'd destroyed his heart—his life—and I wished fervently that I had, because I no longer had a heart to be broken.

My voice dropped to a harsh whisper as tears clogged my throat. *"Why didn't you tell me?"*

He opened and closed his mouth, shook his head, but said nothing. I grabbed my purse, shoved past him and ran for my car. I had to get away from this man who would have been my perfect match. This man I should have loved and now never could.

Away from Bella and her delirious joy. Away from Dux Ducis, the royal family werewolf.

Away from my heart, which was now a cold, dead stone.

Chapter Sixteen

Once in my car, I drove as fast as I could without getting pulled over. With the rage flaming through me, if a patrolman stopped me now, I'd probably take off his head.

When at last I reached the empty countryside, I raced flat out, howling my rage. Bristles stung my skin as I came near to morphing again and again. How could he have done it to me? How could he have destroyed my entire life?

Having enforced myself against the only love I was ever meant to have, I would never be able to love anyone else, and I couldn't love him.

I would be forever solitary. And unloved.

I never wanted to see him again.

I drove back to Lost Canyon where I finally embraced my pain.

I morphed in the most painful transformation I'd ever gone through. As if even my body mourned for that lost part of my life, I went through agony with every lengthening of a bone. Every change of my body's shape. Every bristle pushing through my skin.

And I welcomed it.

Once the change was complete, I ran hard. No warm up. No jogging. I ran until there was no air left in my lungs, no energy in my muscles. I ran until there was nothing left inside me. My pads were bleeding heavily by the time I limped the miles back to my car. When I returned to human form, my palms and soles still bled, but I didn't care.

This new anguish took some of my focus from what was missing in my life.

What would always be missing in my life.

****

I stood at the back of the chapel, clutching the bouquet of highly scented gardenias that the bustling florist had shoved into my hand. The music, almost as sweet as the fragrance causing my stomach to clench, droned on. The dress I wore, which I'd had to pull every string in my arsenal to get in the short time we'd had between the engagement and the wedding, bit into my waist.

As I waited for our cue to enter, I tapped the toe of my Jimmy Choos, trying to work off some of my excess energy. I glanced at Bella, who stood behind me with our dad, glowing in her happiness. It was all I could do to keep from pushing Dad aside so I could smack her.

If she hadn't said yes to Spencer, we wouldn't be here now.

But here we were in a beautiful old church in Round Top, Texas, just outside Austin, waiting to be in an intimate wedding party. Very intimate. Just Bella, Me, Spencer. And Doc.

The rock that had once been my heart weighed like lead as I thought of him.

I wouldn't go through it. I didn't even want to be in the same state as the man who'd destroyed me, much less the same church in a romantic, candle-light wedding.

The minister and Spencer walked out of a door near the front and turned toward the aisle we'd walk down. It was difficult to draw a full breath as I waited for Doc to emerge.

The music started, my cue to drift down the aisle, but I waited until I could fill my lungs then took the first step. Slowly I made my way to the front. As I walked I forced a grin for our sorority sisters who all but filled one side of the chapel, then I tossed a smile to Mom, who was already in tears, while I shook my head. She shouldn't be crying on Bella's wedding day. Bella was getting everything she'd ever wanted. And more.

But once I passed Mom, there was only one place to look. At the front. I swallowed hard, took a deep breath and lifted my gaze. My pride wouldn't let me keep my head down. I tried to keep my focus on the minister, but somehow I couldn't. I let my gaze drift to Spencer.

Then, with a slow, casual turn of my head, I looked at Doc.

The world stopped.

I stopped.

If Dad hadn't tapped me on my nape, I might still be there today, but luckily the big guy was there for me. Somehow he maneuvered me and Bella to our places.

I saw nothing but Doc. Heard nothing but my pulse, whooshing in my ears. And smelled nothing but Doc's scent.

I clenched the bouquet hard as memories drifted through my mind; I took my time examining them. The Halloween party where we met made me feel as if I'd swallowed an atomic bomb, which detonated in my stomach. The dedication ball—when I'd first spent time in his arms.

I tried to force my mind back to minister's droning, but that night on Doc's pool table took over my mind.

Bella's soft but firm voice caught my attention for a moment as she turned to face Spencer, looking up into his face.

A vision of making love with Doc in his bed rose before me, spiriting me away. I relived the breakfast we had at his favorite restaurant, the time we had steak for dinner at mine and—

"—pronounce you man and wife."

I came to with a start. Bella's wedding was over, and I missed most of it. Somehow I held her bouquet along with mine. I returned it to her with a kiss on the cheek when she paused next to me, a knowing smile curving her lips.

Then she was gone, and Doc was there, waiting for me to take his arm. Keeping my touch light, I hoped with everything in me that he wouldn't feel me trembling.

We exited the church, and while the new married couple took the limo to the reception, I drove alone.

When I arrived at the venue, I hurried out of the car and over to a group of our sorority sisters who'd already visited the open bar. Several times.

"Jazzy. The man of honor is one fine looking man," Nicki, the sorority prez our senior year looked around for Doc between sips of her drink. "Is he taken?"

"No." I answered quietly, my jaws frozen. "But you were last time I checked."

Her laugh sounded exactly like a mule's bray. Why hadn't I noticed in college?

Beck, another friend, drew me aside. "Ignore her. Come on, I'll buy you a Mai Tai." Her bright red curls bounced as her green eyes sparkled.

"It's an open bar," I snapped. "Drinks are free."

Beck raised both eyebrows. "Lighten up, Jazz. I was joking."

I shook my head, wishing I could get into a fight with someone to work off some of my excess anger. What I had saved for Doc spilled out all over my friends.

Shrugging, I gave her a light hug. "Sorry, Beck. Mea culpa."

"Not a prob. Let's watch them cut the cake."

I let myself be swept away in the festivities, and before long, confetti was being passed around to throw at Bella and Spencer.

My heart ached as they ran for the limo, which would take them to their flight. Bella and I'd never been separated longer than a few days. Now she'd no longer be living in our apartment. How would I cope?

Beck broke into my thoughts. "You know it's Mardi Gras week."

Who cares? I wanted to ask as I drained my iced tea and set the glass on a nearby urn. "Is it? Bella and I were so busy getting this wedding together in record time, I had no idea."

"Well, it was beautiful. But now it's time for you to celebrate. Why don't you stay a few days with me? We'll party hard. And I'll reserve us a space at the Super Topper on Fat Tuesday."

Super Topper—the celebration we'd started as freshmen at UT. "You're still doing that?"

"Yeah, but it's taken on a life of its own. Not only

the Omegas anymore. Now the famous and infamous around Austin make an appearance."

As soon as Bella and Spencer left in a shower of confetti, I found my parents and told them I'd be staying with Beck for a few days. They were more than happy for me to. And I hoped going to the Super Topper might take my mind off Doc and my dead heart for a while.

The trouble was the parties during Mardi Gras week were never as much fun as the memories. And the memories Bella, Beck and I'd made had been shining for a while now.

****

Fat Tuesday finally arrived. I was anxious for Super Topper to be over so I could go home. Get busy. Maybe if I tried hard enough, I could work Doc out of my mind. The way things were going, I'd never get rid of the pain trapped inside my wall with me. I couldn't stop thinking about him, dreaming about him, wanting the physical part of him.

But I'd never again be able to love him.

Beck and I had great costumes planned for the party. She chose the Queen of Diamonds, and I the Queen of Hearts. With my mood the way it had been since the wedding, I didn't dare choose the Queen of Clubs. It was too big a temptation.

After having our makeup professionally done, we went back to the apartment and got dressed. While still in my bedroom, I looked at myself in the mirror and almost threw up. I didn't look like the Queen of Hearts; with my hair pulled back as it was, I looked like Alice in Wonderland.

Grabbing my makeup bag, I pulled out sparkling

black eyeliner and dark shadow, which I applied liberally. Then I added a set of extra long lashes. With a Darker than Night lipstick, I was almost ready. Except for my hair.

I yanked off the crown, drew in the length and grabbed a tube of sparkling burgundy-colored gel akin to concrete. After applying it liberally and giving myself a few spikes, I replaced the crown with the tiara Beck had received for some honor or other in school.

I replaced the bell shaped skirt with a pencil slim one, slit high enough to make a nun sigh that I'd picked up when we were shopping, tugged the heart-shaped top low and belted it to keep it there. Then I stepped into a pair of nose bleed Monolos and once more looked in the mirror.

Alice doesn't live here anymore. I stepped out of the bedroom, lifted my chin high enough to howl and shot Beck a grin.

"It's good to be the queen," she quipped as she grinned back.

But where's my king? The question came to mind before I could stop it. My smile melted around the edges, but I forced it back into place before Beck could notice. Or comment.

"Jazzy. You look fabulous!" Beck circled me, her string of "diamonds" clacking as she moved. "That's not the costume we rented is it?"

"Some of it is," I answered. "But you know me. I like to be...different."

"Different," Beck said at the same time, her red curls bouncing. "With that makeup job, you won't even need your mask."

"I'll take it anyway." I glanced quickly at the small

mask that curved over my eyes with puffy, sparkling hearts attached on the side like so many balloons. "The taxi should be here," she said, glancing at the glass floor clock, standing in the corner.

Slipping my new spangled bag, that looked like a pair of joined hearts with an arrow piercing them, around my neck and over one shoulder, I tucked in plenty of cash, the key Beck had given me, my ID and my Darker than Night lipstick. If I needed anything else, I'd just have to come back for it.

Like that would happen.

We hurried to the taxi in a flurry, giggling as if we were still freshman. When we were securely inside, Beck opened her mouth to give the driver the address, but the clean cut young man spoke first. "I bet I can guess. It's Super Topper tonight. Right girls?"

"Yes." Beck's voice took on a smoky quality, a sure sign it would be a long evening. Heaviness took some of the excitement from me as Doc's image loomed again. Why couldn't I get him out of my mind?

I glanced out the window, watching as the driver took us to the Warehouse District, the part of Austin recently redone to look as it did over a hundred years ago—almost. Everything looked old, but was new. There was no moldy smell, no missing parts, no crumbling pieces.

It was as if that whole part of the city had come out to play dress up, just like the rest of us.

The party venue was one of the nicest hotels in the city. Entering, we were directed to the largest party room. The Stephen Austin Room. The "room" was arranged on two levels and had several "Bluebonnet Pockets," small areas that opened off the main room for a little privacy. Very little.

The lavish decorations, in the Texas state of mind, were overdone with brightly colored hand-crafted tissue flowers with pearl centers, shellacked to give them stability and shine. The beach ball sized blossoms popped up everywhere there was space. Bouquets of them loomed in every corner. They lined walls, sprouted from spaces between exits and had been wrestled into tall center pieces on a few tables stationed on the far side near the stairway, leading to the upper party area. Under the stairway was a glass pond filled with water plants, floating star-shaped candles and graceful Koi.

Multi-sized star lights had been strung overhead—a mad cartoonist's idea of the Texas night sky.

Beck soon handed me a flute of champagne and looked around, trying to guess who the other guests were. Quickly claimed for a dance, Beck swirled away in the arms of a man in a gorilla mask while I turned to walk off the floor.

Before I could find a place to sit, a man wearing a tuxedo stepped in front of me. His mask covered most of his face, except his chin, and looked made of gold. The shape vaguely resembled a wolf. He waited a long moment before he spoke, but unable to see his face, I had no idea why. "Dance with me."

I tried to draw a breath, but suddenly my animal instincts turned on at maximum strength. Chills raced through me. I couldn't find enough breath to answer, but I'm not certain I could have spoken in any case.

I morphed, but it wasn't my body that changed. Rather than the burn of bristles breaking through or the ache of elongating bones, my mind alone became animal.

Then I focused on the man in front of me. Instinct, knowledge passed genetically through the ages, is a wonderful thing, even when the heart is dead.

****

Chase waited, enjoying the view as he did. She looked gorgeous tonight, but that wasn't unusual. Whether skiing, making love or fighting virus infected werewolves, this woman was beautiful; a beauty of the heart.

Her mask did little to hide her identity. Her tilted green eyes and delicious mouth gave her away.

She moved slowly to him, settling in his arms as if she'd always been there. And would always remain. But he knew better.

At one time he could have made her his life mate. He'd had the ingrained knowledge and the yearning, but he'd let his damned goal—the fire in his gut—deflect him from what was truly right.

And that chance had fled.

But he couldn't help loving her. He always would. Couldn't help wanting to be with her one more time. Again, he always would.

The music had an underlying jungle beat or was that his heart thundering in his chest? What's the difference? She moved against him, knowing his every step before he took it, following him as if they'd danced together forever.

Spying an opening, he slowly moved in the direction of the elevator until it was just to the left. And when the door opened to emit several laughing people, he whisked her inside, immediately pushing the button to close the doors.

As he reached for the button that would take them to his floor, she took off her mask. His heart stuttered.

She gently pulled off his mask. "Hello, Doc."

When the elevator reached his floor, he led her to his suite and quickly unlocked the door.

"You found me." Her normal verve was missing from her voice, but what could he expect?

Heaviness settled in his gut as hope faded. "I couldn't stay away." He tried to think how to explain, but his mind was a confusing whirl, moving too quickly to say only one thing.

"In this city of hundreds of thousands of people, you found me."

He nodded. Swallowed.

"In that crush of masked people downstairs, you came directly to me."

"I'll never want anyone but you. No matter—"

Stepping near enough to feel her heat, she put her hand over his mouth to stop his words. "I told you, it's too late. I performed the Tumuld Argamelino." Her tone was amazingly cool, breaking only once as she spoke the terrible words.

"I know." He fought to stay on his feet as she nodded. If he followed his instincts, he'd be on his knees, wailing his loss of her. The death of her love. Heart breaking, he barely found the words, "But I need to know why."

"Because I loved you too much, and you didn't love me." When he gasped a breath to argue, she closed her eyes. Shook her head. Now even her voice sounded dead. "Not enough. You put your research before me. Held back when we made love. You were in control every single minute.

"We were mismatched. Each time we made love, I had to fight to keep from losing it totally. Morphing. Howl at the moon, toss caution to the wind and changing into the woman-animal I am.

"But I couldn't do that with you. You finished each time with barely a ripple on the smooth ocean of your control. Not a hair out of place or a drop of sweat on your brow."

He gritted his teeth at the pain. "So you honestly did it."

Her face haggard, she nodded. "I read about it in my grandmother's journals. She fell in love with a man who said he loved her, gave her a gold coin set in a necklace to prove it then went away. She had to do it to remain sane. So did I."

What he'd been taught from the cradle had rebounded to destroy his life. A lifetime of indoctrination echoed back to him. *No one must know. The family secret is a royal one, but a secret all the same. Never, never, never let anyone find out. Even another werewolf.* And because he'd learned his lesson so well, he'd lost the only woman he could ever love.

Anger flashed over him, and this time rather than hold back, he allowed himself to change. Why had she done this thing without talking to him? Giving him the chance to explain?

Now it was too late and neither one of them could ever have a happy life. With a howl of deep pain, he fell to his knees. His jaw elongated as his muscles filled with the power he'd so long held back.

Just as his brain slipped from human to wolf, a thought trickled in. *He had the power*. There in the connection between his human brain and powerful animal body, he knew there had to be a way.

His transformation back to human was like a cool mist on a hot summer day. The heat was fantastic, but the mist a welcome change.

"What happened? Just remaining in control?" She didn't add, "as usual," but the inference was there.

They could do this. He knew they could if he could just convince her to try. "I want to try…something. But not here. Will you come with me?"

She drew her brows together, and for the first time, he saw a sign of life in her gaze. "Where?"

"Will you come?"

As she nodded, he caught her hand and dragged her out of his suite, down the elevator and to his Hummer. Unable to concentrate on anything but what he hoped to do, he drove as fast as he could without endangering Jazzy's life.

The drive took too long, but there was no place else he could think of that would suit. After a couple of hours of silence she cleared her throat. "We're going to the farm, aren't we?"

He nodded. "I hope it's okay. I needed someplace where we could be alone, have room to try."

Finally she glanced at him. Her gaze wasn't warm, but even the chill was welcome. "It's fine."

As he pulled into the driveway, the sun edged over the horizon, coloring the skyline pink. After parking near the back porch, he killed the engine.

Thank goodness for the unseasonably warm weather. For what he had in mind, it would make everything more comfortable.

She leaned against the door and gave him her full scrutiny. "We're here. Me in my gown and you in your tux. Nothing to change into. Now what?"

This had to work. He'd never survive the next sixty or eighty years without her by his side, loving him. He didn't answer. Just went to the back of the Humvee, retrieved the blankets his family kept in every vehicle in case of emergency then helped her out. When she started toward the house, he gently tugged her in the other direction.

With a shrug, she went along. The going was slow because she wore a pair of ridiculous shoes with spiky heels that added about nine inches to her height, but it didn't matter. Nothing mattered except making this work.

Finally they reached the pond. He took her to the far side. Young growth next to the water gave them the illusion of privacy where he spread the blankets.

When their "nest" was made, he pulled her to him. "I can't live without you, Jazzy Cannis. I won't. Together, I think we're stronger than any spell you can perform with fire and herbs."

Doubt puckered her brow just above her cold eyes, but he couldn't quit. He had to make this work.

"Will you let me—us—try to undo what you've done?"

After a long moment, she shrugged, then, finally, nodded.

He stepped close enough to feel her body warmth then slid his fingers in her hair. With his palms skimming lightly, he eased his hands to her face, wanting to touch every pore, every particle of her. Like a blind man, he used his fingers to memorize the shape of her nose, her brows, her chin.

His heart thudded hard as he glided his fingers

from her jaw to the length of her neck. With each beat, *I love you, Jazzy Cannis. I love you* drummed in his mind.

He removed her belt and slid his hand to her back to slowly unzip her blouse. When the zipper reached the bottom of its run, he eased it from her shoulders and let the top slide to the ground, then took off her skirt, leaving her with nothing on but a scrap of a panty, practically not there.

She kicked the skirt out of the away as her nipples puckered. At her slight shiver, he took off his jacket, put it over her shoulders but didn't close it, unable to hide her beauty.

He skimmed his hands to her breasts, and as he ran his thumbs over them, savoring the texture, she closed her eyes, her head tipping back. She gasped for breath.

Inching his palms down her sides, he caught her scrap of panty and shoved it down, past her knees. Kneeling, he ran his hand over first one calf and then the other as he took it off.

Unable to stand it another minute, he stood and yanked open his shirt so he could feel her, chest to breast. Belly to belly. Mouth to mouth. Heart to heart.

After way too long, he kissed her. Fitting his leg between hers, he stepped nearer and the kiss morphed into a firestorm. His mind all but blanked out as he held her.

Her hands worked at his trousers, loosening them. He didn't waste any time. He kicked off his shoes, everything else he had on and dragged her to the blankets with him.

Slow down, slow down, his brain pounded. *This could be the last time. The only time. Savor it.*

He tried to draw a breath, but the air was filled with the wild scent that belonged to her accented by the moisture coming from the pond. His heartbeat kicked higher, his emotions denser.

Loving her as he did, he couldn't hold back, but he must. The lesson ingrained since childhood had been *control*.

But how could control rule him when all he wanted, all he'd ever want, was within his grasp?

He raised his head, hoping to find a breath to steady himself, but she followed. Lifting her arms to encircle his neck, she bit him hard on the shoulder, and lapped the pain into extreme pleasure.

She slipped from under him, straddled his waist and eased herself over him. Closing his eyes, he suffered the torturous delight she inflicted. Bristles stung as they tried to charge through, his bones fought to change, but gritting his teeth, he held himself firm.

She gasped as, with a quick movement, he switched places with her. Now he was in charge—but he couldn't dominate her. She moved wildly beneath him, her breaths coming in gasps and snarls.

This woman who lived all out, holding back nothing, made him wish he hadn't learned his family's lessons so well. She'd put herself in danger for those around her. She didn't care who knew what she was, didn't bother holding back if she deemed the reason worthwhile.

In fact, she was proud of being a werewolf. Ready to tell the world.

She was all he ever wanted—and all he could ever want.

He couldn't hold back. With a burning breath, he

pressed his arms into the blankets and pushing high, he tipped back his head high.

He howled.

And with that howl, he released himself to the passion. The stimulation of morphing as he made love was more than he could have imagined. In those moments, his senses heightened to a level beyond imagination.

His heart detonated, the bristles charged and he let them erupt. His elongating jaw changed his kiss, but he barely noticed as her scent became part of the world around them, visible yet transparent. The sparkle, which he could now see gave her the glow that made her so beautiful, was like mini electrical jolts under his fingers, which quickly transformed into paws.

The feel of her beneath him drove him beyond understanding as she, in perfect sync, began changing.

He was lost.

Chapter Seventeen

I dropped on the blanket, exhaustion nearly killing me when I'd changed back to human form. I hadn't known it could be like that. I'd imagined, but I hadn't actually known.

With a sigh of happiness, I looked into his eyes.

And in that instant with my heart thudding and his nearness sending a warm buzz throughout my body, I realized I loved him.

The Tumuld Argamelino—the exact spell Granny used to kill her heart—had been beaten. Overcome.

I struggled to take a breath, and found it rife with his scent. With all my heart I wished I could capture and bottle it, because I didn't know if he could love me forever, knowing what I was willing to do to stop my love for him.

Tears burned the back of my eyes as I envisioned the rest of my life, loving him but being unloved. Never experiencing again what we'd just had.

Unsure I'd be able to survive, I wondered if nuns accepted werewolf applicants.

"I-I have to tell you something." I shuddered at the sound of my voice. It was just like a whipped puppy, all teary and high. That whiny-baby stuff made me want to scream.

If I had the strength, I'd morph again. I'd stand with my legs braced, my toes splayed, every muscle tensed and the hair on my nape rising.

I'd snarl the words and let the body parts land where they may.

But wolf mouths aren't made to pronounce words and my mind, when I'd gone animal, didn't pick up the normal thoughts and subtleties. I might be able to get a few basic words or thoughts, but I wouldn't be able to make him understand.

"Let me tell you first." We sat with me settled in the space between his legs so I could look into his face. "I love you, Jazzy Cannis. I want to marry you."

Marry me? This man who wanted to wipe out the very gene that had made my life—and his—so wondrous wanted to be married to me?

Tears flooded, turning the world into a blurry place. "What about your Syzygia research?"

He lifted his brows in alarm. "No. When I truly thought about it, I knew I couldn't do that—not to *our* children. I wanted them to experience the wonder, the joy of life that you have. Then I questioned if anyone would truly want to wipe out generations of inherited knowledge by getting rid of that gene, so I've given up my quest to wipe it out."

I bit the inside of my lip hard to keep from sobbing out loud. Finally, he understood what I'd been trying to tell him.

"Now I want to find a way to wipe out the virus that creates neophytes, and to stabilize a serum for the infection until I do." He caught my tears with the pads of his thumbs. "And that dream can only come true if you're there by my side, helping me."

"Even after what I've done?"

His frown made my belly tense, but we had to get

it out. Now. "I did the Tumuld Argamelino to kill my love for you. I burned something you'd given me that you truly cared about."

He waited, watching me, his eyes dark. I couldn't tell if he knew what I was going to say or not. I blew out a breath and sucked in a quick one, but could barely manage a whisper. "I burned your granddad's poster."

He stared at me for a very long moment then nodded. Getting up, he retrieved my clothes and handed them to me.

That was it. My answer. He no longer wanted to be with me. His grandfather's poster meant more to him than I did. Blinded by tears, I struggled to get dressed and gathered up the blankets.

He picked up my shoes and held them out to me, but I shook my head. I wanted to walk with the dirt and dried grass of the field beneath my feet. I wanted something beneath me that I knew wouldn't change, no matter what stupid thing I'd done.

As we walked back to the house, I tried to swallow so I could find my voice, apologize to him before we parted, but I couldn't.

Then a miracle happened. He slid his arm around my waist and pulled me against his side. We walked together as one person.

I swallowed. Twice. "You don't hate me?"

His smile was soft, his gaze sparkling. "Never."

We walked on until we came to the house. Going inside, we went to the living room, dropped the blankets in a heap and snuggled into them.

"How were we able to break that spell? I performed it exactly as Granny described in her diary, and she said it was permanent. Could never be undone."

Doc drew me to him. My head went naturally to the hollow in his shoulder as I relaxed against him. "I think no matter how viable the spell or how fervent the wish, we've proven there's nothing in this world stronger than a pair of werewolves in love."

Wanting to tease him just a little, I straightened and met his gaze. "All right, Mr. Scientist. How did we prove that theory?"

The twinkle in his eyes as his lips quirked into a delicious grin sent a thrill through me. "You did, darlin'. You made me howl."

A word from the author...

Unbridled imagination—gift or curse? For me, it's been a little of both. Curse, when the 'nation took over and I lost what the teacher was saying. Gift when nothing interesting is happening, which could be why I lost track of the teacher's words.

Luckily several years ago, I harnessed my imagination and started writing.

When I'm not writing, I'm spending time with my family (both at work and at home), gardening, knitting, or reading.

When I am writing, I'm often on my blog, where I talk about my Small Town World.

http://susanshay.net

I like to hang out at Twitter

@shaywriter

and Facebook, too.

susanspessshay

I hope you'll drop by and say hi!

Thank you for purchasing
this publication of The Wild Rose Press, Inc.
For other wonderful stories of romance,
please visit our on-line bookstore at
www.thewildrosepress.com.

For questions or more information
contact us at
info@thewildrosepress.com.

The Wild Rose Press, Inc.
www.thewildrosepress.com

To visit with authors of
The Wild Rose Press, Inc.
join our yahoo loop at
http://groups.yahoo.com/group/thewildrosepress/